"Maybe your father couldn't be helped,"
Brady s... ...**...ked as if he**
regrett...

"And ma...

She sen... ...le touch of
a finger under her chin, ...back.

"I don't believe that," he said quietly but firmly.

Ashley looked at him, thinking it amazing that a
man in his job could have such warm, kind eyes.
She remembered the first time she'd looked
into them, as he'd pulled her from the car in the
moment before it had slid down the mountain.
She remembered thinking then that those eyes
promised she would be safe, that somehow he
would get her out of this.

And he had. At no small risk to himself.

She couldn't let him risk himself even more.

* * *

Be sure to check out the rest of the books in
this miniseries.

Cutter's Code: A clever and mysterious canine
helps a group of secret operatives crack the case

* * *

Dear Reader,

I usually use this space to tell you something about the story, how it came to be or what inspired it, and I will. But as I write this now, my state is in the middle of an extended lockdown for reasons, sadly, the whole world knows. The thing I wanted to make note of, however, is the good news that so many animal shelters are emptying out as people turn to pets to help ease the isolation they feel. I hope every one of them realizes this is what's been missing in their lives, something that can be provided only by our precious animal friends. And may each of them be the kind of person who will continue to love and care for the creature who has helped them after the crisis is over.

As you can guess from the title, *Operation Mountain Recovery* is set in...the mountains. I love mountains. I don't necessarily need to live amid them, but I will always want to be where I can see them, as I am now. Perhaps it comes from being born in flat, flat Iowa—although I was there for only the first six months of my life. When my wonderful editor expressed a wish for a certain type of story, I sat on my deck for a while, looking toward the snow-covered Cascades, and thought. And now you have the result. I hope you enjoy it.

Happy reading!

Justine

OPERATION MOUNTAIN RECOVERY

Justine Davis

HARLEQUIN
ROMANTIC
SUSPENSE

Recycling programs for this product may not exist in your area.

ISBN-13: 978-1-335-62682-0

Operation Mountain Recovery

Copyright © 2020 by Janice Davis Smith

This edition published by arrangement with Harlequin Books S.A.

For questions and comments about the quality of this book, please contact us at CustomerService@Harlequin.com.

Harlequin Enterprises ULC
22 Adelaide St. West, 40th Floor
Toronto, Ontario M5H 4E3, Canada
www.Harlequin.com

Printed in U.S.A.

Justine Davis lives on Puget Sound in Washington State, watching big ships and the occasional submarine go by and sharing the neighborhood with assorted wildlife, including a pair of bald eagles, deer, a bear or two, and a tailless raccoon. In the few hours when she's not planning, plotting or writing her next book, her favorite things are photography, knitting her way through a huge yarn stash and driving her restored 1967 Corvette roadster—top down, of course.

Connect with Justine on her website, justinedavis.com, at Twitter.com/justine_d_davis or on Facebook at Facebook.com/justinedaredavis.

Books by Justine Davis

Harlequin Romantic Suspense

Cutter's Code

Operation Midnight
Operation Reunion
Operation Blind Date
Operation Unleashed
Operation Power Play
Operation Homecoming
Operation Soldier Next Door
Operation Alpha
Operation Notorious
Operation Hero's Watch
Operation Second Chance
Operation Mountain Recovery

Visit the Author Profile page at Harlequin.com, or justinedavis.com, for more titles.

Black Beauty wasn't a typical rescue. A vet bargained with a pet store to sell any unwanted puppies. I stopped at the store, just to look. The black ball of fluff, with white on her chest, her toes and the tip of her tail, an Australian shepherd/black Lab, captured my heart. As a puppy, she liked riding in the stroller while my nephew toddled alongside. Black Beauty was supposed to reach only forty pounds but grew to seventy-five pounds. On our walks, people often commented, "Nice guard dog."

She was a marshmallow. And smart. When I hid her pills in food, she'd eat the meat, cheese and even peanut butter and spit the pill out, unless it was chunky peanut butter. If I did something wrong, she'd ignore me. She'd bring her rag bone to play tug-of-war as her way of saying all's forgiven. She was my unofficial therapy dog. Seventeen and a half years she graced my life. She's been gone almost as long.

Someone asked, "When you reach heaven, what words do you want to hear first?" I should want "Welcome, child," or "Well done, good and faithful servant." But the first thing I want to hear is "She's waited so long for you. She's right here." I still miss her, every day.

~Judy

This is the latest in a series of dedications from readers who have shared the pain of the loss of a beloved dog. For more information, visit my website at www.justinedavis.com or Facebook at Facebook.com/justinedaredavis.

Chapter 1

"Are you sure you don't mind not going somewhere sunny and warm?"

Quinn Foxworth gave his wife a glance and a smile, keeping his attention on the mountain road. "You're here," he said. "That's all the sunny and warm I need."

Hayley felt the burst of pleasure she always felt when her husband of one year to the day made one of those simple declarations. "We've got two weeks. It's January. Maybe we'll get snowed in."

"I can but hope," Quinn said. "I am a bit nervous, though."

Hayley blinked. "Nervous? You're a year too late for that, aren't you?"

Quinn grinned at her. "Not about us. Never about us. Him." He jerked his head toward the back seat, where their dog, Cutter, was snoozing.

Hayley glanced that way. Some people might think it

odd that they had brought their dog with them on their first-anniversary trip. But those people didn't know Cutter. He looked so innocent, lying there with his dark head on his front paws. People tended to focus on his coloring, black head and shoulders transitioning to russet brown over his back and plumed tail. But they soon learned that behind those pretty looks was an uncanny canine brain.

"He was pretty insistent that we were not to leave him behind, wasn't he?"

"A little too insistent for my peace of mind."

"I'd like to ask what trouble could he get us into a hundred miles from home, but that's tempting fate."

"And this is Cutter."

At the sound of his name, the dog lifted one eyelid to look at them sleepily, then closed it again.

"Indeed it is," she said with a grin. As she said it, she sensed the slightest of slips, and instantly the SUV's speed slowed. She was glad Quinn had spent yesterday afternoon changing over to snow tires in preparation for this trip. "Ice?"

"Just a patch. All it might take on this road, though."

She might have been worried if anyone other than Quinn was driving, for the road did wind around the side of a mountain, with a precipitous drop-off on the other side. Alex Galanis had warned them it could get tricky in winter when he'd insisted they use his cabin up here. Hayley knew Quinn normally wouldn't accept for personal benefit such an offer from someone the Foxworth Foundation had helped, but when the entire Northwest team had united to insist they go, he'd given in.

She looked to her left. Coming back this way, on the outer edge of the road, would be an adventure, though. And if—

Cutter was suddenly fully awake and on his feet. His

ears were up and focused ahead. She looked but saw nothing moving, nothing but empty road until it turned out of sight to follow the contour of the mountain. But then a low rumbling and an all-too-familiar sound issued from the dog's throat. Neither growl nor whine, it was somewhere in between the two—and was a signal they'd learned not to ignore.

"Uh-oh," Quinn muttered.

"Yes. But what, where?"

Cutter was still staring forward. "Ahead, I gather, since he's not battering my eardrum to turn anywhere," Quinn said. They'd learned this as well, that the uncannily clever Cutter was quite adept at getting them to go where he wanted them to go, simply by deafening them until they made the right choice.

The distinctive sound of the studs on their snow tires was quieter at this lower speed. Quinn obviously was taking Cutter's warning seriously. There was something up ahead, and it wouldn't do to go barreling around that curve without knowing what.

"Maybe it's a herd of deer," Hayley suggested.

"You mean a normal dog reaction?" Quinn asked dryly.

"We can always hope."

They exchanged knowing grins, because with their dog, it was very rarely that simple.

At first, when they slowly rounded that curve, it didn't look serious. All Hayley saw in those first seconds was a single, marked sheriff's SUV pulled to the side of the road. Eagle County Sheriff, she noted. But in the next second, three things happened. Cutter's low rumble turned into a loud barking, and Hayley spotted the ominously damaged guardrail and a man in uniform at the back of the vehicle, lifting out a coiled rope.

"And here we are," Quinn murmured. Someone or

something had obviously gone over the side. "Looks like he's going after them."

The deputy looked over at them but quickly went back to fastening his rope to the push bars at the front of his unit. Quinn was right—he was going to go over the edge, risking his own safety.

Quinn glanced at her. She smiled back at him. Her husband was who and what he was, and driving past something like this wasn't in his playbook, even if Cutter hadn't been on his feet and barking insistently.

Quinn pulled over until they were just a few feet from the marked unit, nose to nose. The man in the sheriff's uniform—not the tailored spit and polish of the city but rugged, heavy-duty gear, with boots that looked as if you could climb a rock face in them—looked up again as Quinn got out. Hayley noted he was as tall as her husband and nearly as muscled. He moved with that same kind of powerful grace that spoke of fitness and confidence. His dark hair was a little ragged around the edges for a cop, and she wondered if perhaps they were short of barbers here in the mountains.

Quinn didn't waste time on formalities. "Got a winch," he said, jerking a thumb toward the front of the SUV.

The man glanced toward their vehicle just as Hayley slid out herself. The name patch on his uniform said B. Crenshaw. His eyes were blue like Quinn's, too, she noticed, but a darker shade. She smiled inwardly at herself and how she compared every man to her husband these days. And the best any of them could ever do was to, as this man did, come close.

She saw him look at the winch on their front bumper. Then he looked at Quinn, assessingly. Quinn was silent, probably because he'd be doing the same thing if their positions were reversed. Whatever the man saw convinced him, because a moment later he nodded sharply.

Quinn turned around without a word and came to unfasten the winch cable. Hayley knew it was rated at nine thousand pounds, so they should be fine, although since it was designed for pulling, not lifting, she wasn't sure it would be able to pull a car up that steep a slope. But it would get them safely down to it, and that's what counted now.

"Crowbar?" Quinn asked the deputy.

"Got one. But two might not hurt."

Quinn nodded, and Hayley ran to the back of the SUV and grabbed theirs from the tool bin. Cutter looked over the back seat at her, silent now.

"We'll fix it, boy," she said, and the dog gave a low whine that sounded approving; she'd given up trying not to read humanity into his communications. She grabbed up the chocks next to the bin and brought them, too. She ran back to the man she loved more than life, in no small part because this was who he was.

"Always thinking. One of the many reasons I love you," Quinn said as he took two of them and slid them in front of the back tires while Hayley put the others to the front.

"On the com," Quinn said to her. "And get Cutter out of the car, just in case."

She nodded, picked up her own Foxworth phone and pushed the red button that turned on the walkie-talkie function as he did the same. With a push from the SUV's base system, they should be in full, live communication.

As she got the tense but calm dog out of the car, she told herself Quinn had done much, much worse than this, but still her pulse picked up as the two men vanished over the side.

Brady Crenshaw had been a deputy in this mountain country he loved and where he had grown up for nearly ten years now. And this was not the craziest thing he'd done. Some might think so, trusting a man he'd never seen before, and before he'd even spoken to him. But he'd learned to trust his gut on some things, and a man with such nerve and knowledge in his steady gaze was the kind of man you wanted on your team. Even if you were doing something like going down the side of a very steep mountain.

A glance at size of the winch, mounted on a special front bumper designed for it, told him the man understood the physics of this. A glance at his eyes told Brady he'd seen much worse.

The cable had loops near the end, enabling them to slip a foot in before starting down. Brady pulled on his leather gloves and stepped into the lower loop. The man from the SUV held the remote that controlled the winch in his left hand, stepped into the other loop on the other side of the cable and, once they were set, started unwinding it slowly. The winch motor did it without hesitation, their combined weight nothing compared to what it was designed to do—pull the full weight of a vehicle the size of the SUV it was attached to. He wouldn't be surprised if this guy was smart enough to have it powered by its own battery instead of using the vehicle's; he had the look of a man who thought of just about everything. The kind who would be a help rather than a hindrance when dealing with the chaos Brady's beloved mountains could throw at you.

And a man who obviously loved the woman with him, telling her to stay clear in case the worst happened and the car they were trying to get to went down hard and fast and took theirs with it.

He swore silently at his first clear look at the car below. It was perched dangerously on a snow-covered ledge and looked ready to slide the rest of the way—an almost certainly fatal hundred feet straight down—at the slightest breath of encouragement. The guardrail had likely slowed the descent, but that made the current situation no less precarious.

"Well, this'll be interesting," his new, temporary partner murmured.

"As long as it doesn't turn into a thrill ride," Brady said with a wry grimace, but he gave the man a nod in acknowledgment of his cool. He'd sounded not rattled at all, but just what he'd said—interested.

In the next instant, Brady saw movement in the car below. So somebody who took this sleigh ride was still alive.

"Don't move!" he yelled downward, and the figure froze. But the car shifted, just slightly, the front end now tilting slightly downward.

"It'll go that way if it goes," the man just above him on the cable said.

"Agreed. I don't think we can risk trying to get it hooked onto the frame, though. Could dislodge everything."

"Bumper, then. Front or back?"

Brady looked back at the precariously perched car. "Front, I think. If we use the back, it'll hit with both weight and momentum. Bumper might not hold. Front might not hold, either, but may give us a couple of seconds more."

"Agreed," the man said, echoing him. Then he looked from the vehicle to the shadowy figure inside it. Looked at Brady again. "Your scene, your call."

Brady nodded. "Hook it while I check the doors. Then I'll see if I can get the driver out."

He dropped off the cable just above the vehicle and did it slowly and with exquisite care. The last thing he wanted was to send the thing sliding the rest of the way by dislodging whatever was holding it under the snow. His new partner edged just as carefully toward the front of the car and lowered himself very slowly.

Some part of his mind noted he could see the left front tire, because the wheel was oddly angled, but he was more focused on how the passenger side of the car was badly bent. The question was had that tweaked the frame so much the driver's door wouldn't open? It looked only slightly bent from here, but that might be enough. And trying to yank free a jammed door would likely send the thing down the mountain.

He inched a little closer. Got to where he could see inside, could see the driver. A woman. Wearing a green puffy jacket and with dark hair pulled back. She was at an angle, braced against the center console. He saw the loose end of a seat belt that had obviously been cut free. So he wasn't dealing with a nonfunctional, paralyzed-with-fear person—she'd thought to do that and was apparently prepared enough to have the means to do it. She was shivering, from either cold or nerves or both. He didn't blame her; she was in a hell of a spot.

Then she seemed to realize he was right there, because she turned her head. And looked at him with a pair of eyes that were the most vivid green he had ever seen in his life. Maybe except for his mom's cat, they were nearly that green.

He gave himself an inward shake. This was no time to get distracted. Those eyes were amazing, but they were also full of terrified understanding of how close she was to death.

"We'll get you out," he promised and hoped fate didn't make a liar out of him.

She frowned, as if she wasn't sure what he'd said. He pointed at the window with a questioning look. She got there quickly, but moved slowly—so she wasn't stupid, either—to try to lower it. It went about an inch and jammed, no doubt against the bend in the door. But at least they could hear each other now.

"Are you hurt?"

"A little. Not bad." Her voice was low and remarkably steady, considering.

"What's your name?" he asked.

"Ashley. Ashley Jordan."

"Ashley, we're going to get you out of there," he said again. The moment he did, the car shifted again, slid another couple of inches, but stopped sharply. He glanced over and saw his partner backing away from the front end. The man gave him a thumbs-up to indicate the cable was attached.

"Okay," he told the woman, "we've got a cable attached, so you won't slide the rest of the way." *Optimism is not always your friend.* But it worked—she looked a little relieved.

The man from the SUV worked his way closer, but not too close. In fact, he stopped right where Brady would have, making sure his weight didn't disturb the same section of snow Brady and the car were on.

"Think it'll pry?" the man asked.

"Judging by the way the window jammed, no."

"The window, then?"

"Think it'll have to be. And," he added, looking at the even more precarious position now, "it'll have to be quick."

"Good thing you brought the rope, then. You have a tool?"

Brady nodded. He appreciated the matter-of-fact tone. It confirmed his guess that whoever this guy was, he was the kind you wanted around.

He quickly explained to the green-eyed woman what

they were going to do. Her eyes widened, and she swallowed visibly, but she said steadily enough, "All right."

He gave her a quick, reassuring smile. Then he tied a bowline knot in the end of the rope as he tossed the other end to his temporary partner. Somehow he knew he didn't even have to suggest how to tie it off on the cable for insurance; the guy would know. And he approved when he saw him tie it to one of the foot loops, so the rope wouldn't slide down any farther down the cable if the car shifted again.

"We're going to have to break the window. Move as little as possible, but take your jacket off, put this—" he passed the loop through the window gap "—around you below your arms, put your jacket over your head and shoulders to keep the glass off, then grab the rope."

She didn't speak but quickly did as he'd said. If everyone was this cool, his life would be a lot easier.

"We're going to have to pull you out really fast, so push off with your feet if you can, then just hang on."

"All right." It was muffled by the jacket but clear enough. And still steady, even though she couldn't see a thing. Maybe that helped.

He glanced at the other man, who nodded. He reached into his pocket and pulled out his key ring with the rescue tool on it next to the unit key. He pushed the bolt against the lower left corner of the window and pressed. The bolt shot out, and there was a crack. A small hole appeared, and a split second later, the safety glass shattered.

He tried to get the glass out in a hurry without moving the car and upsetting the delicate balance. He cleared as much as he could before he heard an ominous creak.

"On three," he said, loud enough for the SUV guy to hear.

"Copy" was all he said as he positioned himself to help pull the rope.

"I'm ready," the woman said.

Brady counted down, hoping his last glimpse of those amazing eyes wouldn't be just that—his last.

"Three!"

He pulled, hard. Felt the rope go and stay taut behind him. She moved, and he could feel she'd managed to get some leverage. He went hand over hand on the lead of the rope twice, then was able to get both hands on the loop. He pulled. Felt the strain but kept pulling. He could see her hands, white-knuckled, slender, looking too fragile for this kind of task.

Death grip.

Like hell, he answered that voice in his mind. And put everything he had into the next pull.

Things happened almost simultaneously, the margin between them as slim as the margin between life and death. He was able to reach her arms. Felt the snow slip a little beneath his feet. Heard another creak from the car. Heard the other man's shouted warning. Grabbed her under the arms. Half pulled, half leaned back, using his body mass to move them both.

His feet went. He hit the ground. But he held on. She came down on top of him, a slight weight.

And in that instant, the car went, sliding clear of the bent tree that had been barely holding it. It swung on the end of the cable, slamming into some rocks. There was a loud creak. Then the wrenching squeal of overstressed metal. His racing brain registered they would have had those couple of seconds, but nothing more.

The bumper ripped free, and the car hurtled down the side of the mountain.

Chapter 2

Ashley shuddered at the sounds. She didn't need to see to know what had happened. How close she had come.

She clung to the man holding her. Pressed to his chest, she could hear his heartbeat, slowing now. Could feel the also-slowing rise of his breathing. Crazily, she found herself wondering about the kind of man who chose to wear a badge in this mountain place and thought if he was a typical example, then they were in good hands.

She felt her jacket move, realized he was pulling it off her. She almost regretted it and had to smother a longing to stay in the quiet, warm cocoon of his arms.

"It's okay. It's over." His voice was low, a little rough and incredibly reassuring.

"I know," she whispered, her head still resting on his broad chest. For a moment, just a moment, his arms tightened, and she felt safer than she ever had in her life since her father had died.

It took every bit of internal nerve she had to move. She realized belatedly she was draped on top of him like a lover. The thought shot the heat of embarrassment— at least she thought it was embarrassment—through her.

"I'm sorry," she said quickly, trying to sit up.

"Whoa," he said quietly. "If you move too fast, we both may end up down there with your car." Then, in a wry tone, he added, "And if you move that knee another inch, I'm going to regret it."

When she realized what he meant, that the knee she had tried to use to get upright was pressing against a very intimate part of him, renewed heat flooded her. She couldn't think of a thing to say, so she said nothing as he helped her get off him.

And a moment later, the second man spoke from her right.

"I've still got the rope, so you won't fall. You okay, Crenshaw?"

"I'm good. Get her clear."

The other man—who looked as big and powerful as the deputy who'd saved her life—simply nodded. He spoke into a phone in his hand, telling someone above they were all right, then put it in a pocket and turned back to her. "Keep your hands on the rope. I'll pull, you just get your feet moving."

She glanced back at the deputy—it was B. Crenshaw she now saw embroidered on the shirt of his dark green uniform—who was slowly, carefully getting to his feet. He was bleeding from a cut across one cheek and didn't seem aware of it. "I'll be right behind you if you slip," he said, nodding at her.

She wanted to ask who would help him if he slipped but didn't think it wise to venture the possibility at this moment. Besides, if ever a man had the look of someone who could take care of himself, this one did. He wasn't just tall and obviously strong, he exuded competence and confidence. She could sense he was a man who knew his job and did it. A man who didn't quit when the going got tough.

He was also strikingly handsome.

The moment she thought this, she chided herself fiercely. *Don't be an idiot female. This is not the time to swoon like some love-struck teenager.*

Besides, her life was a big enough mess already. A man like this would likely have little patience with a basket case such as she was right now. And she couldn't blame him.

She concentrated on putting one foot in front of the other until she got to the other man. Looked at him, realizing this would be that teenager's dream come true—two big, hunky guys saving her.

He'd freed the ripped-off front bumper from the end of the metal cable, and once she had a grip on the cable, helped her free herself from the loop of rope. By then her rescuer was there, and she had to resist the urge to ask him to hold her again. She supposed he got a lot of that if he went around saving people like this often.

Then he almost did just that. He slipped an arm around her, at least, startling her into wondering if she'd asked him without realizing it. Dear God, was she that far gone? Had her grip on reality slipped that much? She shivered, and he tightened his hold.

"Just a little longer," he said. "We'll get you up top and on solid ground, and you'll feel better."

She didn't doubt that was true, but it would take a lot more than just solid physical ground to make her feel one hundred percent. There were times when she wondered if she would ever feel whole again, physically or mentally.

He put a foot in a loop that hung off the cable, then guided her to put her foot on top of his.

"I'll hang on to the cable, and you hang on to me."

Nothing I'd rather do.

She managed not to say it, thought about saying, "Yes, sir," but decided another nod was her safest bet. But when she slid her arms around him, and he put his free arm around her to hold her close to him, she couldn't seem to stop herself from thinking how long it had been since she'd been this close to a man. Especially one who looked like this one.

But when the second man stepped into the other loop on the cable, she couldn't help asking, "It will hold us all?"

"It's rated to pull a nine-thousand-pound vehicle," the man said reassuringly. When he clicked a button on what looked like some kind of control he held, and after an initial jerk as the cable tightened, they rose steadily. Dimly, the moment the cable began to move, she heard a dog barking from above. She clung to Deputy Crenshaw tighter, and his arm tightened around her as if to let her know he had her.

And as they went, she wondered how her quiet, calm life had turned into such never-ending chaos.

She seemed to be moving all right, Brady thought as they got to the top and he helped her scramble over the edge. As they'd gone up, he'd noticed a little bleeding from a cut on one hand, and a little more that could have come from a cut on her forehead or have been wiped there by that hand. Now he took a better look at her, ignoring the rather nice feminine curves as he stuck to business. He certainly hadn't seen any indication of broken bones, but if it wasn't a limb, she might not even be aware yet. When the fear and adrenaline wore off, she might go down like a broken puppet.

"You'd better sit down," he said, pulling open the door

to his SUV. She didn't argue but sat on the sideboard, so he gave her points for common sense on that front at least. "Any place hurt more than the rest?" It took her a moment, but he was familiar with the confused thoughts after a crisis. Then she shook her head, albeit slowly.

He was aware of the two people approaching, although he didn't look away from her. The dog that had been in the car was with them; he caught a glimpse of a dark head with alert ears out of the corner of his eye.

Even as he registered it, the dog came forward, not rushing, but clearly intent on getting to her. He almost moved to stop the animal, but his owner arrived beside him and said quietly, "It's all right. He'll be good for her."

He glanced at the man who had, without hesitation or the requirement of duty, risked himself to help. After a moment, he nodded. And watched as the couple's dog came to a halt a foot away from… Ashley, he remembered. She looked at the dog and, slowly, smiled. He was a beautiful animal with his black head and shoulders turning to a reddish brown from the shoulders back. His coat looked thick and soft, and his tail, up and wagging gently as if to signal no ill intent, was full.

"Hi," she said, her voice sounding a little steadier. The wag increased, and the dog stepped forward. He sat down close to her and gently lowered his chin to her knee in obvious invitation. She lifted the nonbloody hand and laid it on the dog's head. Her left, he noticed. She must have hurt the right freeing herself, so he went with right-handed. Not that it mattered, but it was just a matter of course that he observed.

The change that came over her the moment she began to pet the dog was nothing short of remarkable. The confusion left her eyes, she straightened and then she was smiling.

"Wow," he muttered.

"Our little miracle worker," the other woman said, and he turned to look at them both.

"Quinn and Hayley Foxworth," the man said, holding out a hand, adding with a grin, "Better late than never."

As they shook hands, the man's grip strong but with nothing to prove, Brady locked down his certainty that this was a man you could trust. "Brady Crenshaw," he said. His wife's handshake was gentler, but firm, and he had the feeling that she was a power in her own right, in her own way.

He was used to—and good at—making quick assessments. It was a necessity of the job. And the words that came to him about these two were *solid, steady, smart, caring*...and *together*. With a capital *T*.

He felt a jab of...something. Envy? Maybe. His one try at that kind of relationship had ended badly, on several fronts. He wouldn't say he'd given up, but he wasn't looking, either. Because he'd pretty much decided that what the Foxworths had wasn't in the cards for him.

Which right now, looking at them, made him feel pretty damned gloomy.

Chapter 3

"He's wonderful," Ashley said, still stroking the dog's head.

"We think so," Hayley Foxworth said with a warm smile that made Brady like her even more.

He turned back to Ashley. "Ribs okay?" he asked her. "Collarbone? Sometimes seat belts can do a number on you while they're saving your life."

She quickly touched the clavicle on both sides of her slender throat. His fingers curled oddly, and he had to stomp down the wish that he'd checked her himself. Then she tentatively reached down and ran a hand—her right, so it wasn't incapacitated—over one side of her rib cage, then the other.

"Fine," she said. "It'll bruise, I imagine, but I don't think anything's cracked and definitely not broken."

"Where were you headed?"

"Over to Snowridge. To pick something up for my mother."

Perfectly coherent. And it fit; the crash had happened just a quarter mile from the turnoff to the ski town. Another good sign. He pulled his small flashlight off his belt.

"Look at me," he said.

She did, and he saw the stark white of her face was giving way to more normal coloring. She was pulling out of it, both quickly and relatively soon, considering. Her eyes were genuinely amazing. In fact, she was pretty darn lovely all around. But he'd better shove that right on out of his head. Back to business.

He checked her pupils, found them equal and reactive. She tracked his finger when he asked, up, down and sideways, and gave him her name again, her age—twenty-eight, four years younger than he was—and the date, and she knew where they were. It was enough that anything more could wait for the paramedics, anyway.

"Help is on the way," he said. "Medics can look you over and be sure there's nothing hiding. What about your hand?"

She looked at it. "I scraped it on something, I think, getting out."

"Sorry," he said.

"Sorry?" she said, staring up at him. "What on earth for? If you hadn't done what you did, risked your life like that, I'd be down there with the car, and I doubt I'd be walking away."

The impassioned words took him by surprise, but he couldn't deny they pleased him. Also embarrassed him a little. He didn't do this job for accolades, although when they came, he didn't belittle the person's experience by saying it was nothing, either.

"And the übercalm demeanor was just what I needed," she added, with a smile that made him smile back. "You've got that down, Deputy Crenshaw. Thank you."

He supposed this wasn't the time to mention how he'd wondered what would happen if the car went before they got clear or if the cable snapped and took them out like a blunt broadsword.

"Can't argue with her assessment," Quinn Foxworth said. "That was some nice work."

"It wouldn't have gone so well without your help," Brady said, meaning it.

Hayley walked over and sat beside Ashley, putting a gentle hand on her arm and smiling reassuringly. Brady took the chance to walk back to the edge and look down. He could still see the car, upside down now, at the bottom of the slope. He shook his head at the near escape, then walked back over to the woman who had taken that hair-raising ride.

"Where do you live?" he asked her.

"In Hemlock," she said. "With my mother, temporarily. Nan Alexander."

Brady blinked, then groaned inwardly. This was a headache he didn't need.

"What happened?" he asked, rather bluntly.

"The back end just slid on the curve. I didn't see any ice, but there was a layer of fresh snow. Not much, though."

That matched what he'd seen. And it was a front-wheel-drive car, so if it was going to lose traction, it made sense that it would be the rear.

"I don't understand," Ashley said, still stroking the Foxworth dog—Cutter, Quinn had said. "I checked the road reports between home and Snowridge. They said snow tires would be enough."

"They would be, if you had them," Brady said, trying to keep his tone neutral. She might be very attractive, but he'd been at this long enough to find lack of common sense unappealing.

"But...the car does have them. They were put on yesterday."

Brady frowned. Remembered the tire he'd seen and was nearly certain. In the same moment, he sensed Quinn go still. Glanced at the other man, who gave a slight shake of his head. So he hadn't seen snow tires, either.

"I think your other help is approaching," Hayley said, looking down the road.

Instinctively Brady glanced at his watch. "Only twenty-three minutes. That's light speed around here." He shifted his gaze back to Ashley. "They'll take good care of you."

He reached into the front seat for his binoculars, then walked back over to the edge again. He focused them on the car just as Quinn came up beside him. He could see the tires clearly, and there was not only no sign of studs marking them as snow tires or the distinctively more aggressive tread pattern of an unstudded snow tire—in fact they were getting a little short on actual tread.

Silently, he handed the binoculars to Quinn. He took a look, lowered them and with a glance at Brady shook his head.

"'Put on yesterday' is pretty specific," he said.

"Yes." Brady used the binoculars again, this time tracing the marks in the snow the car had left on its way down.

"Ideas?" Quinn asked.

"Wondering if somebody in Hemlock ripped her off. Which would tick me off something fierce. She could have died. But...that makes no sense. Nobody would."

"No town's perfect," Quinn said, his tone neutral.

Brady held the other man's gaze and answered what he hadn't said. "Not saying it is. And although we service Hemlock, I don't live there. But..." He hesitated, then decided after what he'd done today the man could be trusted with the truth. "I realized who she is."

Quinn raised an eyebrow. "Realized? Meaning you know of her, but not her?"

"Exactly." He let out a compressed breath. "She's the mayor's daughter."

Quinn went oddly still for a moment before he asked, very quietly, "Connection, you think?"

Brady liked the way he asked it, as if without even really knowing him he would accept the answer as valid. Truth be told, he simply liked this guy. "All I know for sure is her mother's a...politician. And," he added sourly, "she's fairly tight with my boss."

Quinn held his gaze steadily. "And is your boss a cop first or a politician?"

Yes, he liked the guy. "That you know to ask that means I don't really have to answer, right?"

"My sympathies, Deputy Crenshaw. But it could be worse. At least you don't have to go into town and tell the mayor her daughter's dead."

"There is that," Brady agreed.

"Maybe she'll hang a medal on you."

"No, thanks," he said. "On general principle, I'm much happier when she doesn't even recognize me."

Quinn laughed, and it was full of such understanding that Brady found himself wondering who, exactly, this guy was and what he did.

The lead paramedic finished bandaging Ashley's right hand just as Quinn Foxworth's laugh drew her gaze, and for a moment Ashley just looked at the two men. Something about the sight of them, the sound of that laugh and the deputy's smile, did something odd to her.

"He's got a great laugh, my Quinn does," Hayley said softly.

"He does," she agreed.

"And your rescuer has a great smile."

"He does," she repeated, but although the words were the same, they felt different; there was a little catch in her throat as she said them. Two men cut from the same cloth, there was no question.

"Two of a kind," Hayley said, agreeing with what Ashley hadn't even spoken aloud. "And that's not something I say lightly."

"Deputy Crenshaw," the woman in the county EMS uniform said, "is a peach. The best kind of cop, and a good man besides. If I wasn't madly in love with my husband, he'd be at the top of my list."

Ashley smothered a sigh. It wasn't that she couldn't look at Deputy Crenshaw and see and sense all of that was true, it was the way the woman spoke of her husband that made her ache a little inside. Just as Hayley simply saying that about "her" Quinn's laugh had.

Once, her life was on track to reach that treasured goal, a connection with a man she adored. But now she was in chaos, and Alan had abandoned her for someone closer to his ideal. Which was certainly not a woman who woke up screaming practically every night.

And so here she was, at twenty-eight, broken, broke and living with her mother.

"There you go," said the medic. "I think you'll be fine, but remember what I said about any headaches, dizziness, change in vision or numbness." Ashley nodded. "We'll transport you to the clinic—"

"No!" It came out a bit high-pitched, and she sucked in a breath. "I mean, I don't need to go there, do I?"

"Afraid it's policy. Normally Brady could just take you home, but once we've treated you… I mean, you can refuse, but it turns into a big deal, paperwork-wise, if you do. Not that I blame you. If I were you, I'd rather ride with

Brady, too," the woman added with a wide smile. "By the way, he has a weakness for brownies, if you decide you want to personally thank him for saving your life."

Ashley tried to match the smile but knew she failed. As if her mother would turn her loose in her kitchen. Once upon a time, she'd been a very good baker, but a kitchen fire that had almost gotten out of control had gotten her banned.

The Foxworth dog, Cutter, leaned into her again, as if he'd sensed the despair that threatened. She'd never thought of herself as a stupid or weak person, but in the last six months, her self-perception had been shaken to the core. And she couldn't blame her mother for not wanting to take any chances, not when she continued to do such brainless things.

She reached out to once more stroke the soft, dark fur. And once more, an odd sense of calm crept over her. Looking into the animal's amber-flecked dark eyes, she had the oddest feeling that somehow, some way, everything would turn out all right.

Which was far too much to ask of a dog.

As the medics packed away their gear, her rescuer—"her hero" sounded too much like bad dialogue—came back and crouched in front of her. He reached out to pet the dog, instinctively, it seemed. There was a dog, he should be petted. The thought made her smile inwardly. *A peach indeed.*

Hayley stood up and walked over to slip an arm around her husband as he came back from wherever he and the deputy had gone. But Ashley was focused on the man before her. Which was far from a hardship.

"You said there were snow tires on the car," he said quietly. She nodded. "Did you look at them?"

Her brow furrowed. "No. I mean, I knew they'd been installed, so I didn't bother."

"But…you heard the sound of them?"

"I…didn't really. I was playing music and didn't notice."

"Ashley," he began, and she was too busy realizing how much she liked the sound of her name when he said it for it to register immediately that he was uncomfortable with what he was about to say.

"What?"

When he answered his voice was exquisitely gentle. "There are no snow tires."

She blinked. "What?"

He gestured at the binoculars he'd set down at his side. "Quinn and I both looked. Not only are they not snow tires, but even as regular tires, they aren't in the best shape."

She stared at him. For all their gentleness, his words hit her like a bludgeon.

She'd been having a rough time, she knew that. Ever since the nightmares had started months ago, she'd been off balance. Then they had gotten so bad she was afraid to sleep and spent most nights sitting up in a chair. She had chalked up her lapses in memory to exhaustion, but they had steadily worsened until her mother had insisted she move in with her so she could look out for her. The dreams hadn't improved, but at least she'd felt safer.

Until now.

Now she was face-to-face with reality.

It was true. It was really true.

She was going insane.

Just like her father.

Chapter 4

Brady didn't think he had ever seen a more devastated pair of eyes. The vividness of the green faded just as the color she'd regained in her face did. In mere moments she seemed a pale shadow of herself. She moved, reaching out, and he reacted instinctively, only stopping himself from grabbing her when he realized she was reaching for the dog.

She hugged the animal rather fiercely. Cutter let out a small, low sound that was half whine, half growl. But he didn't move, and there was no aggressiveness in his demeanor, so Brady just kept an eye on him.

Eventually the dog stood, and Ashley's arms slipped back to her side. She was trembling slightly, shaking her head as if in denial. Or exhaustion, he thought as he looked again at her eyes. They were bright, but not in color as they had been. It was the gleam of tears, which made his stomach knot. He was no good with crying women. Hadn't Liz proved that to him?

But the change in this woman, after she'd faced death with such calm and nerve, was really getting to him.

Then Cutter turned and sat at Ashley's feet. The dog looked up at Quinn and Hayley, standing a couple of feet back. No, not just looked. He was staring. Fixedly. Pointedly?

"Yeah," Quinn muttered. "I figured."

"You already knew?" Hayley asked, which made no sense to Brady.

But right now he wasn't thinking about the couple or their dog. He was trying to figure out what he was going to do about the fact that he never, ever got involved in the cases he came across, he always stayed a step back, but… Ashley Jordan was breaking his heart.

He would bet his badge that she'd been completely convinced the car she was driving had snow tires, so much so that she hadn't even looked. And if she hadn't lived here long, if she wasn't a mountain resident, he supposed she should get some credit for even knowing about snow tires. But that didn't explain much.

"Who put the tires on for you?"

"I don't know." Her voice sounded as dull as she had suddenly become. He drew back slightly.

"Ashley," he prompted gently, "I need some answers here."

She appeared to make an effort, but the gutsy, steady woman he'd pulled out of that car was nowhere in sight now. "It's my mother's car. She had them installed yesterday. She told me this morning before she left for her office."

She said it as if reading dry, emotionless words off a page. As the meaning registered, he groaned inwardly.

Great. Now he was going to have to deal with Mayor Alexander directly and personally to get to the bottom of this. So much for his until-now successful effort at flying under the woman's radar.

"Why did you keep going after the car started to slip back there on the bridge?" She blinked, giving him a puzzled look. "I was behind you on the road," he explained. "Since the falls."

And he hadn't seen anything to bother him about the way she was driving for a couple of miles, but there had been a small patch of black ice on the bridge over the creek, and the way the rear end had slipped just slightly had gotten his attention.

"I noticed it, so I slowed down a little more, but when it didn't happen again, I thought it was just because of the bridge."

So she knew that was a common problem, that black ice developed on bridges. What had at first seemed like a straightforward conclusion of driver ignorance was getting more than a little cloudy. He should have known the minute he realized who she was that this wasn't going to be that simple.

The dog made a low sound, a sort of half whine, half rumble. It pulled Brady out of his inner whining, and he stood up.

She had to tilt her head back to look up at him. "Still no dizziness, even with your head like that?" he asked.

"No, none. What…happens now?"

"They'll get you to the clinic, and you can call your mother to come get you, since it doesn't look like you'll need to stay." He didn't think he mistook her wince at the mention of her mother. "She going to be upset about the car?"

"Yes," Ashley said with a sigh. "But then she'll be impossibly kind and understanding."

Not words he would have applied to the status-conscious Mayor Alexander, but he was glad to hear that apparently her daughter got different treatment. That, at least, was as it should be.

He looked over his shoulder to where the medic's van was parked. "Whenever you're ready, she can go," he called out.

"What about you?" she asked, startling him.

Not sure what she was asking, he said, "I need some photos before the tow truck hauls the car up. You'll probably need a copy of the report for insurance, so barring anything else coming up, I'll get that done ASAP."

"I meant your injury."

He blinked. "What?"

"The scrape on your cheek."

He flexed facial muscles, felt the slight sting on the left. He hadn't even realized until she said it, but now a vague memory of dodging a jutting boulder on the way up came back to him. He'd been so busy holding on to her—and carefully not noticing how she felt in his arms—that he'd quickly forgotten.

"It's nothing. I'll deal with it later."

She visibly drew in a long breath. "Then I suppose… all that's left is to thank you. Again."

He smiled at her. "You're welcome. You take care. And take it easy for a few days. You'll probably be really sore after tomorrow."

He watched the medic van—with Ashley thankfully sitting in it, not needing the gurney—carefully negotiate the snow at the edge of the roadway and maneuver back onto the road, heading back toward Hemlock. The Foxworth dog was not happy at her departure and made it known with a series of protesting whines.

"They'll take good care of her, boy," Brady said instinctively. Then, when Quinn and Hayley came up beside him, he asked, "Does he always get attached to people that quickly?"

The couple exchanged another one of those looks he'd seen—and envied a little—from really close couples before. Then Quinn shifted his gaze to Brady. "You've got to wait for the tow truck, right?"

"Yeah," Brady said, puzzled.

Quinn gave him a wry smile. "Then we have time to explain."

"Explain?"

"About Cutter. And the Foxworth Foundation."

Brady drew back slightly. "The Foxworth Foundation? You're those Foxworths?"

"Guilty," Quinn said, sounding cheerful.

"Wait… Quinn Foxworth." It should have hit him before. Must have been the adrenaline surge of the rescue. "You're the guy who took down that cop killer, the case that just blew up all over again last month."

"That would be him," Hayley said, and there was no denying the pride in the woman's voice.

"I looked you guys up when all that hit. The Foxworth Foundation, I mean. Or tried to. You're pretty low profile."

"We work mainly by word of mouth and…a fairly new case finder," Quinn said.

"So you really do…that? Help people with problems no one else can or will?"

"People with a problem we believe in, yes," Quinn said. "Which brings us to Ashley Jordan."

Brady blinked. "Why?"

"First," Hayley said, "we have to explain—and you have to believe us—about Cutter."

The tale they told him then was, obviously, unbelievable. A dog who sensed people in trouble, he could buy that, it didn't seem much farther out there than trained dogs who could sense illness, or impending seizures, or simply pets who knew when their owners were worried or upset and tried to comfort. But what they were telling him went way beyond that. This was a dog sensing not physical things, but things he had no way of knowing or understanding. And that the animal had various ways of letting them know, and his sitting staring at them—and his vocal unhappiness when Ashley had been carted away—were definitely two of them.

"We know how it sounds," Hayley said.

"And nobody was a harder sell than me," Quinn added. "But his record stands. Sixteen months of cases now, and he's never steered us wrong."

Brady had the feeling there was more, something they weren't saying, but they probably realized he'd reached the limits of logical acceptance here. Actually, he had gone a little past those limits. But it was clear they completely believed what they were saying. And what he'd learned about Foxworth from his own sources added up to a stellar reputation. The only people who had anything bad to say about them were usually crooks, or even killers, who bitched from the wrong side of the bars of a cell.

Then, belatedly, it hit him.

"Wait…you're saying when the dog sat there like that, in front of her, staring at you two…that was a signal?"

"It was." Hayley this time. "That's his 'fix it' look."

"Meaning…?"

"She has a problem," Quinn said, deadpan.

Brady looked toward the skid marks and the crumpled guardrail. "Ya think?" he said dryly.

Quinn didn't take offense—in fact, he smiled. "This is where it gets really strange."

"I think we passed that a while ago."

Quinn kept smiling, supremely unruffled. Brady had the feeling he'd been through this before. Perhaps often. Definitely often, if what he'd said about multiple cases was true.

"To clarify, she has a problem Foxworth can help with."

He knew he was gaping at them now, but he couldn't help it. "You're saying your dog can not only tell when someone has a problem, but when it's a problem you can fix?"

"Pretty much."

He turned to look at the dog in question. Who sat watching him as if he somehow knew Brady was the one they were trying to convince. Watching him with those dark, gold-flecked eyes in a way that made him think of animals controlling huge flocks of sheep with the simple power of their gaze.

Now you're off the deep end, Crenshaw.

"But," Hayley said after a moment when he tried to stare down the dog and lost, "that doesn't really matter yet. If nothing else, I get the feeling dealing with her mother the mayor isn't something you're looking forward to. Foxworth can help with that. We've got a bit of a record with politicians."

The rest of what he'd heard and read about them came back to him in a rush. Including the departure in shame of a governor he'd never liked or trusted in the first place.

"Small-town mayor's a bit below your weight class, isn't it?" he asked.

"That's the best part of being Foxworth and independent. We decide who we help instead of having it decided for us."

He smiled at that. But shook his head. "Look, I appreciate it, but she's just a pain, not crooked. She wants to make Hemlock a utopia."

"Utopia tends to be expensive," Quinn said dryly.

"Yeah. And Hemlock's just a typical, decent small town. Nothing big enough to get you guys involved."

"We already are," Hayley said, nodding at their dog.

Brady's brow furrowed. "Let's put it this way," Quinn said. "He will give us no peace until we help."

Brady shook his head again, but this time wonderingly. He just couldn't reconcile this man with being controlled by a dog.

He heard the rumble of a truck coming down the road, glanced up and saw the heavy-duty tow truck approaching.

"Aren't you curious about the whole tire thing?" Quinn asked.

"Of course. I'm going to dig into that," he said, feeling a tiny bit affronted that they'd think he wouldn't. But they didn't know him, any more than he really knew them. It was all first impressions, and as good as he was at that, he wasn't perfect.

"I guessed you would," Quinn said, and the sting faded. "But I'm also guessing your department's stretched a little thin, maybe, and you don't have a lot of time for such things once the initial reports are done. We have resources at your disposal. And we can, perhaps, keep the mayor at bay if you end up treading on her toes."

That alone made it the most tempting offer he'd had in a while.

"As soon as you're done here, why don't we go to the clinic and check on Ashley?" Hayley said. "Then we'll go—or not—from there."

That couldn't hurt, could it? Besides, he'd always had a gut-level feeling that talking to any politician without witnesses was not a wise thing to do.

"All right," he finally said as the truck slowed and began to pull over.

Cutter barked. Short, sharp and sounding almost like he was indicating it was about time. Quinn saw his glance at the dog, and laughed.

"My friend, this is only the beginning."

Chapter 5

Brady was glad to see Ashley sitting in the waiting room when he and the Foxworths arrived at the small clinic in town. That she was already out here indicated they weren't going to hold her. She was signing a form one of the staff had apparently given her, since a woman in the clinic scrubs was standing next to her with a clipboard.

She stood up as the woman left, and he noted she did it easily, albeit carefully. Her forehead was furrowed, though, as if she was still upset. Understandable. Whatever the story was behind the snow tire mix-up, she'd had a hell of a ride.

Then she looked up and spotted them. The smile that crossed her face then did crazy things to his pulse. Which made no sense. She was just another citizen he'd helped—there was no reason for her to have that kind of effect.

"I didn't expect to see you here," she said when they reached her, and Brady didn't think he imagined she was focused on him, although she'd nodded at the Foxworths, as well.

"Just following up," he said in his most professional tone. "They cut you loose?"

"Yes. I'm fine. My mother is on the way. They said I should rest and take these—" she held up a small bottle with some pills "—for the soreness that will be coming."

"Do it," he recommended. "It's a lot easier to stay ahead of the pain than to knock it down once it gets a foothold."

She gave him another of those smiles. And it had the same effect, damn it. "Voice of experience?"

"Yes."

A large knot of people came through the glass doors, and all of them seemed to be talking—loudly—at once.

"I think I'd rather wait outside," she said.

"My feelings about any medical facility," he said, and when that smile came yet again, he couldn't help smiling back.

"Now," Hayley said when they were outside and she and Ashley had taken seats on the bench in the shelter of the portico, "is there anything you need at home? Do you have food that will be easy to fix for the next couple of days? Is there a place that delivers?"

"Benny's," she and Brady said at the same instant. And they both laughed. She looked a little startled, as if she were surprised she was able to laugh.

"I'll be fine. My mother will help. And—" She stopped, turning her head slightly. He'd heard the same thing she had: the insistent barking of a dog.

"That," Quinn said, "will be Cutter. He'll need to see for himself that you're all right."

Ashley laughed again. And again seem surprised by it. Whatever had turned her ashen back on the road was obviously still eating at her.

Quinn pulled out his keys and hit a button on the fob. The barking stopped. Seconds later Cutter was racing toward them. He must have raised the back, Brady realized.

The dog ignored his people and came to a halt in front of Ashley. He gave a low whine that managed to sound worried. "Oh, you sweet boy," she crooned, leaning over as she reached to pet him. The moment she stroked the dark fur, her forehead smoothed out, as if whatever it was had receded, at least for the moment. Crazy, the effect the animal had. Petting any dog always made him feel better, but not to this extreme.

She looked up then and seemed almost normal again. At least, as normal as anyone could be after having been through what she had today. "Thank you all for coming. I feel so much better."

Brady believed her, but *better* didn't mean well, and there were still dark, ugly shadows in those green eyes. The whole snow tire thing had hit her hard, and that made him angry. If somebody here in town had ripped her mother off, telling her they'd installed snow tires when they hadn't, then they'd be getting a visit from him. But he couldn't imagine anyone in Hemlock being stupid enough to try a stunt like that on the mayor, of all people.

A car in a hurry pulled in under the portico and stopped in a red zone.

"She's here," Ashley said just as Brady recognized the woman behind the wheel. He supposed she could be forgiven the parking, given the circumstances. Oddly, he remembered something about her wanting a car and driver but having to forgo it for budget reasons. She must have borrowed this car, since hers was sitting at the tow yard on the other side of town.

Mayor Alexander got out as soon as the car stopped. She

was average height, slim, with jaw-length dark hair. Determinedly dark, he'd heard one of their dispatchers say once.

Ashley stood up. And in the same instant, the Foxworths' dog got to his feet. The animal was staring at the woman approaching. And then his head went down, his hackles went up and a low growl issued from his throat. And he moved slightly to stand between Ashley and her mother.

"Well, well," Brady heard Quinn murmur, almost under his breath.

"Interesting," Hayley seemed to agree.

"It's all right, Cutter, it's my mother," Ashley said. Brady thought it said a lot about her that she wanted to soothe the dog after everything she'd been through.

But the dog didn't appear soothed, and the low, warning growl continued. Then the dog looked up at his people.

"We got it, boy," Quinn said to him. "Stand down. For now."

The dog quieted. Sat. As if he'd understood perfectly. But he kept those dark eyes on the woman nearing them now. What the hell was that about?

He backed away as the mayor approached, giving the woman a chance to assure herself that her daughter was all right. Ms. Alexander gave the dog a wary look, although he was still sitting immobile. But then she turned to Ashley and enveloped her in a clearly heartfelt hug.

The two had a muted conversation, out of which Brady could only hear phrases. "…so worried…you were just confused…don't worry…the car…you could have died."

And a moment later Ashley was pointing to him.

"This is Deputy Crenshaw, Mother. He and Mr. Foxworth—" she gestured at Quinn "—saved my life."

The woman frowned for an instant, but it vanished quickly. "I owe you both a debt of gratitude."

"My job, ma'am," Brady said.

"Yes. Well." She glanced at Quinn, and the frown reappeared for an instant. But then she waved Brady to one side, asking to speak to him privately.

"What actually happened, Deputy Crenshaw?"

He gave her what would be a matter of public record anyway and kept his speculation to himself.

"But...where was this?"

"About three miles east on the highway, just before the Snowridge turnoff."

The woman looked mystified. "But she was only going to the market. Barely a block away."

He frowned. "She told me she was on her way to Snowridge to pick up something for you."

"She...did that two days ago." She gave a sharp shake of her head.

"Could she have gotten turned around? Easy to do if you're not familiar with the area."

The mayor shook her head again. "She grew up here."

Brady's brow furrowed as he tried to remember if he'd ever encountered Ashley Jordan before. Not that he remembered, but he would have graduated the local high school before she'd even started, so that wasn't surprising.

"Please, tell me how it happened."

But by the time he was finished, Ashley's mother was again shaking her head, slowly this time, and to his surprise, there was a sheen of moisture in her eyes. And he chided himself for forgetting this wasn't the mayor he was dealing with at the moment, it was Ashley's mother.

"I was praying this day would never come," she said, almost brokenly. "It's her father all over again."

"Her father?"

Ms. Alexander shook her head as if to clear it. "I must ask you to keep this confidential."

"Of course."

"Ashley…has been having trouble."

"Trouble?"

"Mentally. It started six months ago, but it's gotten worse. She was heading for a total breakdown."

"That's…extreme." And it did not compute, did not fit with what he'd seen today. Surely a woman who could deal so well with what had happened out there couldn't have such a tenuous hold on sanity?

"She lost her job," her mother was saying. "Then her apartment, because there were…incidents. A couple of small fires and water overflows, that kind of thing. She's become very forgetful."

Okay, that was pretty serious. "What was her job?"

"She was working at one of the resorts over in Snow-ridge." She gave him a sad smile. "A friend of mine is a partner there, but I couldn't ask him to keep her on when she made so many mistakes. I finally brought her here to live with me, so I could see to her safety." She shook her head again and sounded wrenchingly heartbroken. "She's seeing a psychiatrist, but there hasn't been much progress. If anything, it's all gotten worse, because she's developed anger issues."

"Anger at who?"

"The doctor. Me. Anyone trying to help her, actually."

This was sounding incredibly grim, but Brady was still having trouble reconciling all this with the woman he'd seen today.

"Tell me about the snow tires," he said abruptly.

Ms. Alexander blinked. "What?"

"Where did you have them installed?"

She frowned. "But… I haven't. Yet. That's why we agreed she would stay in town after the snow."

"Your daughter said it was done yesterday."

She stared at him. Then realization dawned in her eyes. Eyes that were, he noted, brown, far from Ashley's vivid green.

"Is that…what happened? She skidded because of no snow tires?"

"I think it was a large factor, yes. So whoever told you they'd installed them, they have some explaining to do. Tell me who it was…"

His voice trailed away as tears welled up and over now. *Great. Now you've got the mayor crying.*

"Clearly she's become a danger not only to herself now," she said, wiping at her eyes. "Deputy, I told her I planned to have snow tires put on, not that I already had. But she so often hears what she wants to hear. Or what she hears gets changed by the time it gets to her brain. The doctor has a technical word for it, but…"

He drew in a deep breath. Let go of his first perceptions of Ashley Jordan, since clearly they were wrong. Or perhaps it was only because of the high-stress situation that she'd reacted so calmly. Or maybe she was so mentally detached she hadn't realized what danger she was in. It was hard to believe, but obviously something was very wrong.

He watched them both, Ashley without at least any visible qualm, get into the car. They left at a much more sedate pace, her mother apparently calmer now that she knew her daughter was all right.

"Nan Alexander, went back to her maiden name after being widowed two decades ago, current age fifty-one, second term as mayor. That sound right?"

Brady blinked as Hayley Foxworth quoted all this to him from her phone as soon as the car with Ms. Alexander and her daughter were out of sight.

"I guess," he said as he fiddled with his keys. "She was on the city council when I started ten years ago. Didn't know about the name change, although I knew she was a widow." Something occurred to him. "Ashley's father?"

"Andrew Jordan." So she wasn't married. Not that it mattered. Or maybe she just followed her mother's lead and went back to her maiden name. Or never changed it. Or— "He committed suicide when Ashley was eight."

Damn. That sucked. "I didn't know that part, either," he muttered. No wonder her mother was so worried.

"Can screw a person up, I would think," Quinn said.

"Twenty years later?" he asked, rather rhetorically.

"Or maybe all along," Hayley said gently.

"There is that," Brady said. He couldn't share what her mother had told him in confidence, so he said only, "Her mother is concerned about her…state of mind."

"And the snow tires?" Quinn asked.

He could share that much, he supposed. "Mother says she only told her she was going to have them put on, not that she already had."

"Hmm. Could be a simple misunderstanding. Unless she makes a habit of it."

He didn't speak but saw that Quinn understood that was an answer in itself.

It was tragic, sad, poignant and several other things. What it was not was his business. Not any longer.

Chapter 6

Two days later, Brady cleared the scene of a reported vandalism—after convincing the resident that his neighbor putting snow from shoveling his walk in a pile that spilled over onto his property was not, by definition, vandalism—and gave the disposition to dispatch. The voice that came back held amusement, and Brady suspected she had known all along it was a nothing call. But in return he got cleared for lunch, and while he was conveniently here in town so he could grab something decent. And warm, like maybe a bowl of chili at Benny's.

On the way there, he passed the Hemlock city hall, a rather stark, modern building just a couple of blocks from the sheriff's office. And that made him wonder if the mayor was back at work or at home caring for her daughter. Alexander had never seemed the soft, mothering type to him, but what did he know? His own incredibly gentle, loving mother could turn into a wildcat if someone she loved was threatened. Maybe Mayor Alexander was just the opposite.

He made the turn off Mountain View and headed toward Benny's. He should call his mom; it had been nearly a week since he'd spoken to her. Although she was so busy these days—

His thoughts were derailed when he caught a glimpse of the tow yard down at the end of the street. He could see a silver sedan sitting just inside the gate, the driver's window missing.

How was she? She could be really hurting today. The second day after a jolt like that was often the worst.

He made a sudden, impulsive decision, even though he'd been reminding himself for forty-eight hours now this—she—was not his problem. Still, a follow-up couldn't hurt. It was just good PR, and Sheriff Carter was all about good PR. Not that they were in a place that needed it; these mountains generally—his complainant just now aside— bred a tough, hardy lot, and since they only called for help when they really needed it, they tended to respect it when it showed up.

He knew where the mayor's home was. They all knew, because if a call came in from there, it was immediately high priority. Such were the politics of public service. He wondered if perhaps they'd been called out there since Ashley had moved in and he just hadn't heard about it. He tended to tune out the gripes and complaints about such things, since whining didn't change anything. But maybe he'd check when he got back to the station this afternoon. Just to satisfy his curiosity.

When he reached the large, imposing house at the end of Hemlock Hill Drive, he thought not for the first time that it looked like it belonged in the Swiss Alps rather than the mountains of Washington State. He remembered the modest, much smaller house that had once been pointed out to him as where the mayor used to live, before she became mayor. He wondered now if that was the house Ashley had grown up in. The house where her father had committed suicide one dark night, with his child just down the hall.

He knew this because he had looked up the report in the archives. That had taken some doing, since it had been twenty years ago and those files had not been computerized. Sheriff Carter wasn't fast on the uptake, nor did they have the money for all the latest and greatest or the manpower to maintain it, so they had only input the last ten years or so into the system. He'd almost given up the hunt when he'd realized half the files were out of chronological order, but his stubborn had kicked in and he'd kept looking.

Once he'd read the report, he almost wished he hadn't. How do you do that to people you supposedly love? If you can't take any more, fine, but damn, to blow your brains out with your eight-year-old daughter only a few yards away? It had been hard enough when his own dad had died after a long fight with cancer—he couldn't imagine what it must have been like for Ashley to know her father had left her by choice. True, the man's psychiatrist had laid out a diagnosis of various mental issues, but still, to an eight-year-old…

When he got to the door, he almost turned around and left, but again that stubborn kicked in. He'd just check on her and leave. An official visit. Well within his purview as the responding officer, as it were.

When she answered the door, he was sure he probably gaped at her. She looked weary, haggard and much worse than she had after the crash. Her hair was tangled, she wore a sweatshirt so big it came almost to her knees and her eyes, those eyes that had been so vividly green and alive that day, looked…vacant. It took her a moment or two to recognize him, even after he'd reminded her of his name. Her reactions were slow, much slower than they had been that day, and he wondered just how strong those pain pills they'd given her were. He looked at her eyes again, noted the size of her pupils. Could be, he thought. So maybe this was just someone reacting to a temporary medication.

Or not.

Something was nagging at his memory as she hesitantly answered him; yes, she was sore, sorry she didn't remember much, and was it you who pulled me out?

Yes, she had to be on some strong drugs, he thought. And he'd heard a roughness in her voice that made him wonder if she'd been crying.

And then it hit him, what had been tugging at him. Right now she reminded him of Liz. The onetime fiancée who not only couldn't handle his job, but had come to hate him for it. The slightest difficulty had seemed too much for her fragile nature, real difficulty reduced her to near hysterics, and she blamed him for all of it. Or as his mother suspected, blamed him for not letting her manipulate him with her tantrums. Either way, it had actually been a relief when she'd left him for some slick sales type and had moved back east.

There was no way in hell he wanted to deal with a woman like that again, even for work, if he didn't absolutely have to. That helped him shove this right into the slot it belonged in, which was labeled *not in my job description.* Ashley was obviously alive, if not in good shape, but how she chose to deal with her situation was up to her. If he thought he was going crazy, he might self-medicate, too.

"I just wanted to be sure you were all right," he said briskly, professionally.

"As you can see, I'm alive." Her mouth twisted sourly. "Not well, but alive."

"Have you seen your own doctor?" *Not your job, Crenshaw.* "An accident like that can rattle you," he finished neutrally.

"I was…rattled long before that," she said, so sadly it wrenched at his new determination to stay clear. "Don't worry about me, Deputy Crenshaw. There's nothing you can do about what's wrong with me."

An out. Take it and run, idiot.

"What's wrong with you?" he said instead.

She looked up at him, her eyes looking suddenly bright, not because she was any more there than she had been, but with the gleam of tears. "I'm going insane. Just like my father. Goodbye, Deputy Crenshaw. Thank you for… everything."

And then he was staring at a closed door.

I'm going insane. Just like my father.

Was it true? Her mother thought so, and he knew mental illness sometimes seemed to run in families, but that was about where his knowledge ended. His job was to deal with the fallout, not the causes.

He walked back to his unit, got in and sat there in the SUV for a moment. With an effort he put it—and her—out of his mind and went back to work. One shoplifter in custody, a nightmare of traffic control while a semi that had misjudged a turn tried to get out of town without taking half the streetlights down, two stray dogs taken home and he was done. He signed out, got back in the unit—which he always drove, since you were never really off-duty in a place like Eagle County, where they were stretched so thin—and headed for home.

He stopped at his lookout on the way. He got out of the unit and climbed up to the boulder he usually sat on here. It was his favorite place, this cliff-side vantage point only a mile out of town that had an amazing view of his beloved mountains. It was different at all times of the day and all seasons, whether it was with the sun painting the night sky as it rose, the clouds barreling over the top and down in a storm, or just a quiet day where the massive bulk of them cut a jagged line across the sky. Today, on a severe clear Northwest day, wearing their full winter coat of snow, they looked almost unreal, they were so staggeringly beautiful.

Right now he needed the wonder this place gave him. Needed the peace, the solidity. Because he needed to figure out why the hell he always seemed to be drawn to people who needed rescuing. Or who needed it, but didn't want it. Or who needed it, but he couldn't do it.

Hero complex, Crenshaw? Is that what her shrink would call it?

He was staring out over the mountains when he heard a bark. Odd—he usually had this place to himself; there was an official lookout a couple of miles farther down the road, where it was easier to park and there was a marker labeling the peaks you were looking at. He didn't need any labels, he knew them all by name, not just these but everything from Hood to Adams to Rainier to Baker.

The bark came again, this time sounding oddly familiar. He laughed at the idea of telling one bark from another, but stopped when he looked around and saw an indeed familiar dog running right at him. Cutter.

He slid down from the boulder, having to dodge a spot where the snow had piled up beside it. The dog greeted him with dancing delight, as if he were a long-lost friend. It made him smile despite his mood.

"Well, hi there, my furry friend," he said and bent to stroke the dog's head as Quinn and Hayley walked more sedately toward him. Holding hands, he noted, feeling a pang.

They halted beside him, but they were looking out at the mountains. And then Quinn shifted his gaze to Brady.

"Looks like a good place to find it."

Brady drew back slightly. "Find what?"

"Peace."

And it came back to him, the certainty he'd had that this was a man who understood. A man who saw the need for it, who had been on that search himself. Brady's glance flicked to a smiling Hayley, then back to Quinn. "Second only to where you found it."

Quinn's smile could carry no other label than that of a satisfied man. "Yes."

"What made you stop here? People usually head down to the official lookout."

Quinn lifted a brow as Hayley laughed, a light, loving, beautiful thing. "You answered your own question." So they preferred the solitude, too.

"And," Quinn added, "we discovered we're picky about who we share our anniversary with."

Brady blinked. "That's why you're here? It's your anniversary?"

"Number one," Hayley said.

"Of many. Congratulations."

"You sound pretty certain," Quinn said with a grin.

He grinned back. "Buddy, it's written all over both of you. So are you liking my mountains?"

"We're going to look for a place of our own. Alex said we'd fall in love with it."

"Alex?"

"Alex Galanis. A friend of ours. We're staying at his vacation place."

"He's my neighbor," Brady said, and then the pieces fell together. "It was you. Foxworth, I mean. You're the ones who helped him out a few years ago."

"We helped, yes."

"From what he said, it was a lot more than that. You not

only got his son out of that terrorist hellhole alive while the freaking officials sat around scratching themselves, you kept his whole family safe while doing it. Two other kids, in different colleges across the country, each of them being watched and under threat from the same ass—"

"Hats," Hayley supplied with a grin when he cut himself off.

"Yeah," Brady said with an answering grin. "Them." Any lingering doubts he had about these people—there weren't many, and most of those centered on their seemingly exaggerated faith in the instincts of their dog—vanished in that moment. Alex didn't just swear by them, he damned near lit a candle for them at a church he didn't even go to.

"Have you seen Ms. Jordan since Wednesday?" Quinn asked.

Brady sighed. "Stopped by there today. She looks," he said frankly, "like hell. Probably just the pain meds, but…" He shrugged.

Cutter whined, and Brady looked down to find the dog sitting there, staring up at him. Intently. No, not just intent. Intense. He leaned down to pet the dog again. The animal let out a small sound of appreciation, but that look never wavered, the ears never shifted and the tail didn't wag. He just sat. Staring.

"My dog-ese is a little rusty, my friend, so I don't get what you want me to do," Brady told him.

"Fix it."

Brady straightened to look at Quinn, who had said the words simply, as if it were obvious.

"Like I told you that day, that's his 'fix it' look," Hayley elaborated. "He's found the problem, and now it's up to us to fix it. And in this case, that 'us' clearly includes you."

His brow furrowed. "But what am I supposed to fix?"

"I'm guessing it's who," Hayley said softly.

The obvious image came to him, of the woman he'd walked away from a few hours ago. The beaten, haggard-looking woman who had so flatly, openly, told him she was going insane.

The woman he'd sworn was *not* his problem.

Chapter 7

She never should have taken those stupid pain pills in the first place. She was hurting, yes, but they were worse. She hated the disconnected feeling she got from her regular meds, but these made it intolerable. And besides, they made her want to throw up half the time. The half when she wasn't so groggy she could barely move. Her mother, worried by the fierce bruises that had shown up, had pushed her to take them, but this morning she'd finally put them right back in the bottle and set it aside. It had been four days—it was time to get over it.

If only healing the brain was as simple.

She'd had, at her mother's insistence—and expense— three different brain scans in the last five months, and they had found nothing. And that alone told her how terrified she was, when finding a brain tumor would be more hopeful than finding nothing.

But all the clean scans had done was prove that it was

nothing physical, that the chaos her life had become grew solely out of her own mind. Prove that along with his love for baseball, reading and these mountains, her father had also passed down to her the gene or chemistry or quirk, whatever it was, that was sending her down the same path he'd taken. To pure insanity.

The path to the place she had reached yesterday. The realization that because of her refusal to accept what was happening to her, a brave, good man had had to risk his life to save hers. Two good men, one of them an actual good Samaritan who could have passed right on by. But somehow the fact that it was Deputy Crenshaw's job to protect made it no easier to accept that it was her fault he'd had to do it.

And for the first time in her life, she understood, on a bone-deep, visceral level, why her father had killed himself. If this was what he'd been facing…

I'm sorry I was so angry at you for leaving me, Dad. I didn't understand. Now I do.

She not only understood, but for the first time that permanent exit crept into her mind as a possibility. And that was what had her sitting here, shaking like the leaves on a quaking aspen.

She wanted some fresh air. Wanted to be where she could see the mountains, not holed up here in the study like some crazy recluse.

She nearly laughed out loud at herself. "You are a crazy recluse!"

That did come out loud, and it was followed by the laugh, the sad, pitiful laugh she'd stifled before. As the sound echoed in the book-lined room, she gulped in air, trying desperately to beat back hysteria.

She had to get out. She just had to. Surely if she just went for a walk, that would be all right? She wasn't so far gone she would get lost, and as long as she didn't drive, just walked, and if she didn't go in anywhere and embarrass her poor mother by letting anyone see how far gone her crazy daughter was…that would be all right, wouldn't it? She'd have to be careful, very careful. Her mother had been so kind, so understanding about the car, telling her it didn't matter as long as she was all right.

If her mother was here, Ashley was certain she'd try to talk her out of this. But she was doing a ribbon cutting this morning, at the new park at the north end, with the new trail up to the falls that Ashley hoped to hike someday soon.

Well, not if she didn't get herself back in shape. And what better way to figure out how far she'd backslid than to take a nice, long walk around town?

She could do this. She would make an effort to look normal, too. She'd been aghast when she'd awakened this morning and seen her own reflection clearly, without that drug-induced fog, for the first time. It was a wonder Deputy Crenshaw hadn't had her committed on the spot Friday. It had been Friday, hadn't it? She frowned. She clearly remembered opening the door to see the tall, strong man in his utilitarian uniform standing there, looking at her with shocked concern.

No wonder he'd left so quickly. Probably thinking if he stayed any longer he'd end up doing that mental health committal. She remembered vividly the first time they'd taken her father away, remember her mother crying, an event rare enough that it had stunned her, and stopped her from screaming at them to let her daddy alone.

It wasn't until her mother insisted that she move in here with her that Ashley had realized what a nightmare this must be for her. She'd been through it with her husband

and had to be strong for her little girl. And now she was watching that little girl heading on the same path.

And what would it do to her if you took the same way out?

Sometimes she thought that was the only thing that kept her from doing it.

She did what she could with makeup she hadn't used in a while. She dressed with more care than she had in weeks: jeans, but her black ones, a soft alpaca-blend sweater and boots that were a compromise between warm feet and comfortable walking. She picked up the phone her mother had gotten her after she'd misplaced—permanently, it seemed—her own. A bigger disaster than it might seem, since all her contact info for friends was in it, and none of it had downloaded properly when she'd tried to switch over. She'd even had her mother try, only to have her check and sadly say there were no contacts in the cloud to download.

Served her right for not having memorized any numbers except her mother's, for relying on the phone for that. She'd thought of calling the ski equipment store where her best friend, Caro, worked, but she knew she got in trouble for personal phone calls at work.

What's the point? What are you going to say? "Just a hello and goodbye before I completely lose my mind"?

She felt better the moment she opened the door and stepped out onto the porch. And better yet when she was clear of the house and could really see the mountains. She drew in deep breaths of the crisp, cold air, and to her it was like breathing in rejuvenation. By the time she reached Mountain View and downtown, the fog had completely lifted, and her mind felt clear and sharp. It didn't seem possible that her life was in such disarray.

She found herself looking at every shop, reading the signs in the windows, as if to prove to herself that she could. Everything seemed perfectly normal to her. She seemed perfectly normal to herself, if she discounted the various aches from her adventure down the mountainside. The shadows in her mind threatened to return whenever she thought of that, of what others had risked because of her. Especially the deputy, who had gone to the trouble to check on her. He—

He was right in front of her.

For a moment she thought a brand-new facet of her mental problem had manifested; think of someone and poof, imagine they were there. But he reacted when he saw her. Almost a double take, which told her how bad she must have looked yesterday.

And told her he was real.

"Ashley," he said, staring at her. "Ms. Jordan," he corrected himself. Why? she wondered. Perhaps he thought it was no longer appropriate for him to use her first name. Now that they weren't in danger of dying together on a steep mountainside. Her gaze darted to his cheek, where she was glad to see only a faint red line where he'd been bleeding that day.

"Ashley, please," she said. "Let's not go backward at this point."

He smiled. It truly was a wonderful smile, just as it had been out on the mountain. He'd come out of the cell phone store, although empty-handed. Perhaps they'd had a theft.

"You look…like you feel better today."

She smiled back at him. It seemed the very least she could do. "That was very tactful. I know how I looked Friday."

It was out before she remembered her earlier worry. What if it hadn't been Friday? What if she really had lost more time, as she had on occasion? But he didn't look at her as if she were crazy, or even confused, and his smile—

no, she couldn't have seen this smile before; it wasn't the kind she, or any woman, would forget—just widened.

"You did look a little ragged. Understandably."

"It was those pills, I swear. I've felt better ever since I quit them."

That smile again. "You seem to be moving okay without them."

"I am. Or maybe it's just that I'm so glad to be free of the fog, I don't care about a couple of aches and pains."

"Good." He nodded toward the cell store. "If you were headed in there, they're pretty busy. They had an attempted break-in last night and got backed up dealing with it."

"Oh. Thanks for the warning."

"Phone didn't survive the crash?"

"No, it's fine." She grimaced. "Thankfully, since my mom already had to replace the one I lost. I only wanted to see if they could retrieve my contacts from the cloud, since I couldn't get them to transfer to the new one."

The walkie-talkie on his belt crackled, and he said something into the microphone clipped to his shirt. Ten something. Then he looked at her.

"I was going to stop for coffee while I get this report organized. May I buy you a cup?"

She drew back, a little startled; she hadn't expected that. "Seems I should be the one buying you coffee," she said, and then, driven by that overwhelming need for normalcy, she added, "But I'd like that. Thank you."

And that easily, she was in a place she'd never thought to occupy again. Sitting in a coffee shop, across a table from a very handsome man, feeling as if perhaps, just perhaps, she wasn't really going crazy after all.

Chapter 8

Ashley Jordan was in much better shape. She was moving well, and it looked as if her cuts were well on the way to being healed.

She also did not seem in the least bit crazy. Not that he was an expert. He had some training in handling the most common types of issues he came across, and he did his best to get people who needed it help, but that was it.

But she didn't seem like anyone with active problems he'd ever encountered, on the job or off.

She was funny, amusing and rather sharp. Quick. Steady.

This was the woman he remembered from the crash—scared, but thinking clearly.

Scared.

There was still a trace of that, a vibe he could feel in the moments when she seemed distracted, something he caught glimpses of in those vivid, now thankfully clear again green eyes. And she yelped when the barista dropped a pot and it shattered. But hell, that had made him jump, too. By the time he'd checked on the guy and made sure he wasn't hurt by flying glass, she seemed perfectly calm once more.

"Does your job run to rescuing everyone?" she asked in a commendably light tone when he came back to the table.

"Funny," he said. "I spent some time the other day trying to figure that out—if it's the job or just a misguided rescue complex on my part."

He was a little startled that he'd said that. He didn't usually discuss the things he thought about during those times at the lookout. Especially with a near stranger.

Especially one with mental issues?

But she tilted her head and gave him a smile that did... something. He wasn't sure what, except it was odd. New. "You'll pardon me if I dispute the misguided part. As a personal recipient, I mean."

He found himself giving her a crooked grin at the way she put it. "You're allowed a special dispensation, then."

The smile turned almost teasing then, and his insides took a crazy tumble. "Thank you," she said with an exaggeratedly gracious nod.

By then he was grinning so stupidly he made himself look down at the notes he'd scribbled about the attempted burglary. But he couldn't seem to focus on them and gave it up. His laptop was out in the unit—he'd finish it up there, later.

She took a sip of the latte she'd ordered, basic, no frills or extras—one of the cheaper offerings, he noted, except for his plain black—and studied him over the rim of the cup.

"How did you end up here, Deputy Crenshaw?"

He opened his mouth to ask her to call him Brady, but stopped himself. It would not do to get too personal, not with her.

"I was born here," he said. "Literally. Snowstorm, and my folks couldn't make it down the mountain." His mouth quirked. "In fact, I was born in the back of a sheriff's unit on the way."

Her laugh was a light, lovely thing. And it echoed in her voice when she asked, "So your calling was decided that early on?"

"Maybe. My mother thought I'd just heard the story so often it planted the idea."

She tilted her head again as she seemed to consider that. "Does she ever regret that? It's not the safest profession. She says with definitive certainty," she added with another one of those smiles and a glance at his healing cheek.

He nearly shivered. Damn. What the hell was wrong with him? Was he getting sick? He never got sick. And he felt better in winter than any time of the year.

He gave himself a mental shake. "She felt better about it when I got hired here right out of the academy. It's a quiet place, and most of our problems come from mother nature, not human nature."

She grimaced at that but then smiled as she said, "I'm sure they snapped you up. Local boy, knows the territory, not to mention great PR with the whole born-in-the-back-of-a-unit thing."

He laughed. He couldn't help it—he just liked the way she phrased things. "They did like that," he admitted. "In fact, I was sworn in on the day the deputy who delivered me retired, so they had him do it as his last official act."

"What a wonderful story," she said, smiling widely now. "Are your parents still here?"

"Mom spends winters in Arizona since my dad died five years ago, but she comes back every spring for the rest of the year. This place is in our blood, I think."

"That sounds like a great compromise." She lowered her

eyes to her latte, took another small sip. "I'm sorry about your father, though," she said quietly.

He wasn't sure why he'd even told her that, so he only shrugged. But again, he had the thought of how different it must be, for a parent to give up on life—and you—and make that exit by choice. How horrible must it be to feel that lost, that hopeless, that there seemed no other way to end the pain.

"He was the best," he said simply, as he always did. Because it was true.

She gave him a curious look. "Did they ever fight?"

"They disagreed now and then. Everybody does. But really fight? No. Did yours?"

"Sometimes. I think more than I really remember, because... I don't want to. I've always wondered—"

"Ashley! How wonderful to see you out and about!"

A thin, rather round-shouldered man in an expensive suit strode over to them, a wide smile on his face. Brady felt himself go wary the moment he saw—and recognized—him. He didn't care for Dr. Joseph Andler. He'd been called as an expert witness in a trial Brady had been involved in, and trial results aside, Brady's private assessment was the man was both pretentious and arrogant, two qualities he despised more than most.

"Deputy," the man said with barely a glance at him, and in a much cooler tone. Okay, so maybe he hadn't kept that assessment quite as private as he'd thought.

But a glance at Ashley shoved all that out of his mind; it was as if the woman he'd seen on Friday was back, her eyes wide and fearful, her posture slumped, as if all the bright cheer and energy had drained away like melted snow.

Belatedly, it hit him. Andler was a psychiatrist. And he doubted very much if there was more than one in a town the size of Hemlock, or maybe even Eagle County. So it followed that this was who her mother had meant when she'd told him Ashley was seeing a psychiatrist. Andler was her shrink.

He used the term purposely in his mind, remembering the man hated it. He remembered the time in court when another witness had used it, and the man had jumped up and called out "Objection!" as if he were one of the lawyers withstanding in the case. Judge Clarence, who was a good guy, had slapped him down hard, and Brady had enjoyed every bit of it. Small of him, perhaps, but he had.

But what kind of doctor had this effect on a patient? Ashley had practically crumbled the instant she'd seen him. She'd gone from cheerful, outgoing, even happy to a cringing, fearful, broken soul right before his eyes. She mumbled something to Andler so quietly he couldn't hear it even from just across the table.

"You just enjoy your time outside," the man said with a little too much cheer for Brady's taste. "We'll deal with everything at your next session. I'll see you a week from this Friday, as scheduled. Don't forget, now. Do you have the reminder card taped to your door, as we discussed? An alarm set on your phone? We don't want another problem like last time, do we?"

Brady felt himself frowning and relaxed his expression before the man noticed. He was talking to her as if she were a child. And Ashley was reacting like one, chastened, looking as if she wished she could disappear.

"What happened last time?" he asked after the man left. Warnings chimed in his mind even as he asked, reminding him he'd vowed not to get involved in her personal troubles.

"I...got the day mixed up." He hated the way she sounded. So...tiny. As if she were in fact disappearing. "I put it in my phone. I had the little reminder card he gave me taped up, like he said, where I saw it every day. Every time I looked at it, I noted the day in my head. That day, I couldn't believe I'd gotten it wrong. I ran all the way home to look at that damned little card that I swear said Wednesday. But it was Tuesday. It was right where it had been all week, saying Wednesday, but now it said Tuesday!"

Her voice rose a little at the end. Instinctively he reached across the table and put a hand over hers. She went quiet and still. Raised her eyes to his. And the sheer terror he saw there gouged deep, somewhere low and gut-level. A bloody sort of pain swirled in him as he realized the full extent of what she was facing, the sheer horror of a mind slipping further and further out of her control. He'd feel the same way. As her father apparently had. And understanding crashed in on him.

Get off your high horse, Crenshaw. You'd blow your brains out, too, facing this.

And in that moment it felt suddenly all too real to him. He'd had himself half convinced in was a mistake. That there was no way the woman he'd just spent the last hour talking with was crazy, or anywhere close to it.

But the woman he sat across from right now? Maybe. Probably.

He wouldn't go through this again. He couldn't. He'd dealt once with a woman who used her supposedly fragile emotions to manipulate him time and again. And while he had no doubts Ashley's problems were real, not manufactured to that manipulative end as Liz's had been, it made no difference. He was not going there.

Not. Going. There.

No matter how much he liked her when she was…in balance.

No matter how much she made him smile and laugh.

No matter that she sparked something in him that he'd never felt before.

Chapter 9

Ashley sat with her legs curled up in the big leather chair, staring out the window. The carefully landscaped yard looked clean, almost pristine after the fresh snow overnight. It hadn't been much, maybe an inch. Certainly nothing that ever would have kept her inside before. But now it seemed a good excuse to stay inside, as her mother had suggested.

On the thought, her mother came into the living room, holding the two mugs of the tea she prepared every morning. She handed Ashley one, along with her morning medication. Ashley didn't care for tea and would rather have had coffee, but it was a ritual her mother had begun with pleasure, saying what a delight it was to have her here to share it with her, and she didn't have the heart to refuse. Her mother's schedule was so full it was one of the few times they had to spend together, and so Ashley drank the brew.

"You can have a nice, quiet day," her mother said, sitting opposite her on the matching leather couch, shifting slightly to adjust the jacket of her neat pantsuit. "Read, perhaps. You'll be fine."

"Yes."

She took a long drink from her cup. "Or you could watch movies. That would be a lovely snowed-in day, wouldn't it?"

Ashley didn't bother to point out that they were hardly snowed in, since her mother would be leaving momentarily. She glanced outside again, the new snow just enough to make everything look bright white.

"It's lovely," she murmured. And had she thought that before—for that's how her life seemed to be divided now, into before the nightmares and after—she would have been happily donning warm clothes and boots and going out for a walk in it, loving every aspect of how things looked, smelled, felt.

Her mother took another long drink. As if she were in a hurry to finish. And who could blame her? Why would she want to be here with a daughter who was apparently going the same way as her father?

"Or you could think more about your room, how you'd like to redo it."

"The room is fine, Mom."

"But it's not yours," her mother said briskly. "I was thinking perhaps a lovely pale yellow. Very cheerful."

Also, Ashley thought, the color her room had been in childhood. Sometimes she felt as if her mother was trying to go back to that era. As if she wanted Ashley a child again.

And who wouldn't, if your adult child is going insane?

"Thank you, Mom," she said quietly. "I'll think about it."

As if that was all she'd been waiting for, her mother stood. "I'll see you this evening, then. I've got that meeting with the Chamber of Commerce, so I may be late, but there are meals in the freezer. Only the microwave," she cautioned.

Ashley flushed. "I know."

"And don't forget your medication, now."

Ashley nodded, and picked up the pill her mother had put on the table beside her. She had been quite upset when she realized Ashley hadn't been taking them since the accident, although she gently forgave her because of the accident and the confusion from the pain pills.

Her mother still stood there watching. *Like I really am that child, and she has to make sure I do what I'm told.* She popped the pill in her mouth and picked up her tea.

"See you later," her mother said and swept out of the room in that regal manner she had. She always had had it, Ashley thought. She'd just let it show more since she'd been elected mayor, and more so since she'd been reelected last year.

Ashley lifted the cup, grimacing at the thought of the big swallow it was going to take to get that pill down. She hadn't missed that in the days since the accident.

A cascade of images and thoughts flowed through her mind. She lowered the mug. Spat the pill out into her hand. Stared at it.

When she'd been taking the pain pills, she hadn't been taking these. She hadn't really decided on it—it was just that they made her so groggy she hadn't been thinking at all. And when she'd decided that morning to stop the pain pills, she'd felt so wonderful, so clearheaded again, she hadn't taken these. She knew that many of the medications for mental conditions caused such things—fogginess, a disconnected feeling—but she hadn't realized how much they'd affected her until she'd missed them for a few days. And if she'd had any withdrawal problems, they had been masked by the aftermath of the crash and the powerful medication.

And then she'd had the most wonderful day in recent memory.

Her fingers curled around the pill. In her mind she was back in the coffee shop, looking across the table at Deputy Crenshaw. Kind, brave, handsome, strong, humble, with a grin that could knock down trees...what more could a woman ask?

She could ask to be normal, so something might come of it.

And no matter how loudly her common sense clamored that he was just feeling...responsible for her or something, as if saving her life wasn't enough, or as if it connected them somehow, she couldn't seem to stop herself from wondering, if she was normal, if something really might come of it.

Or maybe she'd just imagined that spark she'd felt when he'd touched her. Maybe it was all part of the downward spiral into madness, imagining things.

Although she didn't think she'd imagined how he'd suddenly had to go after they'd encountered Dr. Andler.

Her mood crashed. She'd been so hideously embarrassed by that whole scene. Being treated like such a helpless child in front of a man like the deputy had been utterly humiliating. Especially when she had been feeling so good until the moment when Dr. Andler had shattered the mood.

She should do exactly what her mother had said, stay here, holed up, read a book, binge-watch some movies, something...safe.

Something moved outside, drawing her gaze. She saw a tiny bird on a snowy branch, apparently looking at its reflection in the window. It looked chipper, cheerful, as if this little bit of snow was nothing, even if it was a third its height.

Even this tiny, fragile bird had more strength, more gumption than she did.

She was on her feet and heading for her bedroom and warm clothes before she could talk herself out of it.

And she tossed the pill into her wastebasket.

When he saw Ashley walking toward him on Mountain View, Brady was torn between the urge to go to her and the urge to run the other way. He would do neither. The decision sounded a bit like a stern order in his head, which made him grimace inwardly. But he was doing his monthly security check with the businesses in town, and that's what he would continue doing.

But he could see her face, her expression. It was the same smiling, happy look that had so captured him on Sunday. She was walking with confidence, moving with a grace and feminine sway that nearly stopped him in his tracks. She had the demeanor of a self-assured, at-ease woman, enjoying a walk through the crisp winter air.

A demeanor he'd seen from her before.

A demeanor that had crumbled before his eyes when the peddler had arrived to shatter her calm.

He didn't know what that meant. His gut wanted to make the doctor the bad guy, to believe that instead of helping her he was somehow causing that change, but he was afraid that was because of his own antagonism toward the man. Maybe it was simply that the doctor had reminded her of her problems—maybe she'd been able to put them aside for a few hours. Although he wasn't sure mental disorders worked like that. And not knowing which type she had, he couldn't research it to find out.

Not that he would. He'd warned himself off, right? No

way he was getting tangled up with someone that fragile, whose mental balance was so delicate the simple appearance of her shrink in an ordinary setting could send her off the edge. He didn't ever want to witness anyone—especially the lively, funny, smart, beautiful woman he'd been sitting with until that moment—disintegrating like that again.

The sun broke through the clouds, not in a shaft of light but a full, brilliant explosion of illumination hitting the new snow, and instantly the whole world seemed to glitter and dazzle. Pedestrians stopped walking and looked, one of the things he loved about his people. He heard the light, airy laugh of someone taking a deep sort of pleasure in the suddenly gilded world.

He knew that laugh.

He looked back down the street. Saw her again. And that he'd been right; she was the one laughing, smiling, looking around as if she were drinking it all in with delight.

She spotted him. For a moment she went utterly still. Even from here he could see her lips part, and his imagination supplied a deep intake of breath. And then she was walking again, straight at him, and he was the one frozen in place. She was smiling that smile, as if the sight of him was as delightful to her as that burst of sunshine. And he simply could not move.

"Deputy Crenshaw," she said as she came to a halt before him.

He had to again stifle the urge to tell her to call him Brady. Not that he was certain he could have spoken at all. Her eyes were that rich, bright green again, clear and focused. They were rimmed with thick, dark lashes that had him wondering insanely what they would feel like brushing against his skin.

Okay, maybe *insane* wasn't a good word to be even thinking, given the circumstances.

"You look…well," he finally managed to say. Which was, he realized, one of the greater understatements he'd ever made.

"Thank you, I feel wonderful today." He heard the deep breath this time. "May I buy you coffee today? I'd like to…apologize."

He knew what she meant, and that was murky water he did not want to wade into. He reminded himself of his determination not to get in any deeper with her. "There's nothing you need to apologize for."

"Then perhaps I should apologize for my doctor, who was less than polite to you and managed to reduce me to a quivering child," she said, her tone very dry.

It startled him. He hadn't thought she would have noticed the man's coolness toward him, or at the least toward the uniform. People didn't always notice or care about the person wearing it. He sometimes joked that if society ever went to actual robocops, it wouldn't be much of a change for some people, since that's what they already thought anyway.

"Not your job to apologize for him, either," he said. "But he is a bit…much." He ended with a shrug, keeping his reasons to himself.

"Amazing what putting an Ivy League degree on your wall will do for your ego."

He laughed. Remembered how often he had laughed that Sunday. And how much time afterward he'd spent wondering what he would have done, if she'd been someone else. If she hadn't been that fragile woman on a razor's edge of sanity.

He had a fairly strong suspicion he would have asked her out. Because of how she made him laugh, if nothing else;

that was rare enough in his world. Of course, that she had those eyes and that mouth that had him wondering things he hadn't thought in a long time had nothing to do with it…

"Please?"

He realized he'd never really answered her invitation. And when he did, it wasn't what he'd intended, which had been a polite, tactful refusal. "Only if I buy," he said. "It feels wrong to me to let a citizen buy when I'm on duty."

There. He'd categorized her now. She was a citizen of the county he was sworn to protect, that was all.

"Those are some pretty strong ethics there, Deputy." She sounded half teasing, but also admiring, and that warmed him more than it should have. "To each our own, then?"

At her lead they went into the bakery this time, and he wondered if she was avoiding the coffee shop her shrink appeared to frequent. Or maybe she simply wanted the banana muffin she bought to go with her drink, today hot chocolate. Which suddenly sounded so good to him he bought one, too, although he passed on the muffin.

"If they could bottle the smell of those cinnamon rolls, I think they'd sell it by the case," she said as she walked toward a table in the corner.

"But you didn't get one."

"Only once a month. Waistline," she said succinctly.

"Nothing wrong with yours." *Oh, brilliant, Crenshaw. Way to keep things professional.*

"Or yours." He hadn't expected that. Or her teasing addition of, "You obviously don't fit the old, tired cop stereotype about doughnuts."

He grimaced. "If I never heard that one again, I'd be happy."

He took two long strides around her and reached to pull out a chair at the small table. He gestured her to it then took the other, which faced out into the shop.

"Why do I feel a bit…herded?"

She said it lightly, so he gave her a crooked smile. "Points for noticing. I hate having my back to the door. Occupational hazard."

It was a couple of minutes and about half a muffin later that she asked, "So how does it work, your job here? I know the sheriff is responsible for the whole county, but is it divided up?"

He nodded. "Into ten districts. The county's just under two thousand square miles."

Her eyes widened. "That's a lot. How many of you are there?"

His mouth quirked. "I believe the required answer is 'Not enough.'"

She smiled. It really was a great smile. "Are the districts all the same size?"

"No. Down on the flats, they're smaller, because that's where more of the population is. So there are six districts there, and only four up here in the mountains. Population of the county is just over a hundred thousand, if you're into numbers. But a lot of the cities down there have dedicated police departments, so our jurisdiction is outside those."

"Sounds complicated."

He shrugged. "Only if the maps aren't clear."

"What about your district? How big is it?"

"About two hundred square miles."

She gaped at him. "That's…huge."

"Only about fifteen by fifteen miles. And outside town, the population's a bit sparse, so…" He shrugged again.

"But if you're at one end and something happens at the other?"

He gave her a wry smile. "And there you have it, the challenge. Try it when there's another few feet of snow on the ground."

She went suddenly quiet, her gaze seemingly turned inward. "I...never realized how lucky I was last week, that you were there, behind me, on that road at that moment."

"I'm just glad I was."

He meant it. Especially since the other option would probably have been finding her frozen body days or weeks later, if not next spring. And for all her problems, all her confusion, he wouldn't want to see that.

Chapter 10

Brady hated when things nagged at him. Especially when he suspected he was not being completely honest with himself, something he could usually tell by the way his mind skittered away from certain aspects of the problem.

Like when he kept not thinking about the simple fact that Ashley Jordan had mental health issues.

He'd run into her—and he'd swear it was not intentional, but what was he supposed to do when there was only one coffee place in town?—every day this week since Wednesday, and she'd been that charming, witty, together woman every time. It was like that other woman, teetering on the edge, was the product of his imagination, not the other way around.

And yet…the snow tires, the heading through the mountains when she was only supposed to be going into town, the confusion over the doctor's appointment, the way she'd practically collapsed when confronted with the reminder of her mental state in the person of Dr. Andler, and her family history. And that was only what he personally had encountered. What he'd just discovered now just pounded it all home.

He sat at the computer workstation at the office—their small budget didn't run to a station at every desk—and stared at the screen. He'd resisted doing the search and had only given in after he'd gotten off duty today because it was a quiet Sunday evening and no one would see him doing it. Why that mattered, when there would be a record of his search on the computer, he wasn't sure.

Probably, he admitted ruefully, because he'd been afraid he'd find just what he'd found and wasn't sure how he would react. But apparently all he was capable of was sitting here staring at the incontrovertible evidence. Multiple instances over the last five months, ever since Ashley had come to stay with her mother, that made it clear she was one confused woman. He supposed it was only chance and timing that he hadn't encountered her personally before that day down the mountain.

She'd been found lost and disoriented by some hikers near the falls. The responding deputy reported that she didn't know how she'd gotten there. She'd been found a week later walking along the highway a couple of miles from town. Same answer: she didn't know how she'd gotten there.

Scariest of all was when she'd been cornered by a pair of unpleasant male tourists who'd apparently decided to take sexual advantage of her confusion, until she was spotted by a passing off-duty firefighter who had stepped in.

After that, her mother had realized the seriousness of the situation, and usually she was reported missing before she was found. And as it continued to happen, supplemental reports about her mother's distraught state started to appear. Whatever polished front she presented as a small-town politician vanished when she was dealing with her daughter's obvious and steady decline. Somehow that made him like her better. It couldn't have been easy, being made a single mom by her husband's suicide. Maybe her brisk exterior was just a defense.

He kept reading, reluctantly because the record was chronicling that decline so clearly. And as the weather changed, cooled toward fall, what had been simple became complex, culminating in her being found in the predawn hours outside city hall, without any jacket or shoes on an early October morning, the day of the first frost of the season. Her story then was that she was waiting for her mother to arrive, that her mother had told her she was on the way.

Her mother, the report said, had been sound asleep at home all night. The officer who'd responded to the house had awakened her.

Ashley had spent the morning at the clinic that time, then was transported to a psychiatric facility for observation. She had been released—after her mother's tearful intervention and promise to keep her safe—but the incidents continued.

Brady tapped a finger on the table, still staring at the screen. *Sometimes having influence isn't always for the best. Maybe she'd have been better off...locked up somewhere.*

He had trouble even thinking it, because the images of the woman he'd seen—the other woman, not the broken, terrified one—kept surfacing in his brain. Her bright, clear eyes, that incredible smile, her quick wit, her way of speaking...how could that woman be mentally crumbling?

But then, maybe that was it. Maybe the woman he'd encountered this week was the upswing side, and the one who'd answered the door two days after the crash was the downswing. Or maybe her problem was some kind of multiple-personality thing. Maybe one side of her was that charmer, and the other side was the…basket case.

He cringed at the phrase.

You just don't want that to be her. Because for the first time since Liz, you're actually attracted to a woman. Or are you just attracted to her because she's…troubled? You become a glutton for punishment, Crenshaw?

Maybe he'd just developed some kind of savior complex.

Does your job run to rescuing everyone?

Her teasing words that had brought on an admission he didn't usually make played back in his head. Had she, for all her confusion, nailed him that easily?

Maybe he was the one who was confused.

You're job's not to save all the birds with a wing down. You're just supposed to protect this little corner of the world. Maybe you need to take some time to think about who you are—a good cop—and who the hell you're not—Superman.

But then he thought of the Foxworths. And their dog, supposedly indicating Ashley had a problem. As if he hadn't already known that. But the Foxworths, who were far from fools, insisted Cutter's actions indicated the problem was something they—and apparently he, although how he'd ended up in the dog's calculations he didn't know—could help fix.

Okay, now you're believing a dog's assessment of a situation? Kinda puts your own mental health in question, doesn't it?

By the time he reached this point, his head was spinning. And on impulse he pulled out his phone and made a call. Sergeant Celeski didn't hesitate to give him a few days off, but then he shouldn't; not only were the holidays over, but Brady hadn't taken a vacation in over three years.

And a few minutes after he'd gotten a hearty "Take all the time you need," he was back in his vehicle, wondering what he'd just done to himself.

At least if he wasn't patrolling in town every day, he wasn't going to be running into her.

Nope, just plain running.

He grimaced inwardly at his own self-assessment. He started the motor, despite not knowing where he was going to go. Home? He would, but if he did, there was always something to do to distract him, some repair to be made or maintenance to be done, and he needed to think. Seriously, honestly think. He wasn't real happy with himself right now, felt like he was heading toward disaster with this whole Ashley Jordan thing, and he needed to get his head straight.

And there was only one place to do that, for him.

The weather had cleared, just as a blazingly brilliant full moon was rising. Moonlight on new snow turned the world silver, and he barely needed the headlights to find his way. The roads were practically deserted on this quiet Sunday night, most of the shops in town closed and most of his people home and safe by now. Celeski always reminded him that when he was off duty, they technically weren't his people or his problem, but he couldn't change the way he felt. He loved this place, these people, these mountains, and if somebody was in trouble, it was a gut-level reaction in him to want to help.

But right now, he was the one who needed help. He reached down and snapped off first the radio in the unit, then removed the walkie-talkie and shut it off, too. If they really needed him for some disaster, enough to call him in from off duty, then they could use his cell. He had things to deal with.

The question of the moment was, why was he feeling

so compelled to help someone whose problem was way outside his experience? Simply because she had gorgeous green eyes and a great smile? Was he that shallow?

He tried to focus on the beauty around him as he drove the winding road to the lookout. The unspoiled swaths of pure white snow, the stark relief of the shadows of the trees caused by the silver light that gave everything an unearthly feel—it all should inspire awe, wonder, and yet he was so damned tangled up in his head, he was missing the splendor of it.

When he got to the point of thinking maybe he should call his mother for advice, he burst out laughing at himself. Not that Mom didn't give good—occasionally great—advice, but he knew perfectly well she'd be on the next plane back if she thought he was as…confused as he was.

Thirty-two years old and running to Mom for advice.

The self-chiding didn't work, mainly because of that realization that his mother was far from a hovering mother type, and she was smart as a whip.

Okay, maybe he would call her. Later. If he couldn't work through this on his own. Although he had no idea how he would explain.

Hey, Mom, I've gone from a fragile flower to a diagnosed crazy lady. Ain't that great?

With a great effort, he slammed the door shut on his roiling thoughts and contemplated the landscape as he got closer to the lookout. Last thing he needed was to end up over the side like Ashley had because he wasn't paying attention. It was above freezing tonight, but sometimes it took the ice on pavement a while to get the message.

He slowed, then parked in his usual spot safely off the road. It was above freezing, but not by a lot, so he grabbed his black knit hat and pulled it on. It was one of his most used pieces of equipment during the fall and winter, and he needed to remind his mother, who had made it for him, of that again. She'd done it with some superwarm fiber, knitted in a lining that doubled the warmth and added subtle flaps that covered his ears without making him look like an overaged skateboarder.

It also had a small red heart knitted into that lining, which she'd told him was because her heart was always with him. It had seemed impossibly corny at the time, but every time he put it on, he thought of that, and it oddly made him more determined to live up to her love and faith.

And reminded him of how lucky he was to still have her in his life.

He got out, his breath sending clouds into the night air. He glanced upward. *Miss you, Dad.*

He didn't even need his flashlight, so bright was the moonlight. He walked past the front of the unit toward the narrow, short path that led to his spot, the boulder with the odd shape that was conveniently like a seat, positioned for that view out over the mountains that always brought him peace. It was a fluke, he knew, a happenstance of nature, but sometimes in his more fanciful moods, he wondered if some long-ago denizen of these mountains had carved it out and it had just been smoothed over time. But the origin didn't matter—what mattered was that he could be alone to think here.

Except…he wasn't alone.

He saw the person the moment he rounded the big evergreen. Standing on the edge a few feet from his rock, staring not at the incredible view but downward, and shivering in clothes far too lightweight for a night in the mountains in January. Something about the posture, the set of the head, the slight sway of the body, warned him. He'd seen it before, on a different edge, but with the same sway, as if the person were fighting inwardly. That time it had ended well, and he'd grabbed the young veteran in time.

But this was a woman.

His gut knew—and knotted—before his brain accepted the fact.

Ashley.

But then she turned, looked at him, and something else crashed into his mind. Her shirt, that too-light, almost summery shirt, was stained with something dark, in small spots on the right sleeve at the wrist.

And although the moonlight leached out all color, he somehow knew this, too.

Blood.

What the hell had happened now?

Chapter 11

"Don't, Ashley. Please, don't."

Until he'd spoken she'd half thought she'd imagined him. Why would he actually be here at this hour, on a Sunday night? She supposed she was gaping at him, but she couldn't help it.

He took a step toward her. Instinctively she backed a step away, to maintain the distance. She couldn't seem to think clearly when he was too close, and she needed to think clearly now. He froze, and she belatedly realized that step she'd taken had been toward the edge.

"Why are you here?" she whispered.

"I…needed to think. This is my spot to think."

As he echoed her own thoughts, something curled oddly inside her. "I know. You told me. So I came here. I needed to think, too."

"It's the best spot for it I've ever found."

"I…can see why."

What she couldn't see was why she was even talking to him. Because while she had come here to think, she had already reached her conclusion before he'd arrived. After what had happened tonight, she really had no choice left. This simply could not go on.

She could not go on. Not like this.

"Don't ruin it for me, Ashley." His voice was so soft, so full of pleading it made her ache inside when she thought she had no room for any more pain. "Don't make this a place I can't come to anymore."

She went still. She hadn't thought of this, had been so wrapped up in her own internal pain that she hadn't thought of what this might do to him at all. Which seemed beyond unkind, given that he'd saved her once. Of course, throwing away the life he'd risked his own to save was even worse, she supposed.

Odd how her mind seemed to still work so reasonably, so logically on one level while descending into utter chaos on the other, the one she had to live with every day.

"I...wouldn't want to do that to you."

He gave her an odd look. "How did you get here?"

The ordinary question startled her. "I...walked."

"Nearly a mile? Dressed like that?"

"I...didn't think to grab a coat."

"Come get warm in my car."

In that moment she wanted nothing more, but something held her back, some tug of a decision made, of a conclusion reached...oh yes. That. She had made that decision. It was going to end, all the pain, all the confusion, all the horror at an even worse future barreling down on her.

"No," she whispered. Because if she did that, she would change her mind. Just being with him now was tempting, so very tempting...

"Then take this."

He was pulling off his own heavy jacket. He held it out, taking a couple of steps toward her as he did. She'd swear she could feel the warmth of it—his warmth—even from here. And it was irresistible.

She took the jacket. It was much heavier than she'd expected. Insanely—God, how often people threw that word around—she wondered what he had in the pockets. Moving on instinct more than anything, she slipped it over her shoulders. And smelled his scent, that mix of pine and crispness, as if he'd absorbed the scent of this place he loved so much. Then the warmth enveloped her, the heat he'd given her, cousin to the heat he roused in her in very different ways, and she couldn't help herself—she closed her eyes for a moment.

Only a moment, but it was enough.

She heard him move, heard the faint crunch of the snow in the split second before he was there, beside her, his arms wrapped around her as he pulled her gently back from the edge.

And she found herself saying the only words she could find, the only truth she was sure of in this moment. "I don't know what to do."

"It's all right. We'll figure it out, Ashley. Come on."

It was so soothing, that voice, that deep, solid voice she could almost feel rumbling out of his chest, the broad, strong chest her cheek was pressed against. So soothing she almost believed him, that it was all right, that there was hope for her. But she knew better. Didn't she? Hadn't these past few months taught her well enough what was in store for her?

She was vaguely aware they were moving, walking back the way she had come. Vaguely, because all she could really think about was how good it felt to be warm again. Very, very good.

The only thing that felt better was him, and his arms so steadily, strongly around her. And when he urged her into the front seat of his SUV, then left her to get in and turn on the motor and the heater, she missed those arms with an ache she shouldn't have the capacity to feel right now.

Then he came back around to her side, reached in to adjust the heater vents to blow warm air on her, then leaned in and asked gently, "Where are you hurt?"

"What?" she said, feeling disoriented again.

"There's blood on your shirt."

Reality slammed back into her mind with the ferocity of a charging bull. "I…it's not mine."

She saw her words register in his sudden, rigid stillness. She knew what she sounded like. Begging. Pleading. And what she—what all of this—looked like. Her out here, like this, blood on her shirt. Blood that wasn't hers. She was certain she was about to be arrested.

That it was this man, of all men, who would do it seemed, in that moment, the most horrible thing of all.

Brady was swearing silently, mostly aimed at himself for letting her somehow get a grip on him. If he'd kept her at arm's length, this would be no different than any other case. Potential suicides weren't frequent around here—the one he'd remembered while staring at her was only the second one he'd ever handled. The first had been an after the fact, when he'd been left to merely wonder how bad it must have been for the man to eat a shotgun shell and be glad he didn't have to do the actual cleanup. Sometimes gallows humor was all they had to get through things like that.

But he hadn't kept her at arm's length. He'd let her creep in. The moment he'd had her in his arms, he'd known, with grim, fierce certainty, that somehow this had gotten much more complicated than a simple urge to rescue and protect. Because what he'd felt when he'd held her was much more than an urge—it was a compulsion he'd never felt before in his life.

Now here he was, looking at bloodstains she said weren't hers, wondering who they were from, what she had left behind, and dreading the moment he saw heading straight for him when he was going to have to arrest her. He would—

He heard the barking at the same moment he heard the car. Startled, he pulled back out of his unit and straightened up in time to see a familiar SUV, a dark one with a heavy-duty winch on the front, pulling over behind them.

Oddly, the first one there was the dog, who had quieted the moment the Foxworths had pulled off the road. The animal was out of the vehicle—what, did they let him out before they even stopped?—and racing over to them before Quinn, who was behind the wheel, even turned the engine off.

Cutter brushed a nose across Brady's hand as if in acknowledgment, but he clearly had a different goal in mind. The dog jumped up onto the front floor of the unit, and Brady, remembering how the animal had comforted her before, instinctively moved to give him room in the small space.

Ashley looked bewildered, but when Cutter nudged her hand, she laid it on his head. And as if it were a visible thing, Brady saw some of the dead look leave her eyes.

Damn dog's a miracle worker.

He nearly grimaced at his own thought. And then Quinn and Hayley were there.

"Let me," Hayley whispered to him.

"Let her," Quinn recommended, just as quietly. "She's got the knack."

Brady went with his gut—and perhaps a bit of his inner

reluctance to see any more of Ashley's pain up close—and backed away a couple of steps to stand beside Quinn.

"What are you doing here?" he asked the man.

"Cutter brought us."

Brady blinked. "What?"

"I told you he was…unique." He explained how the dog had erupted into fierce barking and refused to stop until they got into the car, and then "guided" them by more barking whenever they weren't going the right direction.

"So…he's quiet as long as you're going where he wants, but if you miss a turn…"

"Chaos."

Brady looked over to where Cutter and Hayley were gathered around Ashley, who looked, amazingly, much calmer. Then he looked back at Quinn. "You're not saying he…knew, are you? That she was here, about to—"

He cut himself off, unable to form the words even in his mind.

"Was she? That bad?"

"I think so. But there's more to this, and it's not good."

The moment the words were out, he wished he hadn't said them. He didn't really know this guy, only knew of him secondhand, and no matter how upstanding he seemed he shouldn't be sharing details of what was obviously going to have to be an official investigation with him. The bloodstains weren't extensive, more smears than anything, so he was hoping there wasn't a body lying somewhere, as yet undiscovered.

The blunt realization drop-kicked him back to reality. "I need to make some calls."

"I know you don't know me," Quinn said, so eerily echoing his thoughts Brady stared at him, "but I guarantee you Foxworth won't get in the way of your duty."

"What, exactly, are you saying?"

"That she—" he glanced at Ashley "—needs help. That there's more to this than meets the eye. That Foxworth specializes in righting wrongs."

"Look, Mr. Foxworth—"

"Quinn, please."

"All right, Quinn, I know a bit of your reputation, and I know Alex would swear you're golden, but this is different."

"And you're a straight-arrow cop. I get that." Quinn kept his gaze on him, although Brady suspected he was very aware his wife had left Ashley and was headed toward them. The dog stayed put.

"I'd love to chat about ethics and duty," Brady said dryly, "but there's some urgency involved here."

"If you mean the blood," Hayley said as she got to them, "it's not hers."

He somehow wasn't surprised at her quickness. It would take a smart, steady woman to keep up with the likes of Quinn Foxworth. "So she told me. That just means there's somebody bleeding somewhere else."

"Her mother."

Brady drew back, rather sharply. "What?"

Hayley glanced at her husband, who nodded, then back to Brady. "It's her mother's blood."

Brady swore, low and harsh.

Chapter 12

Ashley was pondering how odd it was, with everything that had happened tonight, that a dog—well, this dog—could still make her feel better. Although Mrs. Foxworth—or Hayley, as she suggested she call her—was really good at comforting. There was something innately calming about her, not as if she didn't ever get excited or upset, but as if she'd been through enough that she knew when it was warranted and, more importantly, when it was not.

As she thought it, the woman came back.

"The place we're staying at isn't far," Hayley said. "We'd like to go back there, get you out of the cold and maybe get something warm to drink for all of us? Then we'll figure out what to do."

Some part of her brain that was hyperaware of what had almost happened, what she'd almost done, laughed rather sourly at how good that sounded. *You were about to put a final end to this, in a very cold and painful way, and now you're wishing for warmth and comfort?*

"Brady will follow us," Hayley said.

Brady. The *B* in B. Crenshaw stood for Brady. How had she not known that until now?

You almost went to your death not knowing it.

And in this moment, that seemed the greatest shame of all of this.

The Foxworth dog unexpectedly insisted on staying with her. She had the crazy thought that at least that would keep… Deputy Crenshaw from carting her off to jail. She wasn't sure why he hadn't already, anyway.

She stole a glance at him as he got into the driver's seat. Funny how every time she saw him she was struck anew by how…amazing he was. Not just his height and obvious strength, or his breath-stealing looks, but that steady, solid core of him that fairly radiated. It was as if each time she saw him, it was new, as if her tortured mind refused to accept he was real and so was surprised all over again when confronted with the proof that he was.

He didn't say anything until they were rolling again. Then it was in a low, rough-edged voice that made her think he was fighting to keep it level.

"It's your mother's blood?" She nodded, clenching her teeth to keep from letting out a moan of pain, pain that wasn't in the least physical. "What happened?"

"I don't…know. Exactly."

"Ashley—"

"I know, I know how crazy that sounds, but what I remember…makes no sense."

"Is she dead?"

Ashley gasped, and her chest spasmed into a tightness that made it almost impossible to breathe. She had just enough air to get out a strangled "No!"

"Well, that's a start," he muttered.

"I didn't. I would never."

"You'd never what? Kill her? Or kill anyone?"

"Unless my life depended on it."

"But you were ready to jump. To end that life."

"I'm nothing if not a paradox, it seems," she said, trying not to sound bitter but not succeeding very well.

He didn't say anything more. The dog at her feet nudged at her, and she petted him again. And again it was oddly, strangely soothing. That or the warmth blowing out from the vehicle's heater was thawing her out to where she felt normal again. At least, as close to normal as she ever got these days.

When she saw the Foxworths slow, then turn, she looked around. They were pulling into a long driveway that wound through some trees, toward a lovely, lodge-style home that looked back the way they had come, down the moonlit mountain.

"Nice," she said.

"Yeah."

He stopped behind the Foxworths, who had pulled into a large garage that also held an ATV and a skimobile. For some reason Quinn Foxworth gestured Brady to also pull into the garage. After a moment's hesitation he did, and she suddenly understood this would hide his marked sheriff's vehicle from any casual passerby.

He turned off the motor and turned in his seat to look at her. "Are you going to run?"

The thought of taking off again into the cold night made her shiver, even though she was warm now. "No. Are you going to arrest me?"

"I'm not doing anything until I know what happened."

She suppressed another shiver that she knew had nothing to do with the chill outside. He was going to question her, that was obvious. Only to be expected. It was his job, after all. And after he'd now saved her life a second time, she owed him answers, didn't she?

She'd be more certain of that if she had any answers to give him—answers that would make sense, anyway.

And if she was certain her life was worth saving.

Brady hung up the phone and for a moment just stood there, staring at nothing in particular, his consciousness turned inward. He'd made the call at Quinn's request, after doing a news search on a sheriff's detective from their home county, Brett Dunbar. The name had rung a faint bell, and the instant the first entry popped up, an in-depth article on the toppling of their corrupt governor nearly a year ago now, it fell into place. Dunbar was the man who'd done it, who had unearthed the truth along with a dead body. Brady had read this exact article when it had come out, and he remembered mentally congratulating the man and noting his stellar record.

And wondering whom the civilian assistance he'd mentioned but not named was.

Now he knew. That assistance had been Foxworth. Quinn and his organization had helped take down one of the scum of the earth, a crooked, corrupt and murderous politician.

"I trust them more than I do some cops," Dunbar had told him in the call he'd just ended.

"I got the vibe."

"It's for real. I've never regretted trusting them, with whatever it takes. They're the best help you could have. They want the results, not glory. Helps if you don't ask every question that comes to you about how they get the job done, though."

"As in nonofficial channels?"

"That are deep and wide and will get you where you need to go a lot faster. You got Cutter?"

Brady had blinked. "I… He's here, yes."

He could almost hear the smile in the man's voice. "Hardest—and smartest—thing I did was learn to trust that dog. He doesn't just know what he's doing, he knows things he has no way of knowing."

"So they've said."

"Believe it. Your life will be a lot easier if you just quit fighting it."

And so, as he put the phone back down, it was the dog he looked at. The dog who was once more sitting at Ashley's feet but looking at him. Steadily. Insistently.

Fix it.

Yeah, he could see it in those amber-flecked dark eyes, even if it did make no sense at all. But that was crazy— he was still a dog.

"I know it's a cliché about a dog being able to judge, but he knows people. We've learned we can trust him," Quinn said quietly, as if reading his wavering. "And we trust that he's not wrong about Ashley."

He turned to look at the man. Quinn held his gaze steadily, without flinching.

Quinn's the guy you want at your back. He was that in the Rangers, and he's that now. I would trust him with my life. And have.

Dunbar's heartfelt words came back to him. There was no doubting he'd meant them. Between that and his neighbor's oft-repeated declaration that the Foxworths had his undying gratitude, Brady made his decision.

"I need to interview her," he said, looking across the room to where the woman and the dog sat.

"Of course. Suggestion?"

"What?"

"Let Hayley stay with her. You'll get more."

Brady glanced at the woman beside Ashley, then turned back and studied the man for a moment. "How'd you find her?"

He hadn't meant to say that, but they were so perfect together, not just personally but clearly professionally as well, that he couldn't seem to stop himself.

Quinn gave him a rather devilish grin. "I kidnapped her. And her dog."

Brady blinked. Glanced at the woman and the dog, then back to Quinn. "A tiny bit of elaboration would be helpful."

The grin widened. "No choice. Classified operation she stumbled onto."

Foxworth, it seemed, was even more than he'd suspected.

He walked over to where Ashley was sitting beside Quinn's wife. He noticed a couple of pillows that looked as if they belonged on the sofa were tossed on the floor as if they'd been in the way, and next to them lay a sweater and a sock tangled together. He guessed what the Foxworths had been up to when Cutter had demanded they follow him. And wondered what it must be like to still be so crazy for each other after a year that you couldn't make it to the bedroom.

Alarm bells clamored in his brain. Sex on a couch should not be on his mind right now, especially with this woman here on said couch.

He sat on the sturdy, lodge pole–style coffee table across from Ashley. "I'm listening," he said, keeping his voice low.

She gave him a glance that held as much fear as anything else, and he didn't like it.

"Why don't you start with this morning?" Hayley suggested quietly. "When did you get up?"

Ashley looked at the other woman, seemingly surprised by the simple question. But she answered it easily. "Kind of late. I…didn't sleep well," she said, with a glance at Brady he couldn't quite interpret.

"What did you have for breakfast?"

Again she looked surprised. Brady saw what Hayley was doing, both lulling her with the ease of the questions and getting her into the rhythm of answering them. Together with her unthreatening demeanor, he could see it was effective. Just as Quinn had said. Even the dog seemed now content to turn it over to her. Cutter rose and walked over to a bed they'd obviously brought for him, given Alex didn't have a dog, and plopped down with seeming contentment. Although he kept that rather unnerving gaze steadily on Hayley and Ashley as his chin rested on his forepaws.

"Breakfast? I…a muffin." She glanced at Brady. As if she were remembering that day at the bakery. Or as if she'd had the muffin because she remembered it. That unsettled him somehow.

Hayley led her through what seemed like a routine, if quiet, day. Brady let her, although he had to rein in impatience for the good of the final goal, which was finding out what the hell had happened with her mother.

Ashley answered a couple more ordinary questions, then Hayley, with a glance at Brady, asked quietly, "Where was your mother today?"

"Oh!" Ashley sounded startled. "I should at least text my mom. She's probably panicked by now."

Brady frowned as something occurred to him. He knew from being on the other end how easy it was to track people via their cell phones these days. In fact, he'd be surprised if, under the circumstances, her mother hadn't made that easily possible.

"Let me see your phone," he said.

She'd told them the phone, and the house key, had been in her pocket by force of habit when she'd gone on what she'd intended to be that one-way walk. Looking puzzled, she pulled it out and handed it to him. He swiped to the apps display and scanned until he found a version of what he'd been looking for.

"It's there?" Quinn asked. Brady looked up and met the man's steady gaze, saw that he knew exactly what he'd been looking for. He nodded.

"And active," he said.

"What?" Ashley asked.

"A tracking app," he said.

Her brow furrowed. "A what?"

"To track your phone's location. Like parents use to keep track of kids."

"But I never…" Her voice trailed away. Then, in a much smaller voice, she said, "My mother."

"Probably." Brady glanced at Quinn again. "Off?"

"For now, I think. Until we have a better idea of what we're dealing with."

Brady nodded, powered down the phone, then pulled out the SIM card. And Hayley repeated her question about Ashley's mother. He sensed her increase in tension, but she answered easily enough. "She went to a charity dinner event. A fundraiser for the Civic Improvement Fund."

Hayley continued with a few more ordinary questions about the fundraiser. In the exact moment when he practically bit his tongue to keep from taking over this interview—she was getting answers, after all, and rational, calm ones—Hayley gave him another look and a slight nod, as much as saying, "Over to you." And in that moment, he envied Quinn Foxworth tremendously.

"When did she get home?" he asked, making certain to keep his voice gentle, nonthreatening, as Hayley's had been.

Ashley was looking at him now, and in those green eyes, a touch of pleading had joined the fear. He didn't like that, either. "About eight thirty. I know because I'd just watched…some old video and was surprised at how late it had gotten."

"Old video?" He wasn't even sure why he asked, it surely didn't matter.

"Of…my father."

There was such heartbreak in her voice, in her eyes, that his stomach knotted up again. He'd long ago had to accept that some sad stories hit him harder than others, but he had no explanation of why hers had nailed him to the wall. Or why her visible steeling herself to go on tugged at him so.

"I really should let her know I'm all right. She worries so much."

Brady was pondering offering his own phone when Quinn pulled his out. He noticed now it was a rather distinctive device, with a set of physical buttons across the bottom, including a red one. Quinn pressed one of the others, opened an app, then held it out to Ashley.

"Now untrackable," he explained.

Both Brady's and Ashley's brows lifted in surprise. He knew his own reaction was at the equipment, and his guess about hers was confirmed with her shocked words.

"What are you saying?"

"Nothing, except we need time to assess everything before we do anything that leads anyone straight to you."

"But…my mother?"

"If she's reported you missing, she may not have control of what's done any longer," Brady explained quietly. Not when Ashley would undoubtedly be reported as an at-risk missing person.

"Oh." Her voice had gone small again. He couldn't

imagine what it must feel like, to have so totally lost control of your own life.

But she input the number and tapped in a message.

The response was almost instant, and Brady guessed her mother had been anxiously hoping for contact. The exchange went back and forth several times before Ashley rubbed at her forehead as if she had a headache.

"Sign off," Hayley suggested. "Tell her you'll be in touch, but for now, stop."

Ashley looked almost relieved and did so. She handed the phone back to Quinn.

Brady wasn't sure what made him ask, "Do you mind if we look?"

Ashley looked puzzled but merely shrugged. "Go ahead. You won't see anything you don't already know."

Quinn was already scanning the texts. Without a word he handed the phone to Brady.

Hi, Mom.

OMG, honey, where are you?

Somewhere where I can think. And rest.

Whose phone are you on?

A friend's.

What friend?

It doesn't matter, Mom.

You need to come home. You need help.

I'm fine.

Clearly you're not. Don't be irrational.

I'm perfectly rational right now. I just need to think.

It will be all right. We'll just forget about what happened.

What happened?

Just come home now. Dr. Andler is here.

Brady guessed that had brought on the headache.

I will. In a while. I just wanted you to know I'm okay.

The string ended there. Brady frowned at the screen for a moment, thinking. Then he went back to his questions.

"What happened when she got home from the fund-raiser? Walk me through it, step by step."

"She seemed wound up, but she always does after those things. She has to be on all the time, you know, and it's hard to come down from that. So I offered to fix her something to eat, because she rarely does at such functions. People are always wanting to talk to her, so she barely eats a thing, even at dinner functions."

There was a familiarity in her tone that made him ask, "You've gone to these with her?"

She nodded. "When I first got here, I went to a couple. Before…" She let out a weary sigh. "Before things got too bad."

Before I got too bad.

He heard what she'd meant as loudly as what she'd said. But he just went on, listening to her describe fixing the salad her mother had requested, slicing tomatoes, chopping onions.

"After she finished, I started to clean up. I was going to run the dishwasher, then remembered I'd left the knife I'd cut everything up with on the counter." She stopped then. Lowered her gaze. "I'm…not sure how it happened. We must have both reached for the knife at the same time. It was strange, she kind of grabbed at me when I picked it up. She got cut, and I tried to help her. That's when I got her blood on me. I let go of the knife, of course…but… she acted like…she backed away, just staring at me with this awful expression."

She let out a long sigh. And suddenly Brady thought he understood. "You think she was afraid."

"Yes." She looked up then, and he saw tears welling up again. "She's been afraid for me, for a while now. But this was the first time I ever realized she was afraid *of* me."

"And that," he said gently, "is what sent you to the lookout tonight? That had you thinking that was the only way out?"

She nodded, and she looked so utterly broken it was all he could do not to pull her into his arms again. He'd always had the need to protect, to help, but he'd never felt anything like this fierce need to comfort. It was so overwhelming he had to stand up for the distance it put between them.

He had to look away from her as he thought, tried to work through his unexpected emotional response to simple facts. He wasn't sure how long it had been, but he was almost grateful when his cell signaled an incoming alert, giving him an excuse to turn and walk away a few steps.

He pulled it out and tapped on the icon for the county alert system. As the app opened, he wondered what could be happening worth a county-wide alert on what should have been a quiet Sunday night.

It was an all-points bulletin. But not one relayed from another agency, as they usually were here. This one had started not only here in this county, but in Hemlock itself. A felony want. Assault with a deadly weapon. One victim, minor injuries.

And he stared as the bulletin scrolled past on the screen.

Her mother's text had said, We'll just forget about what happened.

And Ashley had seemed to have no idea what that was referring to.

But this APB was for a knife attack.

And the suspect was Ashley.

Chapter 13

Ashley knew something else bad had happened by Brady's expression when he saw whatever it was that had come across his phone. And then he turned to look at her, and she felt a chill unlike anything she'd felt yet. The Foxworth dog was on his feet in an instant. The animal came back to her and sat, as he had before, at her feet, facing toward the deputy. As if he'd felt the need to put himself between them.

And when she got a better look at the man, at his eyes, she understood why Cutter had moved. Crazy as it seemed, this dog she barely knew was protecting her. Because this was the man bad guys saw, she guessed. Tough, cool, capable and strong enough to do what he had to do.

"What is it?" She hated how quavery her voice was, but she couldn't seem to help it. Not when he was looking at her like that.

"An APB. All-points bulletin," he added.

She sighed. "My mother had already reported me missing again before I texted her."

"Not exactly."

He took a deep breath, then read what was on his screen aloud. "'Wanted on suspicion of third-degree assault with a knife, Ashley Jane Jordan, female Caucasian, five two, dark brown and green. Last seen at the scene of the assault, the home of the victim, her mother, Hemlock mayor Alexander. Weapon is in custody, but suspect may still be armed.'"

Suspect may still be armed.

Somehow it was that last sentence that sucked all the breath out of her. That warning of danger. They were warning the people looking for her.

Her.

They were looking for her.

She lifted her gaze to his face, knowing she was probably gaping but unable to care. He'd lifted his gaze from the screen and was looking at her, his expression utterly unreadable to her, his blue eyes frighteningly steady and assessing as he watched her. As if he expected her to...what? Run? Try to escape? Or, more ridiculous, attack him?

Suspect may still be armed.

At least they hadn't said the old cliché, armed and dangerous. But then she supposed it was implied, if you believed she'd already assaulted someone. Quinn Foxworth had come over to stand beside him, and suddenly Ashley felt very confined.

She felt the creeping advance of panic, but at the same time, she nearly laughed at the absurdity of it; they were ordering everyone to search for her when Deputy Crenshaw already had her practically handcuffed.

Cutter moved then, leaning into her, and she desperately threw her arms around the dog's neck, hugging him close, seeking, needing that odd sort of comfort he seemed able to give.

After a moment Brady looked back and tapped the phone a couple of times, then held it to his ear. He didn't bother to walk away, so obviously he didn't care if she heard.

More likely he just doesn't want "the suspect" out of his sight.

"This is Crenshaw," he said into the phone. There was a pause, then, "Yeah, I'm off, but I just copied the APB. I'm familiar with the suspect. What are the circs?"

That's what she was to him now, obviously. She wondered what they were telling him. Cutter gave a low, sympathetic-sounding whine. And Hayley Foxworth put an arm around her and spoke softly.

"You're not alone, Ashley. Whatever happens, you're not alone. We'll help. It's what we do."

Who were these people? They were taking the good Samaritan bit a little far, weren't they? But more importantly, how on earth had a simple accident ballooned into this? Did the deputies make some crazy assumptions because her mother had reported her missing and had a couple of cuts on her hands? Had they—

He ended the call. Shifted his gaze to her face again as he slipped the phone into his shirt pocket. She saw his jaw was tight again as he walked back and resumed his seat on the table, directly in front of her. When he spoke, his tone was calm, businesslike, and she found that somehow steadying. Which she needed, in light of what he said.

"Your mother reported the assault."

"She…reported I assaulted her? My mother?"

He nodded. "Claims you came after her with a kitchen knife. That she tried to grab the knife, tried to fight you off, which resulted in her injuries." He held up a hand when she started to speak. She fell silent, decided he was right, she should hear it all first. "They wanted to go with second degree, which is a class-B felony, but she insisted on third, a class C, saying…you weren't in your right mind, and you didn't mean to seriously injure her. Her proof of that was that you dropped the knife and ran when you realized you'd sliced open her arm."

She'd been wondering what the difference was between class B and C, and wondered how the human race had gotten to the point of needing such classifications when the last thing he'd said registered.

"Sliced her arm? She only had a small cut on one finger from when we both reached for the knife at the same time."

"So you're denying you attacked her?"

"Of course I didn't attack her!"

"Easy," he said. "I need you to stay calm and think. Is there any way she could interpret what happened as an attack?"

Again she nearly blurted out a denial but reined it in and tried to do as he'd asked—stay calm and think. She ran it through in her mind at least three times before she spoke.

"We both reached for the knife at the same time. I got to it first. I never expected her to try and grab it, like it mattered who put it in the dishwasher. So I kind of jumped, and that's when her hand got nicked. So there's no way I can see she should have thought that."

There was a moment's silent pause before he said quietly, "Unless it was already in her mind for some reason."

She was feeling even more bewildered now. "But why would it be?"

For the first time, he hesitated. He even shifted his gaze down to Cutter, making her realize just how tightly she was clinging to the dog, who had made no effort to move and made no sound of complaint. Still, she eased up a little. And the dog swiped the tip of his tongue over her hand. It was unexpectedly comforting, as everything about this dog was.

"Why would it be?" she repeated, and he lifted his gaze back to her face.

"Because, according to your mother…your father went the same way."

A brutal chill swept over her. The memory, *that* memory, of the discussion she'd not been meant to overhear. Her father's—and now her—psychiatrist sadly advising her mother that his violent tendencies and fantasies were worsening, and that her father was having great trouble dealing with them. The very idea of her gentle, loving father having any kind of violent ideas had seemed insane to her, even at her young age.

But he had been insane.

And whatever mental or genetic glitch he had had, she had it, too.

But… "I didn't," she whispered. "I didn't cut her, not like that."

"She was taken to the clinic for multiple stitches." He said it almost sadly.

Nausea seized her, violent and sudden. "Bathroom," she barely managed to get out. Instantly Hayley was on her feet and leading her out of the room. She barely made it, and the waves of upheaval continued to grip her long after her stomach was empty.

"She's terrified," Quinn said.

"I know." Brady also knew he would never in his life forget the memory of her face.

Brady was still staring down the hallway where the two women—and the dog, glued to her even now—had gone. He tried to shake off the queasy feeling he himself had developed at her expression of pure horror. Whatever her illness was, she knew where it was going. And she was appalled by it. He couldn't begin to imagine what it must feel like. Going deaf or blind would be awful, but there were ways to compensate. How did you compensate for losing reality?

"What was wrong with her father?"

Brady shrugged. "There, I'll have to show my ignorance. One of those combinations of three different mental disorders, with names I can't remember or pronounce, from manic this to dissociative that, from what I was able to find. Apparently his suicide wasn't a surprise to anyone."

"Except maybe her," Quinn said softly, also looking down the hall.

"Eight years old," Brady said, shaking his head. "And now thinking she's going the same way…"

"It's amazing she's functional at all, let alone so normal seeming."

He nodded. "I just can't believe…" He stopped himself, knowing what he should have said was *I don't want to believe.*

"What do you want to do?" Quinn asked.

"Go back to two weeks ago?" he suggested sourly.

"If only," Quinn said, but with humor.

"I know what I'm bound to do," he said reluctantly. *Cuff her, take her in, turn her over to the system.*

"But that isn't always what you should do," Quinn said, in the tone of one who had had to make this kind of decision.

Cutter appeared out of the hallway. He walked over to his master—Brady had the odd thought that a dog like this would have no master except by choice—and sat, looking up at him.

"I know, boy," Quinn said quietly.

"That 'fix it' look you talk about?"

"Yes."

"And just how are you, or any of us, supposed to fix this?"

"That," Quinn said with a long-suffering grimace, "is for us less clever humans to figure out."

Brady grimaced in turn. "Great."

Quinn turned to look at him. "You're the only one of us who has seen her on a downswing. How bad was it?"

"Bad," he said grimly, describing the time he'd gone to her mother's house, and then her crumbling at the coffee shop.

"Could that have been the pain meds they put her on after the crash?"

"I thought—" *hoped* "—it might be. But this, tonight… she was going to jump. I could feel it."

"I believe you. Cutter made it clear it was urgent we get there." Brady looked down at the dog again. Cutter met and held his gaze as if Brady were some stubborn sheep. "Hayley agrees she meant to jump. Because she didn't even bring her purse."

He looked back at Quinn. "Her purse? Seriously? I mean, I know they always carry them around. Never understood why."

Quinn's mouth quirked. "I suggest you don't question Hayley about that, unless you want a full lecture on the lack of pockets in much of women's clothing."

Brady studied the other man for a moment. "You were a Ranger, Dunbar said."

"Yes."

"And your parents were killed by a terrorist bombing."

"Yes."

"A couple of very large doses of reality."

Quinn smiled. "So why am I doing something so unreal as putting such faith in the instincts of a dog?"

"Exactly that," Brady said, looking back at Quinn. A pair of steady eyes looked back at him. "You're saying he's never been wrong?"

"He's never been wrong."

Chapter 14

"We're what?" Ashley looked at Brady blankly as she sat up on the couch in the large great room, where she'd fallen into an exhausted sleep. She didn't know how long ago.

"Staying here for a while."

She stared up at him. She'd expected him to take her into custody—had in fact thought of herself as in custody since he'd shown up. Expected him to drag her back to town at any moment, had even been grateful he'd allowed her to sleep for a while first.

But he hadn't done it.

She knew he couldn't possibly believe her, not when her mental state was so clearly deteriorating. And yet... her memories of last night, of what had happened with the knife, were so vivid, so clear. As clear as her mind had always been before the fog-inducing meds.

She had never understood why people on those medications for mental conditions would stop taking them when they were the only thing keeping their illness at bay. How many times had her mother told her that if her father had started taking them sooner, he might have been saved? But she understood now. She'd do almost anything to stay out of that fog. Except without those meds, it seemed she conjured up innocent explanations for what she'd apparently done. Or severely distorted what had actually happened.

To her own mother.

What she didn't understand was what this man was doing.

"We're…staying here?"

"They won't look for you here. There's no connection to follow."

"But aren't you…they?"

One corner of his mouth quirked almost sourly, and he let out a compressed breath. "Yeah. And believe me, harboring a fugitive is something I never thought I'd be doing."

Then why are you? she wanted to ask. Almost did. But some combination of hoping he was doing it for very personal reasons and that it might not be the best idea to make him explain and then maybe question his own actions stopped her.

Hayley stepped into the room and gave Ashley a sympathetic look. "I'm thinking you'd like a nice, long shower. And I've got some clean things you can put on. How does that sound?"

"Heavenly," Ashley admitted, getting up quickly. As she did the brightly patterned throw that had been tucked around her slid away. She wondered who had done that. For that matter, the last she remembered she'd been sitting upright. She felt an odd little leap of her pulse as she shot a glance at the man standing there, watching her. Had he done it? Raised her feet and tucked her in like the fragile person he no doubt thought her?

Then she noticed another blanket and a pillow on the floor beside the couch. Her breath caught. Had he slept there? Right beside her? In the first instant her heart leaped, then thudded back down.

Harboring a fugitive.

That was what she really was to him. A fugitive. Whatever his reasons were for not dragging her in immediately, she was still wanted. The phrase made her think of Wanted posters in the post office, and she wondered crazily if everybody who ended up there felt as bewildered as she did. Which didn't change the simple truth.

He'd stayed here, with her, not out of any desire to be close, or protect. He'd done it to make sure she didn't run. And that stiffened her spine.

"Is it all right if I accept Hayley's kind offer, Deputy Crenshaw?"

He looked taken aback for a moment, whether by her words or her very formal tone, she didn't know. And told herself she didn't care. "Of course." Then, rather wryly, he added, "But I think you'd better call me Brady, or it's going to be a very long…however long this is."

"All right," she said, still coolly. "Brady." She got it out without betraying how good it felt to say by calling herself seven kinds of a fool for feeling that way.

"Then let's get you going," Hayley said cheerfully. "And we'll figure the rest out when you're ready to tackle it."

Ashley wasn't sure what there was to figure out, except how to accept the grim truth that was staring her in the face—that she could no longer trust her own mind, her memories, even her way of thinking. Because she was losing her grip on all of it. It was progressing. Getting steadily worse.

Just as it had with her father.

* * *

Brady glanced up as Hayley came back from the bathroom. He was seated at the granite counter of the large kitchen island, working on his second cup of coffee of the morning. It hadn't exactly been a restful night for him, and sleeping on the floor had little to do with it. No, it had been the sound of Ashley's quiet breathing, the constant awakening to check that she was all right—hell, anyone in her situation would be prone to nightmares—and the frequent arrival of Cutter, as if the dog, too, wanted to check on her.

He found himself smiling as he remembered the moment, sometime well after midnight, when the animal had quietly padded over to him, leaned up to sniff at Ashley as if to make sure she was sleeping peacefully, then plopped down beside him and rested his chin on Brady's chest. He'd instinctively lifted a hand to stroke the dog's head and immediately felt an odd sense of calm. This must be what she got from this, he'd thought, but almost immediately he had—finally—gone to sleep.

He noticed that Hayley was carrying the shirt Ashley had been wearing. And his training and instincts suddenly snapped back to life. "That'll need to be saved."

She nodded. "I assumed. I'll bag it. Alex has a safe in his den—we'll put it in there. It registers times of opening and closing, so there's a record."

"Still shaky on the chain of custody," he said wearily. "Good lawyer would get it tossed. And it'd be my fault."

"Let's not worry about that just yet."

He took another long sip of the coffee. Quinn had made it, Hayley had told him, and the man obviously went for a more powerful brew, just as he himself did.

"Where's the dog?" he asked now.

"Quinn's outside with him," Hayley said as she topped off his mug.

"Heck of a way to celebrate your first anniversary," Brady said, nodding his thanks.

"We're getting our celebrating in." She grinned at him. She really was a beautiful woman. "But then, we don't need an occasion, because every day is special."

Brady drew in a deep breath. "I envy you. Both of you. You've so obviously found it, that holy grail of relationships."

Her grin widened. "Oh, now that's the way to put it." Then she gave him a considering look. "So, haven't found it for yourself yet?"

"Yet. If only," he muttered. Then, managing a smile, he said, "Not many women like you around."

Quinn and Cutter came in the back door in time to hear his words.

"Amen to that," the man said and walked over to plant a rather fierce kiss on his wife, who reached up to cup his cheek as she returned it.

"Chilly out," she said.

Brady had felt the brush of cold air as Quinn had passed. When he bent to pat Cutter as he paused beside him, he could feel the chill on the dog's thick fur. Then he watched as the animal proceeded down the hall and stopped outside the bathroom door. He cocked his head and his ears swiveled forward, as if he were listening intently. Brady stifled a smile. But then he thought of what the dog was likely hearing, which sent him into thinking about what was going on in there, and images of Ashley with water streaming over her naked body slammed into his mind again.

His grip on his coffee mug tightened as he pondered just what he'd let himself in for. Not just violating his oath and his personal code by ignoring an APB, but staying under the same roof with the first woman who'd awakened certain body parts in a long time.

Apparently assured that she was safe, Cutter quietly came back and sat in front of Hayley and Quinn. And then, rather comically, he tilted his head back, back, back until he was looking at Brady. Upside down. He couldn't help chuckling, and the building pressure in his chest eased a little. The dog's silly look didn't do anything for the rest of him, however.

"You have a decision to make," Quinn said.

Brady's mouth quirked. "Thought I already did that. We're still here."

"Yes. But once we have a detailed conversation with Ashley, and if she wants Foxworth to help, then you've got another one. Because our goal isn't yours."

He blinked at that. He would have sworn Quinn, and Hayley, too, for that matter, would be the upright-citizen type. As if she'd read the thought, Hayley said quietly, "Your goal, your job, is to uphold the law and follow legitimate, valid orders. Our goal is to help Ashley. They may not always coincide."

"So you have to decide how involved you want to be." Quinn lifted a brow at him. "There's a lot to be said for plausible deniability."

Brady let out a sour laugh. "Sure. 'Yeah, boss, I found her about to jump off a cliff, got the APB on her, then turned her over to these folks I met maybe ten days ago and walked away.' Sounds a bit short on plausibility to me."

"Point taken," Quinn admitted, but he was smiling.

"Just how," Brady asked, "do you think you can help her?"

"We start with the assumption she's not guilty."

He opened his mouth to say something pithy about the presumption of innocence in the justice system, but shut it again without saying it. But he couldn't resist saying rather bitterly, "Why don't you go all the way to assuming she's not mentally ill, either?"

"That may well be part of it."

Brady drew back slightly. "Wait...you think...but she's got a psychiatrist—"

He stopped when Quinn held up a hand. "What I should have said was that we will verify her exact situation."

"How? Doctor-patient privilege and all?"

"We'll work that out if and when Ashley gives us the go-ahead. But let me ask you something. The way she reacted in the crash, did that seem to you like someone mentally incapable of handling herself?"

Brady sucked in a deep breath as Quinn landed upon exactly what had been bothering him the most. "No. And people usually show their true colors under that kind of stress. But how a mental disorder might affect that, I don't know. I just don't know enough about it."

"Exactly," Quinn agreed. "And so we will dig into that, as well. We have people who do know."

He didn't say any of this, Brady noted, like someone who was winging it. He said it like a man with a plan, and more, the wherewithal to carry it out.

"What, exactly, is Foxworth?" he asked warily.

"Just what we told you."

He thought about that takedown of the governor, and the other cases he'd read about when he'd done that bit of research. Including Quinn's role in taking out a cop killer. "And you have what, endless resources?"

"Not endless, but sufficient," Quinn answered. Then, with a half grin, he added, "Let's just say our finance person is an utter genius."

He gave the man a doubtful frown. And then Hayley said proudly, "Quinn and his sister founded Foxworth on their parents' life insurance and built it into something amazing. And now, between that financial acumen and the goodwill and eagerness of those we've helped to help others, we have as close to endless resources as is possible for a private entity."

"Life insurance," Brady murmured. "The bombing."

Quinn nodded. Brady thought a little more, searching his memory. Quinn stayed silent, letting him.

"That back-room deal, where they let the guy go back to the warmth and welcome of his terrorist buddies," he said slowly. Quinn lifted a brow, but still said nothing. "That was…so wrong," Brady said. "And all his victims couldn't do a thing about it."

"Exactly," Quinn said, nodding his head in apparent approval.

"That's the kind of thing you fight? Try to make right?"

"It is. The circumstances vary greatly, but that is what we do."

Hayley offered him more coffee. He thought he might need the jolt to wrap his mind around all this, so he said yes. She poured, and he thanked her. Ordinary. But there was nothing ordinary about any of this.

Then Hayley said with a smile, "As one of our recent clients put it, we help people in the right turn lost causes into wins. And we do it without taking anything more from them."

It seemed impossible to believe that there were people who made that their business, yet sought no glory or fame for it.

"So, what do you say?" Quinn asked. "In or out? Or do you need time to think about it?"

Brady sighed. Set down his coffee mug. He didn't really need time. He knew he'd already made the decision when he'd brought Ashley here instead of taking her in.

"I think I'll go get my civvies out of my unit. Maybe I'll feel less guilty about this if I'm not in uniform."

Quinn grinned at him. "Whatever works."

"You can change in the media room," Hayley suggested, gesturing to a doorway that closed off a room that was apparently better for the purpose than the multiwindowed great room. "Ashley's going to take the second bedroom, but there's a foldout bed in there that's probably a lot more comfortable than the floor," she added.

Brady was still shaking his head—whether at the existence of Foxworth or his own craziness at accepting all this, he wasn't sure—as he opened the back of the unit and grabbed his go bag.

He headed back inside. Saw that Cutter was back down the hall, sitting beside the bathroom door. As if he knew Ashley would be coming out soon.

Brady closed the media room doors behind him and quickly shed his gear and uniform, then got out the jeans and sweatshirt he always carried in the bag. Silly as it was, it did make a difference, he thought as he pulled the jeans on and reached for the sweatshirt.

And tried not to think of possibly similar actions going on just down the hall. Tried not to picture Ashley naked, or in some lacy confection, as she pulled on her borrowed clothes.

He failed utterly, and zipping up his jeans was an interesting proposition.

Chapter 15

Ashley felt decidedly odd. As if she were living in the snow globe her father had given her, complete with the snow. A small, contained world where nothing bad could ever get in. Peaceful, quiet and safe.

And remember what happened to it.

It had been the first day she'd truly had to face the truth about her father. She'd come home from school to find her mother cleaning up the shattered globe, giving her the saddest of looks as she explained that Ashley's father had once more lost control and this time destroyed her most precious belonging, which he himself had given her.

And he had committed suicide barely a month later.

She shook off the painful memory as she stood staring out the window at the fresh snow that had fallen overnight. But that only made room for more painful thoughts—that she was following the same path. That she had lost control enough to have attacked her own mother, then manufactured an innocent scenario that her miswired or off-kilter brain seized upon as reality, so vividly it was impossible for her to believe it wasn't true.

Delusional. That's what she was.

She turned around to face where Quinn, Hayley and... Brady were waiting. The Foxworths were seated, but Brady was on his feet, pacing, as if he were too restless to sit. She was startled by how much different he looked in civilian clothes. Minus the bulk of his gear, she was able to clearly see how lean and trim his waist and hips were, and how broad his shoulders and chest. The jeans he'd put on did crazy things to her pulse, and as he turned to go back the way he'd come, she found herself watching those back pockets in a way that would no doubt embarrass both of them if he turned around and caught her.

She yanked her gaze away from him and sat down as Quinn and Hayley started to explain in detail who they were and what they, and their foundation, did. She was puzzled but listened because it was fascinating. Who'd have thought there was a group dedicated to such a thing? Lost but righteous causes?

It wasn't until Hayley paused and asked if she was with them so far that she realized this wasn't just getting-to-know-you chitchat—this was specific.

"I'm following. And I think what you do is wonderful. But why are you telling me all this?"

"We're offering Foxworth help, Ashley," Hayley said.

She blinked. "To me?"

"Yes."

"But...nobody can help me." It sounded so forlorn, it embarrassed her. And that put an edge into her voice. "I don't have that kind of problem. Don't you understand? I'm going crazy, just like my father did, and there's nothing they can do about it."

Brady spun around on his heel, startling her. "Did you get a second opinion?"

She stared at him. "What?"

"First thing you do when you get a killer diagnosis is get a second opinion. Did you?"

"I… No. I mean, we know Dr. Andler. He treated my father."

"Not very successfully," Brady said sourly. She stared at him. He couldn't have chilled her more if he'd thrown her out in the snow. He grimaced and closed his eyes for a moment, then met her gaze. "Sorry. That was a lousy way to put it."

He meant it. She could hear it in his voice, see it in those clear blue eyes. The chill faded. "Yes," she agreed. "But you have a point."

"I freely admit I don't care for the man."

"I… You know him?"

"Two years ago I was involved in a trial where he was called as an expert witness for the defense."

"Mind telling us what bothers you about him?" Quinn asked, his tone casual.

Brady looked at the other man and said flatly, "He manipulated the jury. Cleverly, but still. His testimony was instrumental in getting a rapist off."

"You were the arresting officer?"

"I was."

"But if he was found innocent," Ashley began with a slight frown.

Brady's voice went harsh then. "He felt invincible after he walked free. So he raped three more women in the first week he was out, one of them a fifteen-year-old girl. And that's in large part on Dr. Joseph Andler."

She felt herself go pale. "My God. No wonder he practically ordered me to get a birth control shot after one time I ended up in…a bad place, with two strange men."

"Of course," Brady said, still with an edge. "He knew there were men like that out there, because he put one out there."

"But naturally," Hayley said sourly, "being only a witness giving his opinion, there were no repercussions for him."

"Naturally," Brady said, echoing her tone.

"I…didn't know this," Ashley said, sounding as shaken as she felt.

He turned to look at her then. And his voice was gentle, with that soothing tone that eased her fears, when he said, "Not your fault. You trusted his credentials."

"And my mother's recommendation," she murmured, almost to herself. At Brady's sharper look, she realized how that had sounded. "She said he truly tried to help my father and that he was devastated when he committed suicide. Took it as a personal failure."

"Maybe your father couldn't be helped," Brady said, then looked as if he regretted saying it. She lowered her gaze and softly voiced what she guessed was the reason for that feeling.

"And maybe I can't be, either."

She sensed him move, then felt the gentle touch of a finger under her chin, tilting her head back.

"I don't believe that," he said, quietly but firmly.

She looked at him, thinking it amazing that a man in his job could have such warm, kind eyes. Beautiful, deep blue eyes. She remembered with sudden vividness the first time she'd looked into them, as he'd pulled her from the car in the moment before it had slid down the mountain. She remembered thinking then—rather inanely, given the circumstances—that those eyes promised she would be safe, that somehow he would get her out of this.

And he had. At no small risk to himself.

She couldn't let him risk himself even more.

"I can't tell you what that means to me," she said softly. "But you've already done enough. More than enough. I don't want to…entangle you in my mess when there's nothing to do about it."

His tone went harsh. "Except jump off a cliff?"

She didn't even wince. "Most of my life I've been hurt and angry about my father. Angry *at* my father, because I thought he was a coward. Because I couldn't understand why he did it. How he could leave me. Now I do."

"Ashley—"

"It's too much, Brady. And if the alternative is being locked up somewhere, drugged up but always knowing every day I'll lose a little more reality, then…" She ended with a shrug.

Hayley rose and came to her. The woman's eyes were warm, gentle. "You've been alone, Ashley. You're not anymore."

"I've had my mother. She tries so hard, but—"

"Your mother has your father haunting her, as well," Hayley said. "What happened has to color her thinking, just as it does yours." Ashley had never thought about it in quite that way. The tumult inside her calmed a little as Hayley continued. "But it doesn't color ours. At least let us try."

"But why? Why would you?"

Oddly, the woman glanced at Cutter. But she said only, "It's what we do."

"And what if you conclude I can't be…fixed?"

Quinn spoke for the first time in a while, and his voice echoed with both certainty and command, just as Brady's sometimes did. "Then we'll still be there with you, every step of the way."

Ashley was certain she looked as doubtful as she felt. But then Brady said, very quietly, "Ashley, if there's even a chance…you have to take it. You can't give up until you do."

Her gaze shifted to him. He was looking at her with those eyes, steadily, with none of the wariness or repulsion she often saw in the expressions of people who knew she was having mental issues.

"Brady," she began, but her voice faded away as no more words came to her. As if merely saying his name was all that mattered.

"What do you have to lose?" His voice was even softer now.

And he had, she realized, a point. What did she have to lose? She'd nearly made that fatal leap last night—what could possibly be worse than that?

Being locked up somewhere, unable to end the nightmare? Living for years in a drug-induced haze? Unable to end it even if she wanted to?

She heard a faint whine, realized Cutter had once more stationed himself beside her. As if he were showing her he, too, was with her against the world, if need be. The fanciful thought would have made her smile if her mind hadn't been whirling into chaos.

As he leaned against her knees, she reached out to stroke the dog's head. And yet again that calm stole over her, as if there were some soothing magic in his soft fur. And something in those amber-flecked eyes calmed the turmoil, until the truth of what Brady had said was all that remained.

What did she have to lose?

Chapter 16

Brady didn't understand the picture that was emerging.

Ashley didn't fit neatly into any category he knew. In fact, if he had to base an assessment on the last couple of days since they'd been holed up—something that would likely cost him his job if this went sour—in Alex's place, on the hours on end he'd spent with her, watching her, talking with her, he would say she seemed perfectly normal for the circumstances. There was no forgetting, no confusion, no misremembering. No odd tangents or impossible-to-follow thought processes.

Quinn had asked her to recount her entire life, it seemed, from the time the breaks in her mental state had begun. And she had done it, starting with when the recurring nightmares had started. She'd sadly admitted some days were shrouded in a befuddled fog, and a few hours here and there lost altogether. Yet she still managed to give a reasonable account of the timing of everything, from the onset of the problems, through when she'd begun therapy with Dr. Andler, the medications he'd put her on, to having to leave her job because the confusion was getting worse, until she started blanking out on hours at a time. Finally, after the incident with the potential rapists, having to get the birth control shot for her own sake. That had been a severe wake-up call, and the pressure to come and stay with her mother had become too much and she'd agreed.

It was a sad tale, and one that made him feel this was at best foolish, and at worst a lost cause.

But hadn't Hayley said lost causes were Foxworth's specialty?

Just as he thought it, Hayley somehow found something to say that made Ashley laugh. He looked over at them, at Ashley, and was slammed anew with the realization she was beautiful. And that he'd give a great deal for that smile, that cheer, to be her permanent state. When that thought registered, the only words that came to this mind were *slippery slope.*

He turned away.

Do not go there, Crenshaw. Do not read into that little smile she gives you, those shy glances, that she's feeling anything more than grateful that you didn't drag her off to jail as you should have. Because even if she feels the same pull, even if there was genuine invitation there, it's not one you can accept. Not when her life is in such chaos. Haven't you had enough experience with a fragile woman to last you a lifetime?

Quinn, who had been standing across the great room on the phone, ended his call and walked over to where Brady stood looking out the window at the snow continuing to fall. It was a good thing the Foxworths had gone on that shopping expedition yesterday, picking up clothes and necessities for both him and Ashley. He'd thought about going back to his place for supplies, but after he'd made that call and mentioned being familiar with the suspect, he thought it might be better to stay out of sight. He might be ending his career by this decision to not take her in, but that didn't mean he had to hurry it along.

He looked at Quinn, who had just called to let the people back at their headquarters know they wouldn't be back as scheduled. "Sorry about that."

"Our people get it. They're as committed as we are."

Brady believed it. They had spent these two days talking with Ashley, and he had been amazed. He generally didn't have time for slow reveals—once the initial case report was done, that was usually the end of it for him—but he was suddenly seeing the appeal of genuine, careful detective work.

"There's one thing I'm already mostly convinced of, though," Quinn said.

"What?"

The man looked over to where Hayley and Ashley were sitting on the couch, Cutter plopped on their feet. "That woman is as clearheaded as you or me."

Brady let out a long breath. "Yes. She is."

"I haven't seen a single break in her stability. Have you?"

He shook his head. "Not a one. Her mind seems crystal clear."

Quinn nodded. "Ty—he's our dig-deep guy—is going after what we can get on her father. And mother." The man gave Brady a half smile. "And one of my local guys is working up some info on your favorite shrink."

Brady drew back slightly. "Is this one of those times Dunbar warned me about, when I shouldn't ask questions about how you do…what you do?"

"You might be happier if you didn't. It helps," Quinn

added with a wry smile, "when you don't have to worry about it standing up in court."

"Normally I'd protest that. The system isn't perfect, but it's all we've got."

"I'd say the concept is, but it doesn't always work, because people aren't perfect."

"I can't argue with that."

"Foxworth tries to help with those times when it malfunctions."

"All right. No questions. For now." Quinn nodded as if he'd expected nothing less.

A while later, coincidentally—or perhaps not—when the snow had stopped, Cutter showed in his polite way that he needed outside. Brady, who had been restlessly pacing again—this violating his oath had him on edge—quickly offered to take him.

He hadn't expected Ashley to jump to her feet and say she'd go with them, that she wanted to go out in the fresh snow. A glance outside at the now solid three feet told him she was unlikely to try to take off, so he merely nodded. And pondered the fact that she sounded...different. He wasn't sure what it was, but her voice, her tone, seemed different. Maybe just relief at this respite from her troubles, he decided.

They'd been using the back door for the dog, since it opened onto a covered patio that was sheltered from the snow. Still, the flakes had drifted up along the sides, practically enclosing the space in pristine white walls. Cutter plowed forward, undaunted, and disappeared behind a particularly tall drift.

Brady was just thinking that it wasn't nearly as cold as he'd expected when Ashley said, "It's practically warm out here. This must be how igloos work."

Startled, he looked around at the surrounding snow.

"I think you must be right. It's acting as both windbreak and insulation."

"Do you think we could sit out here for a few minutes?"

He gave her a quizzical look. "Cabin fever?"

"More a case of giving Quinn and Hayley some alone time," she said. "It is their anniversary trip, and I feel guilty about intruding on their celebration."

"Hayley said every day's a celebration for them," Brady said.

She gave him that smile that made it so hard to believe there was anything seriously wrong with her. "I believe it. They're amazing together, aren't they? Especially given how they started out."

They sat down on a bench he brushed clear of the snow that had made it through onto the patio. "Hayley told you, huh? About him kidnapping her and Cutter?"

She grinned then. The doubts her smile instilled were nothing compared to the crazy tumble his insides took at that grin. For a moment he couldn't even breathe. "Yes. With the proverbial unmarked black helicopter."

His mouth quirked. Quinn had left out that part when he'd told him how he and Hayley had met. "That's when I first realized Foxworth is a lot more than I ever imagined."

"I think they are, too."

He realized then what he was hearing in her voice, what that different, new note was.

Hope.

He felt a sudden qualm. What if they were building that up in her and it turned out that it was false hope? Wouldn't that make it all even more devastating? It seemed she had reached, if not peace, at least acceptance, of her condition, before.

So much that she was ready to die to end it.

The memory of that heart-stopping moment when he'd

seen her teetering on the edge at the lookout slammed into him, and he knew anything that forestalled that was worth it.

Even false hope.

"Do you ski?"

The unexpected question snapped him out of the unaccustomed emotional turmoil. "What?"

She looked at him, her green eyes looking as serene as he'd ever seen them. "I just thought since you grew up here in the mountains, maybe you skied."

"I do. Not as much as I used to, but I try to get out a couple of times a season."

She nodded. "My dad skied."

Brady went still. Tried to remember if she'd ever brought the man up on her own, without referring to the mental illness that had stolen him from her.

"Did he?" he said carefully.

"He was going to teach me, starting on my tenth birthday."

A birthday the man hadn't lived to see.

He didn't know what to say. He didn't want to disrupt the normalcy of this, the way she sounded like nothing more than someone missing their dead father. He tried to think of something…neutral.

"So he was a good skier?"

"Very. He thought about competing for a while, when he was young, but decided it might take the joy out of it for him."

"I get that," Brady said, but he was frowning inwardly. That didn't sound like a guy with a messed-up brain, any more than she did. But she'd said that came on later.

"He was a wonderful man. Strong. Kind. Loving." She gave a faint smile then. And he could almost feel it all creeping back in on her. "I adored him and thought he adored me."

"I'm sure he did," he told her, thinking it rather lame even as he said it.

"I always believed that. That's why I couldn't believe for years, and never, ever understood why he committed suicide. Until the other night."

He couldn't stop himself from grabbing her hands. Her bare fingers were cold despite what she'd said about the temperature out here. "Ashley," he began, but stopped when she turned on the bench to look at him straight on.

"It's all right," she assured him, as if she were the steady one. And at the moment he wasn't sure she wasn't right. "I won't try that again. I don't feel so alone anymore."

He wrapped his fingers around hers, trying to warm them. She curled her hands in turn, as if she welcomed the feel of his. That gut-level part of him responded as if hers was the touch of a lover, something that had been lacking in his life for a long time. He tried to quash it, because what he'd thought earlier still held; he had no right to take advantage of the situation. The problem was, the more time he spent with her, the harder it was to suppress his response to her.

Afterward, he wasn't sure how it had happened. He didn't think he'd done it, but how else had she ended up in his arms? And the way she clung to him, how the hell was he supposed to push her away?

He told himself it was her fragile state of mind that kept him from doing just that, but deep down he knew he hadn't because it felt so damned good. Not only good, having her warmth pressed against him, it felt right. Very, very right.

And when she looked up at him, something in those green eyes made him want…everything. Everything that was possible between a man and a woman. He wanted to start with a taste of those sweet, tempting lips, but he knew if he did, he would not want to stop there.

You're an ass, Crenshaw. Three days ago she was on the verge of suicide.

He was not—was *not*—going to take advantage of the situation, even if it did seem she wanted the same thing he wanted. Because right now she couldn't possibly be sure what she really wanted. Maybe that hunger in her eyes was simply because she hadn't taken that jump, because she was still alive. Maybe it was all just reaction to that.

The only thing he wanted more than what she seemed to be offering was to never see regret aimed at him in those vivid eyes. Not that that made it any easier to tamp down his body's response to her closeness, to that heated gaze. He had to get past this. He had to quit watching her, sneaking looks at her and most of all wishing the situation was different. That she was well and could make rational, fully aware decisions about what she wanted.

And that she'd decide she wanted him.

None of which was reality. And being snowbound here with her was no help at all.

Chapter 17

Ashley awoke the next morning feeling better yet again. As she had been every day. Underlying was the lingering, niggling fear that the only reason she was feeling better was that she hadn't been taking her meds. They were still sitting at home, where they'd been, untaken, since the crash. She'd left them there that night, since she obviously wouldn't be needing them any longer after...

She calculated the timing. Ten days. Ten days since she'd stopped her regular pill. Minus the days of utter fog on the pain pills, when she'd felt so ill from them that even the pain was better. But once that had cleared... there wasn't a moment missing since. She remembered it all, clearly.

But are you remembering it right?

What her mother had apparently claimed had happened that night with the knife was so different from what she remembered. Yet the memory was so clear to her. It had to be her that was mistaken, her confused brain that was responsible. Didn't it? And yet…

Brady hadn't taken her in. It had been three days since that bulletin naming her as a suspect in an assault she would swear hadn't happened, and he hadn't yet arrested her. Even knowing her mind was damaged, and the official version quite possibly true.

Quite possibly? Don't you mean probably? Definitely?

How could it not be true? She was the one with the befuddled brain, not her mother. But could she really have manufactured such a clear memory? She must have. Her mother would never make up such a thing.

But perhaps somehow she had, as Brady had said, misinterpreted what had happened.

Because she'd been through it before. Had probably been expecting it.

Ashley couldn't think of anything more grim that watching, waiting for someone you loved to go over the same edge that had cost you someone else you loved.

A polite tap on the door made her finish dressing quickly. It had to be Hayley; Brady's knock was decidedly more…male. And when she opened the door, it indeed was Hayley.

"I brought coffee," she said, holding out a steaming mug.

"Bless you," Ashley said fervently, taking it.

"Thought you might need it before you sit down with Dr. Sebastian."

She nodded. When they had first suggested an online session with yet another friend of theirs, a psychiatrist, she'd been wary. But Brady had done some research on the woman, and everything he'd found indicated her reputation was stellar. She was on the board of two major hospitals and three mental health organizations and had spent several years on the faculty of a prominent university.

They went into the kitchen, where Brady was working on his own coffee, and to her surprise Quinn was busy fixing up something that smelled luscious.

"Well, that's unfair," she said.

Brady gave her a puzzled look, but Hayley laughed. "It is, isn't it? No man who looks like that should be able to cook, too."

Ashley grinned at her and once more savored something that had been missing from her life for months now—the ease of simple, uncomplicated interaction, especially with another woman.

"Hey," Brady protested, "that's sexist. Or something."

She looked at him, saw one corner of his mouth twitching. "If you tell me you can cook, too, then I may have to change my assumptions."

"I'll have you know I make a great beef stew, better garlic chicken and a truly wicked barbecue sauce."

She raised her brows at him. "Consider my assumptions changed, then."

The twitch became a grin. "Might want to hold off on that. They're also the only things I can make."

"Just means your looks have to carry more of the load," Hayley teased.

"Not a problem for him," Ashley quipped, then looked away quickly before she could see his reaction to her words.

After the breakfast that tasted as good as it had smelled, Quinn led her into the media room, where he'd set up his laptop and mirrored it on the flat-screen television on the wall.

"We'll run a test when we first connect, make sure everything's working right, then leave you in private," he said.

"How do you know her?" she asked as she tried to ignore the fact that Brady had been sleeping in here. There was a small stack of freshly washed clothes on one end, the shirt the Foxworths had bought on top, and that brought on more imagining, like how her pulse had kicked up the first time she'd seen him in civilian clothes. Those jeans, just snug enough...

"We helped her with a family situation," Quinn said. "Something she needed closure on."

"Oh."

"Ready?" Hayley asked gently.

Ashley suppressed a shiver. They had warned her some of the questions Dr. Sebastian might ask could be uncomfortable, and that she would probably ask about her father.

Brady's words echoed in her head. *If there's even a chance...you have to take it. You can't give up until you do.*

She drew in a deep breath to steady herself. She had already signed a waiver allowing the doctor to share all information before starting this. She'd decided if she was going to do this, if she trusted Foxworth—and Brady— enough to do it, she wasn't going to hold back. And so she said firmly, "Yes."

Quinn reached out and tapped some keys on the laptop. A moment later, the flat screen flashed to life. And Ashley braced herself for the first question.

"What's bothering you the most?" Brady stopped his pacing to look at Hayley, who held out his refilled mug of coffee and...a cookie. She smiled at his expression. "I bake when I'm restless. Quinn cleans. You, apparently, pace."

"Kind of useless by comparison," he said as he took both items.

"We're in one of those stages of a case where it's up to

someone else," she said, "and at that point, it's whatever gets you through."

He bit into the cookie. It was soft, sweet, delicious and still warm. "Wow. That's really good."

She smiled. "Thank you. So what is it? That we're on hold for the moment? Or that you're afraid it's all really true?"

"All of that," he agreed, "but...what's really bugging me at the moment is that text exchange. I mean, I get that her mother's worried, but it seemed a little..."

He trailed off, unsure of how to describe what was nagging at him.

"Hasn't settled into words yet?"

"Exactly," he said, a little relieved she understood. He finished the cookie, took a swallow of coffee.

"I did wonder why her first question wasn't if she was all right, but where she is," Quinn said as he joined them, sipping from his own mug of coffee after popping an entire cookie into his mouth and chewing it with obvious enjoyment.

Brady nodded. "That's part of it. Although if she's really afraid of her, I guess that would make sense. But why the need to constantly remind her...of the mental issue? Ashley obviously isn't so far gone she'd forget that."

"Impartiality would say that perhaps we haven't seen her at her worst, but her mother has."

Brady's grip on his mug tightened. "But even as bad as she was that day I saw her after the crash, she knew." It still ate at him, her flat, dull acceptance. *I'm going insane. Just like my father.*

"I think we should let that rest until we have Dr. Sebastian's assessment," Hayley said.

Brady drew in a deep breath and relaxed his hand. Then

nodded. And managed not to glance yet again toward the closed door of the media room.

The room where he'd been sleeping on the foldout couch, now that it seemed clear Ashley was not going anywhere. Not that she could, through all the snow.

So in essence, she was in his bedroom. The bedroom he'd claimed, leaving empty the actual third bedroom in the place, because it was the next room beyond where Ashley was sleeping. And no amount of telling himself he'd done it because she'd have to go past the media room door to get out of the house, so he would likely hear her, was really working.

He was glad when Quinn spoke and yanked his brain off that path. "But dealing strictly with physical observations, I would have thought that if it happened the way her mother said, she'd have had more blood on her."

Brady looked up to meet Quinn's steady gaze. "Yes," he said, the same thought having occurred to him the moment he'd heard the description of the altercation. "The physical evidence that we know of supports her story."

"Then that, combined with her obvious stability right now, gives us inconsistencies that need looking into, explaining."

Brady nodded. "Although it could well be she dodged the blood somehow and there was a puddle on their kitchen floor," he said, feeling grimly obligated to point that out. "The report wasn't final yet, so I didn't get all the details."

"And I think you calling back for more wouldn't be advisable just yet," Quinn said.

"Kind of like running up a flag to announce I know something," he agreed sourly.

Quinn gave him a steady but empathetic look. "I realize this goes against the grain."

"It goes," Brady said flatly, "against everything I believe in."

"I know." Quinn said it like someone who had walked the same path.

Brady rubbed at his eyes. "I'd never even consider it, if I hadn't…if I didn't…"

"Think there was more to this?" Hayley said quietly.

He nodded, slowly. "My gut's yelling there is, no matter what my brain says."

Quinn smiled then. "Welcome to Foxworth. Sometimes that's all we have to go on."

"But it's not what a deputy sheriff in Eagle County is supposed to rely on."

Quinn nodded. "If it comes down to you needing a defense to keep your job, we've got a guy."

"It well may, so I hope he's good." Even as he said it, a memory jabbed at him, from the stories about the aftermath of the downfall of the governor last year. His gaze narrowed. "Hold on. You're not talking about Gavin de Marco, are you?"

"As a matter of fact, I was."

Brady let out a low whistle. "Yeah, that oughta do it."

"Gavin has that effect," Hayley agreed blandly.

Just the thought of having the world-famous attorney on his side was heartening. But then something more important occurred to him. "If they end up pushing the criminal side of this, Ashley might need some legal help."

Quinn nodded. "She'll have it."

And Brady stopped his pacing and sat down, marveling at the whims of fate. The Foxworths' arrival at the scene of Ashley's accident had been the most serious case of right place, right time he'd ever encountered.

Chapter 18

Brady was glad for the warning Dunbar had given him not to think too much about how Foxworth got things done. But surely Andrew Jordan's own child would have the right to access his records? And she'd given them permission, so perhaps it wasn't a violation to be sitting here reading about a man long gone.

But more disturbing, to him, were the similarities between the cases of father and daughter. The same sort of deterioration, from occasional breaks in stability to progressively more serious problems with confusion, memory and perception.

"We're working on the official report on the suicide," Quinn began, but Brady shook his head.

"Don't bother. I read it."

Quinn gave him an assessing look. "So your gut's been talking back on this for a while, then."

He didn't see any point in denying that he'd dug into this

more than he normally would. He just hoped they didn't push for an answer beyond that gut feeling, because he was afraid he didn't have one. At least, not an answer that didn't involve emotions that, in his experience, did more to cloud judgment than hone it.

"Yes. He was found in his den, one gunshot to the head, gun on the floor beside him, only his prints on the weapon." He hesitated, then realized he was already in so deep it would hardly matter. "It was cut-and-dried. Nothing unexpected or odd. And with the supplemental, it was pretty clear."

The supplemental report was an addendum to the official report, and it was often held back and kept confidential for varied reasons. In this case it was speculation on the impetus for Andrew Jordan's suicide. Quinn didn't push, which made it easier for Brady to go on. "Apparently the shrink—Dr. Andler—was going to have him committed."

"Involuntary?" Quinn asked. Brady nodded. "He could have fought that."

Brady sighed. "Maybe he didn't have any fight left in him by then. He'd been going steadily downhill for nearly a year." He met Quinn's gaze then. "Ashley said she could never understand why he did it...until she reached that point herself."

"There are a lot of similarities between their situations," Quinn said.

"Yes."

Logic told Brady that the mental problem that had driven Ashley's father to take his own life could indeed be something hereditary, some genetic quirk passed on from father to daughter. And with that admission came images, imaginings he could well have done without, of arriving at the lookout too late, of her broken, lifeless body at the bottom of the drop-off.

He suppressed a shudder, a reaction that was a warning in itself.

Just means your looks have to carry more of the load. Not a problem for him.

If he'd needed any further proof that he was tumbling down a rabbit hole, Hayley and Ashley's teasing exchange slamming into his mind just then would have sufficed. The simple fact that his pulse had kicked up and his stomach had knotted at the idea that she liked his looks was a warning that screamed far louder than that little voice in the back of his mind.

He felt the sudden urge to bail on this whole thing, to grab his stuff and get out. Go home, where he should have been and stayed. If he'd gone straight there Sunday night, he never would have gotten sucked into this.

And Ashley would be dead. Lying crumpled and broken and probably frozen by now. A lump of dead meat, with no life in those vivid green eyes.

He felt a nudge—a wet one—on his hand. Looked to see Cutter there, staring at him with those uncannily clever eyes. Again the dark nose nudged, harder, until he wasn't sure if he'd lifted his hand to the dog's head or the animal had just managed to slide his head under his fingers. And it was second nature to give the dog what he wanted, so he stroked the soft fur.

Only then did he remember his earlier thoughts about how odd it was that petting Cutter seemed to make problems fade. Petting any dog helped, but this one was…different. He felt the peace steal over him, as if the animal were somehow communicating that everything would be all right. As if he had a certainty his human companions lacked about how things would turn out.

"So we follow your lead and everything comes up roses, is that it?" he murmured to the dog.

The dog made a low sound that sounded oddly like approval and followed it with a tilt of his head and a swipe of his tongue over Brady's wrist. He couldn't help smiling and gave the dog a scratch behind the ears. Cutter sighed happily and leaned into the touch.

"Crazy, isn't it?" Hayley said. "How much better he makes you feel?"

Brady could only shake his head in wonder. "Where'd you find this guy?"

She sat down beside him. "I didn't. He found me." He raised a brow at her. "He just turned up one day on my doorstep. At a bad time in my life. I'd just lost my mother."

"Damn."

"Yes," Hayley said simply. "I genuinely tried to find his owner, ran ads, made calls, but by the time it became clear that wasn't going to happen, I couldn't imagine going on without him."

"So he stayed."

"I don't think I could have gotten him to leave if I tried."

"He can obviously be very…determined."

"And persistent."

"Like the Colorado River was persistent?" he asked dryly.

"Carving out the Grand Canyon?" Hayley grinned at him. "Exactly like."

Brady looked back at the dog, who now was looking at him with his head tilted and what looked absurdly like a smile. If he were human, Brady would have said it was a "Good, you finally figured it out!" expression.

But he was only a dog.

"Dr. Sebastian is…very different," Ashley said.

"From Dr. Andler?" Hayley asked, and Ashley nodded. "How so?"

She glanced at Brady, whose jaw was tight, as if he were keeping his mouth shut with an effort. It nearly made her smile, because she knew his opinion of Dr. Andler and could only imagine what he'd be saying if he did speak.

She felt a little guilty for saying it, but Dr. Sebastian had impressed upon her the importance of being honest with them. "She listens. Truly listens. Dr. Andler mostly talked. And…he basically assumed he knew what was wrong with me. That it was the same thing as my father. She did not."

And the woman had made her feel better after one encounter, online, than Dr. Andler ever had. Admittedly, it had been one three-hour session, but still. Ashley wondered what the doctor and Quinn were discussing back in the media room—Brady's bedroom. She'd given her consent for full disclosure, and the doctor had asked for a private moment with Quinn.

"She's very aware how easy it is to misinterpret or miss things altogether," Hayley said. "From personal experience."

Ashley gave the woman a steady look, wanting her to know she was able to talk about this rationally. "I gathered. She told me about her son. That he killed himself at seventeen."

Hayley's expression was sad. "It was tragic."

"She said she blamed herself for missing the signs. That it's what led her to specialize in at-risk patients."

"Yes. And she's helped a great many."

"She also told me what Foxworth did for her."

Hayley nodded. "That was Liam Burnett and Ty Hewitt. They dug deep, Ty online and Liam on the street." She smiled. "Liam can look like a teenager if necessary, and he used that to good effect."

"She said they found a friend of her son's who was able to help explain what had happened, and who told her that the only reason he made it as long as he did was because he didn't want to hurt his mother. That he'd loved her and knew she loved him. It didn't make it right, but it helped her heal a little. Gave her a reason she could accept, even amid the grief."

"And now she's helping Foxworth?" Brady asked. "Because of that?"

Hayley turned to look at him. "Yes. It's how we work, since we don't charge money for what we do."

"Only in help for someone else down the line?"

Hayley nodded. Ashley found herself watching Brady rather intently, curious what his reaction would be. And felt a sweet sort of warmth when he shook his head almost in wonder, and there was a matching tone in his voice when he spoke.

"That's enough to almost give me hope for the human race," he said.

"Another reason we do it," Hayley said. "So people like you don't lose hope."

He blinked. "Like me?"

"The good guys," Ashley said.

Brady's gaze shot to her face, but before he could speak, Quinn was there. He walked over to Hayley and brushed his fingers over her cheek. Ashley had noticed he always did that when he'd been away, even if it was only in the next room—he went to his wife and made contact in some way, a hand on her shoulder, a touch to her hand or that brushing of fingers. As if it were his way of assuring the connection between them was still there, still strong. And Ashley felt a hollow sort of ache inside, both at having never known that kind of link with someone and at how close she'd come to throwing away even the chance for it someday.

And she managed not to look at Brady as that thought

crystallized, and along with it the acknowledgment that the closest she'd ever come was when she'd been in his arms. Those moments on the patio, in that snow-secluded spot, had become a touchstone amid the chaos. She'd wanted more, so much more. She'd wanted him to kiss her, for starters, and wanted that to be just that, only the start.

But he'd pulled away. And when she protested, asking if he didn't want what she did, he'd quietly said, "What I want doesn't matter. What matters is I'm not taking advantage of the situation."

And she'd known then he was indeed what she'd just called him. One of the good guys.

Chapter 19

"**O**bviously it would take more than one session, but Dr. Sebastian says she would question your situation enough to ask to see your records," Quinn said.

Brady saw hope flare in Ashley's eyes again and felt a gut-deep hope of his own, that they weren't building dreams that would turn into more nightmares for her. Even as he thought it, the flare faded and her brow furrowed.

"But why would she think anything different than Dr. Andler, given my father's history?"

"That's just it," Hayley said. "She didn't know your father's history beforehand."

Brady went still. Said slowly, "So she didn't go in expecting to find the same thing."

"Exactly," Quinn said. "That doesn't mean it's not there, but it's human nature to find what you expect to find."

"I thought that's what all that education was supposed to beat out of you," Brady said dryly. Ashley laughed, and he felt an odd tingle down his spine.

"Dr. Sebastian would agree, I think," Hayley said with a smile.

"She did say," Quinn added, "that if she had to judge based on this one session, she would greatly hesitate to put you on medication just now. She believes in spending enough time looking for the source of the problem before deciding on that."

Ashley's brow furrowed again. "Dr. Andler put me on meds after our first session. In fact, he had it ready there in his office, he was so certain I'd need it."

"He dispensed it? Directly?" Quinn asked.

"Yes."

"He can do that?" Hayley asked in turn.

"Any licensed physician in the state can, and without a pharmacy permit," Brady said. He grimaced. "It's a big added revenue stream for a lot of them."

Quinn looked thoughtful. "Does he charge more than a pharmacy?"

Ashley looked embarrassed. "I don't know. My mother takes care of the bill and often picks up the pills for me, since his office is right down from city hall."

Now that was a thought, Brady mused. He wasn't sure exactly what the possibility meant in relation to Ashley, but it was a blip on the radar, and he noted it. Psychiatrist as drug dealer. Pushing pills for profit. It was a refrain he'd heard before.

"Are you seeing this guy because you trust him or because your mother does?" Brady hadn't meant it to sound like an accusation, but that's how it came out. He was usually pretty good at questioning people, at taking the right approach, the right tone, but he seemed to have lost the knack with her.

"I...trust him," she said, but he didn't miss the hesitation.

"Why?"

She blinked. "What?"

"Why do you trust him? For that matter, why does your mother? He didn't save your father."

She drew herself up and faced him steadily despite his tone. And the part of him that wasn't trying to figure out why he was suddenly pushing her was cheering for that.

"Sometimes there's no saving someone. Or you're too late. If you hadn't arrived in time to stop me the other night, should my mother have blamed you?"

I would have. "That's different," he muttered.

"Why? Some would say you both failed at your job."

"I would say that," he snapped.

"I know." She said it softly, quietly, but his anger, or whatever this was, drained away as surely as if she'd punctured him with the words. Somehow she had turned it all around on him.

He heard a low chuckle and looked up to see Quinn smiling. "She's got teeth. Good to know."

"Good to see." He said it as quietly as she had spoken. And he meant it; it was very good to see that spirit in her, see her stand her ground. He wasn't sure how he felt about the fact that color tinged her cheeks at his words. As if they'd pleased her.

"Now what?" she asked Quinn.

"Dr. Sebastian will be going over your father's records. Just to see if anything strikes her beyond the obvious similarities."

"You mean she's going to decide if Dr. Andler is right in assuming I have the same problem?"

"She'll give us her opinion, always limited by the fact that she's only had this short time with you, and not in person."

"Does that make a big difference, not being in the same room with her?" Brady asked.

"It can," Hayley answered. "Dr. Sebastian is amazingly adept at reading people, but that's a talent better utilized face-to-face." Brady lowered his gaze to his hands, to where his fingers were tapping restlessly on the arm of the chair he was in. "And yes," Hayley added quietly, "she blames herself for not reading her son in time."

Brady grimaced. "Was I that obvious?"

"Only to be expected, given your recent…discussion," she answered, with a glance at Ashley.

He was saved from having to answer by the ringing of his cell phone. It was on the kitchen counter, so he got up to get it while Hayley rose and went to open the door for Cutter, who had been outside.

A glance at the screen told him it was the detective lieutenant. And for the first time in his career, he hesitated in answering a call from a superior. Because usually vacation days were inviolate, unless the interruption involved an active case. And while it could be any of a number of things, the most likely one was sitting across the room from him right now.

He closed his eyes for a moment as he let it ring, his jaw tight as he fought the instincts and training of ten years on the job. The ringing stopped as it went over to voice mail. He tried to tell himself he'd listen immediately, but that didn't ease the knot in his gut.

Quinn came up beside him. "I once ignored a call from an area commander because I knew it would be a kill order on a guy we'd captured. A guy I was sure we could get more info out of."

"Did you?"

"Yes. And it saved lives. Sometimes you just have to go with your gut."

Brady let out a long breath. "And what did it cost you?"

"I took some heat. Worth it." Quinn shrugged. "Helped

that coms were sketchy in the area. Kind of like cell reception in some spots here in the mountains."

Brady knew it was the perfect out, but it still took him a moment to quash the guilt. But it helped that Quinn clearly understood how he was feeling. Sometimes you had to make tough decisions.

And take the heat afterward.

Of course, if he was wrong about this, and the county spent a lot of man-hours searching for Ashley when he'd known where she was all along, it would be more than heat. And it hit him anew that he was risking the only job he'd ever wanted, the only thing he'd ever wanted to do in his life.

When the chime signaling a new voice mail sounded, he picked up the phone. A moment later he was listening to Lieutenant Becker's voice. Which, thankfully, didn't sound angry.

"Hey, Crenshaw, sorry to bother you on a v-day since you never freaking take them, but word is you've had some prior contact with an outstanding missing person. Ashley Jordan. Since she's the mayor's daughter, you can imagine the heat. She's leaning on the boss now, so we're covering every base. If anything about where she might go comes to mind from your contact with her, let me know ASAP."

Quinn didn't ask, but now that he knew what it said, Brady played it back on Speaker.

He heard a low, distressed sound and turned to see Ashley with her hands over her face. That muffled her words, but they were still clear enough. "She must be so worried. I should just go home."

The only one that beat him to her side was Cutter. The dog leaned in and put his head on her knee as Brady sat beside her. She lowered her hands, but unlike before, she didn't reach to pet the dog, and he could see tears glistening in those green eyes. It reminded him of how she'd looked before, which emphasized the contrast of how she'd been these last couple of days. It also sparked in him a powerful urge to push back this tide that seemed to threaten to swamp her all over again.

Pushed by an instinct he didn't question, he took one of her hands in his own and gently tugged the other over to rest on the dog's head. He wasn't about to question the animal's knack for comfort just now. In fact he was fairly convinced it was much greater than his own.

"We'll do whatever you want, Ashley," he said. "But there's something off about this. All of it. Let us figure it out."

Her expression was anxious as she looked at him. "But won't you be in trouble if they find out you've known where I am all along?"

That she'd even thought of that made him feel...he wasn't sure what. "Not your problem."

"You're doing this for me, so yes, it is."

He gave her a crooked smile. "As someone recently said to me, some pretty strong ethics there."

He got a half smile back for that, and it was enough.

Chapter 20

Brady felt the tingle at the back of his neck that told him someone was there. His fingers tightened around his cell phone reflexively.

He didn't need to look. The quickening of his pulse told him who it was. Her voice, that voice that did crazy things to the nerves along his spine, whispered over him. "I'm sorry. I didn't mean to intrude on your call."

"It's all right." He tapped the icon that ended the call. "We were done." He turned around and managed a smile and a gesture toward the snow still surrounding the patio. "It's weird, sitting here amid this, talking to someone who's in Arizona in eighty degrees."

"Some would say they're wiser."

"My mother among them," he said, gesturing with the phone before he slid it back into his pocket.

"You're close, you and your mother?"

He nodded. "Oh, we had our moments when I was

growing up, but since I hit the age where I realized I didn't know nearly as much as I thought I did, and she knew a lot more, we've done great. Especially since my dad died."

"That part still sucks," she said.

"Yours was worse," he answered quietly.

"Because he left me by his own choice? Maybe. The end result is the same, though."

"I had mine a lot longer, too. I was an adult when he died. You were only a child."

"Even more pitiful, huh?" she said with a grimace.

"You're a lot of things, Ashley Jordan, but you're not pitiful."

She smiled, although it looked like an effort. "So did you tell your mother you're harboring a fugitive?" That caught him off guard, and he looked away. "I'll take that as a no."

"If this blows up, I don't want it to touch her."

He looked back when he heard her gasp. "I didn't think of that," she said, her eyes wide. "Could it? It's bad enough for you, but—"

He held up a hand to stop her. "Don't start worrying about that on top of everything else. She'll find out eventually, but she'll be fine."

"Will she be angry with you when she does find out? Will it damage your relationship with her?"

He gave her a crooked smile. "They couldn't accuse me of anything big enough to make her turn on me."

Ashley smiled back, but it was a sad smile. "That's how I used to feel with my dad. He told me once I could never disappoint him."

He felt one of those clicks in his mind. "Why?"

"What?"

"What brought on him saying that?"

"Oh." Her mouth twisted wryly. "I got into a fight with

a girl at school. My mother was furiously upset because I made a scene, but my dad just said he'd have been angry if I hadn't stood up for myself."

"Was your mother always...critical?"

"Kind of," she said, although she sounded uncomfortable. "Back then, anyway. But like you and your mom, after my father died, we did much better."

He wasn't sure he liked the analogy. He and his mother had bonded together because they were all they had left. But he wondered, given the way she'd said her parents often argued, if her mother hadn't been glad. But that didn't seem quite fair, either. If her father had already been well into his mental decline, he couldn't imagine what her mother had endured—maybe she had the right to be relieved when it was finally over, even in that ugliest of ways.

Cutter suddenly appeared at the edge of the patio and sat in the snow, looking at them rather assessingly.

"Ready to go back in?" Brady asked the dog, then laughed inwardly at himself for having picked up the habit of talking to the animal as if he understood. Cutter merely tilted his head, watching them intently. And never moved. Which Brady supposed was, in effect, an answer.

"He's so funny," Ashley said.

Brady chuckled, then looked back at Cutter. "You're going to give new meaning to the phrase *freeze your ass off*, dog," he said wryly.

Ashley laughed, then looked back over her shoulder as someone else came out. "He's just sitting there, watching us," she said to Hayley.

"What he's doing," the other woman said with a grin, "is gauging whether he can lure either of you into a snow fight."

Brady drew back slightly. "Okay, if you're going to tell

me that on top of everything else, he can make snowballs and toss them, I'm going to have to jump off this train."

Quinn had stepped outside in time to hear that and laughed. "No. The snowballs are your bailiwick. He catches and eats them. And when it's his turn, he just digs up snow in a big spray at you."

Ashley laughed again, and for a moment it was as if they were simply a gathering of four people and a clever dog who seemed like a person, a group that liked each other and were content to just spend time together. Friends. And he was startled at the sudden tightness in his chest as he sat there stupidly and wished it was true.

Ashley paused in the entryway to the great room. Brady was on the couch, his long legs stretched out with his sock-clad feet on the coffee table—his boots were on the floor next to him—and what looked like Quinn's computer on his lap. She stood there for a moment, just looking at him. Which, she thought with a wry inward smile, she could happily do for a very long time.

Cutter, who had been stationed outside the bathroom when she came out—and probably would have been inside if she hadn't laughingly shut the door on him—nudged her as if to prod her forward. She stroked his head, marveling anew at the comfort the simple gesture gave.

"Did I hear a car leave?" She thought she'd heard the sound of tires crunching on snow.

Brady looked up and smiled. She had the crazy thought she should freeze that image in her mind so she could hang on to it in more desperate moments. It was the best smile she'd ever seen.

He put his feet down and set the computer on the end table at his elbow. "The snowplow finally made it up here, so Quinn and Hayley decided to see if they could get to town. And if they can, then I can try to make it to my place up the road here. I'd like to see how it did in the snow."

She blinked. "You live up here?"

He nodded. "About a half a mile farther up."

"I...didn't realize."

The smile again, a little crooked this time. "Believe me, my place is nothing so grand as this. Alex Galanis pulled out all the stops."

She walked toward him, paused and looked around at the great room. "So you know the guy who owns this?"

"I do. He's half the reason I trusted the Foxworths, because I knew what they did for him."

"What did they do?"

"His son ran afoul of some terrorist cabal down in Mexico. They held him for ransom. The government was 'negotiating' when he got a finger sent to him, with threats that they'd take his other two kids. Foxworth got his son out and kept the other two safe even though they were in college two thousand miles apart."

She knew she was probably gaping at him. "I... Wow."

"Yes." He gave her a wry smile. "Amazing what you can do when you're not crippled by regulations."

And she had these people on her side?

Cutter came up behind her, between the couch and the coffee table. The dog apparently misjudged the distance, because he bumped her rather hard behind the knees, and she half sat, half fell onto the couch. Beside Brady.

But not too close. Not as close as she'd like to be.

"What's with you?" she asked the dog. "Cranky because they didn't take you with them?"

"I gather that was his decision," Brady said, his tone amused. "They asked if he wanted to go, and his answer was to go lie down outside the door of the bathroom where you were."

Ashley laughed. "He is…unique."

"They said he'll be watching over you for the duration."

Will you? Or will the call of duty overwhelm you and make you do what you should have done the moment that wanted bulletin came out?

"I'm so sorry," she said softly.

He blinked. "What?"

"Helping me has put you in an awful position."

He let out an audible breath, and his lips compressed for a moment, telling her how accurate her observation had been.

"It's a first, anyway," he muttered.

She couldn't help herself, she reached out to brush her fingers over his unshaven jaw. His hand came up, caught her wrist. But instead of pulling her hand away as she'd expected, he held it there. He closed his eyes, and she felt a muscle jump under her touch. Her breath caught, held.

There was a sudden movement as Cutter jumped up on the couch. It threw her off balance once more, pushed her toward Brady. His eyes snapped open. They were mere inches apart.

"It was the dog," she explained. Or tried to. Her voice broke in the middle as his closeness seemed to swamp her. Things she'd never felt before were swirling through her. Heat, urgency and a kind of need she couldn't even name.

He was just looking at her, staring, his blue eyes overwhelming, fierce somehow, as if he were feeling the same kind of turmoil she was.

"Ash," he murmured, as if the second syllable was too much. She liked the sound of it. Face it, she liked everything about this man, from his looks to his ethics. If he'd had no second thoughts about what he was doing, she doubted she would be so attracted. She was nothing if not a contradiction.

"Yes," she whispered back, and as soon as the word escaped, she realized it was the answer to just about anything he might ask of her.

And then he was kissing her, his lips warm and as fierce as that look in his eyes had been. She realized everything she had been feeling had been merely prelude. His mouth on hers was the spark, and her body responded with an explosion of sensations that was nearly overwhelming. Deep, powerful, irresistible. This, this was what all the fuss was about. It made sense of so much even as it threw her into chaos.

He deepened the kiss, and at the first touch of his tongue against hers, she felt another surge of heat, and the only thing she could think was that if this was what a kiss did, sex with this man would shatter her completely. And right now she wasn't sure what, if anything, would be left of her afterward.

She wasn't sure she cared.

With a low, rough groan, he pulled back. He swore under his breath, as if helpless to stop it. For a moment he stared at her, and she saw all the same fire and tumult she'd been feeling in his eyes. He swallowed visibly, as if his throat were as tight as hers.

"That," he said, his voice none too steady, "should not have happened."

She understood. Why would someone like him want to get involved with a basket case like her? No matter how much better she was feeling, she had to remember that it was only temporary. That her life—her miswired brain was too much for her to handle, so she could hardly ask someone else to deal with it.

None of which changed the wonder of what she'd just experienced.

"You're right," she said, a little amazed at how steady her voice was. "But forgive me if I'm not sorry it did."

His eyes widened for an instant before he said, rather grimly, "I think I likely will be."

Chapter 21

He took his sweet time refilling his mug of coffee. And he needed every second of it.

Getting up and walking into the kitchen had been an interesting proposition. It had been a long time since he'd been that aroused, and he didn't think he'd ever been that hot over just a kiss. He lectured himself that it was only a kiss and it wasn't helping. Neither was remembering what she'd said about Andler making her get a birth control shot, just in case. Although it should, since it was a reminder that she was not in control.

You can really pick them, can't you, Crenshaw?

He kept stirring the coffee, although the teaspoon of sugar had dissolved at least a minute ago. He was stalling. He knew that. And it irked him. He wasn't usually a coward about facing situations. But this was different, and on some deep, buried level, it scared him.

You couldn't just fall for Ginny at the coffee shop. No,

you have to get tangled up with a woman whose life is an utter mess.

Steeling himself, he walked back into the great room. Ashley was still where she'd been on the couch, petting Cutter, who had sprawled out and plopped his head in her lap.

An enviable position, dog.

He nearly groaned out loud at his own thought.

But unlike him, Ash seemed to have regained her equilibrium by the time he came back. No, Ashley, he told himself firmly. Another barrier between them, not using that too-familiar nickname he'd let slip out.

As he set down his refilled mug, she gestured at the laptop on the table. "What were you looking for?"

He glanced at the screen as he sat down, hesitated, then shrugged. "I was looking up the medication Dr. Andler had you on. For side effects."

"Dr. Andler gave Mom a flyer, the kind that comes with a prescription. She showed it to me." She sighed. "It might account for some of my…symptoms, but far from all of them."

"I know. I read the list." He picked up the laptop, resumed his former position with his feet up again and denied to himself that he was using both computer and position as a barrier. "I know those drugs help people, but…"

"I hated taking it. It made me so foggy all the time. Not like the pain meds did, but constant. Like there was a layer of gauze between me and the world. Even the colors weren't right. The sky wasn't as blue, the trees as green or—" she gestured toward the patio "—the snow as white. Not like they are now."

"And that's when you started having memory problems," he said, remembering the chronology she'd written out at Quinn's request. "After you started taking it."

"Yes. But Dr. Andler said I'd be having those anyway, as things…progressed. Just like my father did."

"Just like he expected you to have," he corrected, thinking of what Quinn had said about Dr. Sebastian and not going into this with any preconceived ideas.

Ashley got it. "Do you really think she's right?"

The hope welled up in her voice and her expression as she looked at him. He hated to quash it, but he felt required to point out the obvious. "I'm not qualified to judge that."

"But you have instincts. Good ones. Those gut feelings, right?"

"Yes, but they're unhelpfully nonspecific. All they're telling me is that there's something off about all of this."

Cutter's head came up, and he let out a short, sharp yip that sounded weirdly like agreement. Ashley obviously thought so, too, because she smiled and said, "He agrees, I think."

"I'm getting to the point where I don't put anything past that dog," Brady said. Then, after a few moments while she stroked the dog and leaned over to nuzzle him, and he fought down the wish that she'd do the same to him, he asked, "It's been how long off the meds now?"

"Today is day twelve." She gave him a rather wan smile. "I guess I was lucky about the pain pills. If I had any withdrawal symptoms from the other meds, they were hidden."

"Traded one fog for another, huh?"

"Exactly," she said, relieved he understood.

"And you haven't felt…worse? Shakier? I mean, you don't seem at all confused, or uncertain, but I'm not in your head."

For an instant her eyes widened and her breath caught. As if she'd stopped herself from saying something. After a moment, steady now, she answered. "No. I feel…wonderful, all things considered. Mentally I feel sharp, clear-headed, and my memory's been fine."

He nodded. "That's how it seems."

She grimaced, and from her tone when she spoke, he guessed she was feeling compelled to be honest, just as he had been. "But Dr. Andler told me if I stopped taking the medication, it would seem that way…until my next break. Which would likely be worse than ever before."

"Are you feeling like you need to go back on them?"

"No!" She grimaced, as if the very thought made her shiver.

He looked at her for a long, quiet moment. "Promise me something?"

"Anything." She gasped, and her eyes widened even more this time. "I didn't mean… I…"

He waved off her protests. But inwardly he was acknowledging that he was slipping downhill like a skier on the downhill course over at Snowridge. Because he was wishing she'd meant that "anything."

"Not going there," he muttered.

"I'm still not sorry," she insisted.

"I never should have…kissed you. I had no right, not when you're mired in such chaos. I was taking advantage of your situation."

"You were not. I didn't stop you," she pointed out. "And I know that much about you, Brady Crenshaw. If I'd asked you to stop, you would have."

He frowned. "Of course."

"And that," she said with emphasis, "is why I didn't."

He blinked. Cutter made a low sound, something he'd have sworn in a human would be a chuckle. "That made sense to you, dog?" he asked wryly.

"Obviously," Ashley said, and she was smiling now, a small, sweet smile that nearly undid him all over again.

"Then he's better at understanding the female mind than I am."

"I think he's better at understanding people than most people."

"That, at least, I understand," Brady said.

Her smile widened. And after a moment she asked, her voice fairly level now, "Promise you what?"

He drew in a deep breath. Met her gaze and held it. "If you have the slightest thought about hurting yourself, about ending it, if it even flits into your mind, even if it seems like the most logical, most obvious solution…tell me?"

She looked startled. "I haven't," she said. "Not since that night." She paused, then added almost shyly, "Not since I've had you all on my side."

"But if it comes back," he began.

"I promise," she said.

She lowered her eyes, as if she couldn't hold his gaze. He understood. That damned kiss had rattled everything, and her balance was already so precarious, she could lose it at any moment.

She looked around, seeming almost desperate, then latched on to the laptop screen as a likely distraction. "What did you say were you looking up?" she asked as she studied the photo on the screen.

"Just your meds," he said.

She frowned and leaned in closer. He saw her read the caption under the small picture on the right side of the column of text. She stared at it for an oddly long time.

"Ashley? What is it?"

"Can you enlarge that?"

He tapped at the touchpad. The image of the two small pills snapped out to fill the screen. One side of the small round pill showed a number he knew was an identifier, and the other showed a score at the midpoint, making it easier to break the pill in half for a smaller dose.

She looked at him then, her brow furrowed in puzzlement. "I don't understand." She gestured at the image. "I know what it says, but…that is not the pill I've been taking."

"What?"

"It's not the same size or shape, and it's not scored like that." She gave a shake of her head. "I must have been taking a generic version. Although I'd think Dr. Andler would have mentioned that."

Brady noted that she spoke in the past tense, as if she had no intention of starting the medication again. But that didn't matter now, not yet. His voice was tense when he asked. "You're certain?"

One corner of her mouth quirked. "Every day for five months? Yes, I'm sure. My pills are bigger—uncomfortably so—oval and unscored. So it must be a generic."

Brady quickly rescanned the entry, down to where he'd read what he was looking for. Confirmed what it said. Then he shifted to look at her straight on. "Ashley, there is no generic. It's still protected. Whatever you're taking, it's not what he told you it was."

Chapter 22

"There it is."

Ashley's voice was tiny, and even she hated the sound of it. Cutter suddenly abandoned his relaxed pose and sat up on the couch cushion. He nudged her to pet him, but at the moment she didn't have the energy for even that.

"There what is?" Brady didn't look at her as he spoke, he kept studying the computer screen, as if looking for something, anything, that would make this not true.

"What I've been waiting for. Afraid of. Proof that... I'm not okay."

His head snapped around, and he did look at her now. "What do you mean?"

"It's obvious, isn't it? Just like with the knife, I've replaced reality with my own version. Taken something I've done every day for months and the glitch in my brain changed something as basic, as simple as what the pill looks like."

Brady drew back slightly. She didn't blame him. "That's what you think?" he asked.

"What I think," she said wearily, "is that the last two weeks, two weeks of clarity and functional memory, were a dream. A hope I manifested just like I did with what those pills look like. I even imagined they were big enough to hurt going down."

Cutter nudged her again. She didn't oblige; there was nothing the dog could do to make her feel better right now.

"Why?"

"What?"

"Why would what the pills look like matter enough for you to…mentally change what they look like?"

She gave a bitter laugh. "If only it made that kind of sense. But it doesn't, Brady. That's why they call it crazy."

He stood up abruptly. Set the laptop back on the table. Stepped out into the open room and began to pace. She still didn't blame him for wanting some distance between them. He was probably regretting kissing her even more now.

On top of the flood of weariness, the feeling of inevitability that had returned, she felt an aching sadness at never having known what could really happen between a man and woman before. Never having known what it could feel like, what the songs and symphonies and poetry were about. He'd given her a taste of it with that kiss. But only a taste. She still didn't know what slaking that urgent, imperative need would be like.

Now she never would.

This time when Cutter nudged her, she gave in, but only because she thought he could be an anchor that would keep her from flying apart right here, as her world—and the hopes she never should have allowed herself—were flying apart. And stroking his soft fur was soothing, beyond soothing, but as much as she'd come to like the dog, she would trade all his comfort for being in Brady's arms again.

His words came back to her. *You don't seem at all confused, or uncertain, but I'm not in your head.*

And what she'd nearly said aloud rang in her ears now as if she had. *The heck you're not.*

She watched him pace, some part of her reeling mind vividly aware of how much she liked the way he moved, the long-limbed, well-muscled grace of him. She couldn't help picturing the body beneath the jeans and long-sleeved T-shirt, wondering if he could truly be as beautiful as she imagined. Wondered what it would have been like, if they'd gone beyond that kiss.

Now she would never know. Now—

He spun around abruptly, cutting off her unruly thoughts. "Why do you assume that?"

"I...don't understand. Assume what?"

"That you're wrong about the pills."

Her brow furrowed. She gestured toward the laptop. "Because that's from the manufacturer, right? They obviously know what the pills they make look like. I'm the one who has the...the malfunction."

He crossed the room in two long strides, and sat on the coffee table right in front of her. "You're doing exactly what we talked about, what you said Dr. Andler did."

She blinked. "What?"

"You said he assumed you had the same disorder your father did."

"Because there's research showing it can be hereditary."

He waved that off. "But now you have the opinion of an even more qualified doctor who didn't make that assumption."

She knew she was slipping again, because she couldn't

seem to grasp what he was getting at. "Brady, whatever you're trying to say, please just say it."

"The picture of the pills doesn't match your memory. So you assume your memory's wrong."

She sighed. "Because it so often is. I'd hoped, when things were so clear the past couple of weeks—"

She stopped when he reached out and put a hand over hers. The heat of him seemed to radiate through her, even from that small connection. She stared at their hands, wondering how that was possible.

"What if," he said quietly, "you didn't make that assumption? What if you instead assumed your memory was right?"

She lifted her gaze to his face. The intensity of those blue eyes was nearly as heat-inducing as his touch. She tried to concentrate on what he was saying, but his closeness, his touch, was making it difficult. She was further gone than she'd thought.

"If my memory was right," she said slowly, to make what seemed obvious to her clear to him, "then I was taking something else. But that can't be. I even have the printout he gave me."

"Is there a picture on it?"

"No."

"Was it from the drug company?"

Her brow furrowed as she tried to bring the image of the sheet of paper to mind. "I don't think so. There was no logo or anything on it. And he printed it right there in the office. Of course, he could have downloaded it from the company."

"Did you ever fill the prescription at a pharmacy?"

She shook her head. "He said he was happy to do it for me, so I didn't have to...try and interact if I was having a bad day. And it was so easy for Mom to just pick it up, I never questioned it. Why?"

He pointed at the image still up on the laptop screen. "What other explanation could there be, if this isn't what you were taking?"

"That…he made a mistake? Gave me the wrong meds? Is that what you're getting at?"

"Not exactly."

Before he could go on—and likely confuse her further—Cutter's head came up and he gave a rather rhythmic bark that was clearly one of welcome, not warning. Quinn and Hayley must be back.

After greetings and putting away the supplies they'd brought back—including, to Ashley's amusement even now, carrots that were apparently for Cutter—they returned to the great room. Hayley looked at them both assessingly and glanced at her husband, who lifted a brow. She nodded. Ashley had never really observed that kind of nonverbal communication between spouses before, but these two clearly had it down pat.

"So," Quinn said conversationally, "want to tell us what you were deep into when we got here?"

She let Brady explain, hoping perhaps as he did she would figure out what bone he'd latched on to. He did it in the manner of a police report: short, concise and impersonal. That her meds had always come directly from Dr. Andler, that her mother had usually picked them up, that the flyer she'd been given had no image and that they had just discovered her memory of the pills she'd been taking did not match the image from the manufacturer.

At that, Hayley picked up her cell phone and rose. "I just want to check something." She walked into the kitchen.

"Do you have any of the pills with you?" Quinn asked Ashley.

Ashley grimaced. "No. I didn't expect to…" *To ever need them again.* She heard a low sound from Brady, and his expression looked as if he'd heard her thought.

"Don't," he said, his voice nearly hoarse. "Don't ever think that again, Ashley."

Crazily—that word yet again—the first thing she thought was that she didn't like that he'd gone back to her full name. She much preferred that taut, urgent way he'd whispered "Ash" in the moment before he'd kissed her. She wished he would say it again.

She wished he would kiss her again.

Hayley came back, stopping her from doing something unwise like kissing him. "Dr. Sebastian told me treating mental illness with drugs is always tricky. Finding the right medication, or combination, at the right dose. That sometimes the wrong medication is worse than no medication."

"She have anything to say about giving out one medication and saying it's another?" Brady asked sourly.

"She did. And it was rather colorful. But she can't say what effect the wrong medication might have without knowing what it is."

"And I heard from Ty." Quinn's tone was grim. "I may have a couple more things to add to that list. One, Dr. Andler gets paid an exorbitant amount for being an expert witness."

"They usually do." Brady grimaced. "Unless they're testifying for the prosecution."

"Well, he's high priced for a small-town guy." Quinn looked at Ashley and asked, "Who was paying him for your therapy?"

Her mouth twisted sadly. "My mother's paying for it. I should at least text her again. Let her know I'm still all right."

"I don't think turning on your phone again is wise," Brady said.

Tracking. She'd forgotten. But then Quinn spoke. "You can use one of our phones again, with all ID and location masked. It might be useful to know what's going on on that end. All we heard in town is that the search is on and the mayor is nearly hysterical."

Ashley felt a horrible jolt of guilt. All her mother had ever done was try to help her, and she was putting her through this.

"Please, yes," she said, almost breathlessly.

"All right," Quinn said.

Brady felt a little qualm at reading over her shoulder, but not enough to look away. He needed to think of this as part of an investigation, not snooping into the private business of a woman he…what? Was worried about? Sure. He had been since he'd found her in that car. Cared about? Of course. He'd care about anybody who was going through the hell she was going through.

Wanted? Oh yeah.

He tamped down his body's instant response to just the thought. Maybe there was something to that old saying about if you save someone's life, you're connected forever. Maybe that's all it was.

Sure, that's all it is, Crenshaw.

He focused on the screen on the phone she was holding. After a greeting where he could almost hear the other woman's cry of relief, the exchange rolled on.

We've been searching everywhere, honey. The sheriff, the fire department. Where are you?

I'm safe. Call them all off, it's a waste of time and money.

Brady found it interesting that she thought of that, considering the stress she was under.

You need to be home with me. I'm the one who has your best interests at heart.

I know that, Mom.

I'm the only one who truly loves you.

Brady frowned but kept reading.

I just needed to get away for a little while.

You shouldn't be alone.

I'm not.

He frowned at that, too. Maybe she shouldn't have said that.

What? Who are you with? You have no friends. You know they couldn't deal with your condition.

That was cruel.

Brady's jaw tightened. It was more than that.

You're too sensitive. And defensive. I wish you could discuss this calmly, rationally.

I just wanted you to know I'm with friends, and I'm fine. I'll be home soon. We can talk then.

You're being irrational, Ashley. Making things up again. Like about the snow tires.

She rubbed at her forehead, and Brady guessed her head had started to ache, because so had his. And the next line was an abrupt sign-off from Ashley.

He looked at her. "Is this how it usually goes with her?"

She nodded. He glanced at Quinn and saw an expression he guessed probably mirrored his own. He had a suspicion now, and it wasn't one he much liked.

Ashley had the feeling the others had seen something she hadn't. But that was hardly surprising these days. They didn't say anything, and right now she didn't have the energy to ask. After she had ended the text conversation with her mother—who would give her a lengthy lecture on manners and parental respect the next time she saw her—it had been all she could do to hold off a tension headache.

Quinn had booted up his laptop, that industrial-looking thing that appeared as if it would have survived a drop down the mountain much better than her mom's car had. And after a moment of moving through whatever program he'd opened, he went very still, reading intently. Then he looked up and spoke.

"Ty discovered the doctor has a sizable offshore account." Ashley didn't know much about such things, but they'd always sounded faintly illicit. "Which in itself isn't suspicious, but the fact that there have been big deposits after cases he's testified in is…interesting."

"But you said before he gets paid a lot," Ashley said.

"Yes. And his agreed-to payment for that is deposited in a bank account here. Openly."

Brady went still. Stared at Quinn. Ashley wondered briefly how on earth Quinn had found that out. Clearly

Foxworth had many sources and resources, in many places. Brady was right—they were a lot more than she ever would have imagined. And belatedly the actual meaning of what they'd discovered hit her.

"Wait…you mean he was secretly paid over and above what he got for testifying?" she asked.

Quinn nodded. "It was all masked fairly well, several layers deep, and it wasn't the only money in the account, but at the end of the trail, in large part the money came from either attorneys or agents for the people he was testifying for."

Brady swore under his breath. "Bribed. The ass—he was bribed for his testimony to go a certain way."

"Looks that way. Including in that case you mentioned, the rapist."

Brady spun around to look at her. Ashley saw an odd glint in his eye, an almost triumphant gleam. Not surprising, after what he'd said about Dr. Andler at that trial and what had so awfully happened afterward.

But when he spoke, it wasn't about that at all. It was about her. And he nearly spat out the connection she, still reeling a little, hadn't quite made yet.

"So there you have it. Your doctor, the guy who declared you mentally ill, is a damned, crooked liar."

Chapter 23

Ashley was stunned, Brady could see that. Understandable, of course, given she'd just learned the man she'd trusted her very sanity to was a lying, corrupt bastard.

"We can't prove any of this yet," Quinn cautioned. "Right now this is mostly speculation."

"Based on fact," Brady said flatly.

"Yes. But not enough fact for a court."

"I'm not worried about a court right now," he said, and something like surprise flickered in Ashley's eyes. What did she think, that he was going to be strictly by the book here? Hell, he was so far off even the last page of that book now that he'd be lucky to not end up in jail himself. And he didn't care about that, either. Which should rattle him a lot more than it did.

"Lay it out," he said to Quinn, trying to keep from sounding as angry as he was. "All of it." He wanted her to hear it, every bullet point, in succession.

Quinn seemed to understand, and began the list. "He has an offshore account. Not huge, but sizable. He was given additional payments by entities and parties who had already paid for his testimony, so it was possibly to influence that testimony, since that money and the sources were hidden. If we are correct in that assumption, he played a part in the release and/or exoneration of not only that rapist, but an embezzler, a disbarred attorney and a driver accused of manslaughter. In which case, by the way, he testified that the victim was in such a state of confusion he should not have been allowed out by himself at all, let alone onto a busy street."

"'Keep her home, Nan. Don't let her out alone.'" Ashley whispered what were obviously remembered words, but Brady heard them. And the anger he was trying to suppress ratcheted up another notch. His suspicions were growing, and he was beginning feel the urge to hunt down this slimy excuse for a human and take him out.

"We're digging deeper, going back further," Quinn said, "but as good as Ty is, it still takes time."

Brady gave the other man a glance. "I'm really glad I was warned not to think about how you get things done."

Quinn smiled easily. "For somebody used to going by the book, it's usually best."

"I don't mean to sound selfish here," Ashley said, "but I still can't help wondering what this all has to do with me."

"You're not being selfish at all," Hayley said reassuringly. "We need to tie this in to you and your situation."

"But I don't see any connection. I mean, it's disgusting and devastating to learn the truth about Dr. Andler, but that's just money. Does it mean he's a lousy psychiatrist?"

Brady spun around. "Do you really want to take the

word of somebody who can be bought off to let a rapist go free about your mental state?"

"But it's not just his word. I was having trouble before I ever started seeing him."

"The nightmares."

She nodded. "It was so bad I was afraid to go to sleep. I was awake most of the night most nights."

"And lack of sleep can cause half those problems," Brady pointed out. "We had a horrific brushfire the entire county was called in on a few years ago. I didn't sleep for more than an hour or two for nearly seventy-two hours. By that time I was loopier than a drunken ferret. I was surprised I knew my own name."

She was staring at him rather oddly. "Sometimes," she said softly, "I think we all forget."

His brow furrowed. "What?"

"How much we owe men like you."

"Amen," Hayley said.

"Not my point," Brady said with a shake of his head. "I just meant—"

"I know what you meant," Ashley said. "But since you won't trumpet your laudable acts, somebody needs to do it for you."

"She has a point," Quinn said mildly.

Brady gave him a look over his shoulder. And took a stab at what he guessed was probably fact. "Drag out all your medals to wear on special occasions, do you, Foxworth?"

For the first time since he'd met the man—damn, was it really only two weeks ago?—Quinn appeared nonplussed. And Hayley was laughing.

"Gotcha," she said cheerfully. "Nicely done, Brady."

The immediacy of his anger drained away; it was impossible to maintain in the face of Hayley Foxworth's grin. Even Ashley was smiling, which under the circumstances was amazing. And once the anger had ebbed a little, his brain kicked back in. And something that had been tickling the edge of his memory for a while surfaced.

"You have an appointment with Andler tomorrow, don't you?"

She nodded. "At four o'clock." There was no confusion, no forgetting, he noted.

He turned to look at Quinn. "He's got to know she's not showing up."

"I'm not?" Ashley asked.

His gaze snapped back to her. "Hell, no. You don't really want to go, do you?"

"No. I don't." Her expression turned very odd, almost wondering. "It's been a long time, or feels like it, since what I wanted had anything to do with…anything."

"Well, it does now," Brady said rather fiercely.

The smile she gave him then made every last bit of his fury fade away.

The snow was starting to melt. Not quickly, since it was still in the thirties, but it was several degrees above freezing and so the trickles were appearing, and bare branches here and the green of an evergreen bough there were beginning to show through. Ashley felt unexpectedly sad about that as she sat on the patio bench, realizing this spot would soon be just a normal patio again, open and no doubt with a lovely view, but no longer with this feeling of privacy and seclusion.

She'd been glad when Hayley had suggested she take a break from it all. She'd gratefully come out here, followed by Cutter, who was now sitting at her feet with his chin resting on her knee. The dog really was an amazing comfort and a stalwart companion as she tried to sort out the mass of information and emotions that had enveloped her.

His head came up, and she saw the wag of his tail. A moment later the patio door opened, and Brady stepped out. The dog had no doubts about Brady, obviously. But then, neither did she. Not about who he was at the core, a good, decent, brave and on occasion heroic man. It was no surprise that she was attracted to him. What woman wouldn't be?

She saw he was carrying two steaming mugs. He sat down on the bench—close, but not too close, meaning not close enough for her taste—and held one out to her.

"I think I may be coffee'd out," she said; she'd had several cups trying to jolt her brain into moving faster on all this.

"It's not coffee," he said. "Hayley seemed to think chocolate was called for, so she picked some up when they were out."

"Bless her," Ashley said, meaning it as she took the proffered cup.

She took a long, slow sip, savoring the rich taste, then the warmth as it went down. He took a swallow of his own, then cupped his hands around the mug. She thought of how his hand had felt on hers. Which led to how his lips had felt on hers. And in that moment there was nothing she wanted more than to taste his mouth again.

"I'm sorry," he said. She blinked. He'd already apologized for kissing her, an apology she'd hardly felt necessary. "I lost my cool in there, and I shouldn't have."

Ashley felt color rise in her cheeks, and she looked down into her mug as if the rising steam could mask it. He'd probably long forgotten that kiss, while she couldn't seem to get it out of her mind. But then the sense of what he'd said registered.

"Do you have any idea how long it's been since any-one was angry on my behalf? How long it's been since anyone thought of me as anything except someone to be pitied or avoided?"

"Too long," he said gruffly.

"Yes. So please, don't apologize for that." She took an-other swallow of the rich, sweet brew before she asked, "How did you know Quinn had medals?"

He snorted, meeting her gaze with a grin that warmed her more than the chocolate. "Seriously? That guy? He's got *hero* painted all over him."

"Yes, he does." She waited a moment before adding quietly, "Just like you."

He looked startled, then shook his head. "I'm just a guy trying to do a job in a place where it's not usually too hard."

"But when it is, you're there and you deal. What else is a hero?"

Brady lowered his eyes, as if embarrassed, but Cutter let out a short, sharp bark that she supposed would be called a yip but sounded crazily like "Yep!" She'd never realized dogs made so many different kinds of sounds, and how expressive they could be.

Brady reached out to give the dog a scratch behind the ears. To do it he had to lean over her, and his arm brushed over her breast. Even though the touch was clearly acciden-tal, it sent a jolt through her, leaving her very skin tingling.

And that quickly she was thinking about that kiss again. He might regret doing it, but that didn't change what it had been. Not for her, anyway. Maybe it simply hadn't been that hot, that consuming for him. Maybe he kissed women all the time. Maybe he kissed one particular woman all the time.

No. He would never have kissed you if there was a permanent partner in his life. That's not the kind of man he is.

And she was more certain of that than she'd been of anything in her chaotic, ridiculous life lately.

Chapter 24

"**Y**ou've got two choices," Brady said, sounding more grim than he'd meant to. He was pacing again, now that they were back inside. It had started to rain, accelerating the melt, and they'd managed to get back in before they— or the dog—got too wet.

"Only two?" Ashley said rather dryly.

He turned back to look at her. Smiling despite the problem they were chewing on. Because more and more sparks of humor and wit were breaking through, and he liked seeing it.

"Two that lead to all the rest," he elaborated.

"Naturally." She sighed. "Go ahead."

"Either Andler knew or didn't know. About the meds."

She nodded slowly. "If he didn't, he's incompetent. But if he did… I don't know what that means."

"We need to know what he did give you before we can guess at that."

"And how do we do that?" Ashley asked. "There must be hundreds of plain, big, white, oval pills out there."

"We need a sample," Hayley said. "We have people who can figure out what's in them."

"Of course you do." Ashley gave the other woman a smile. "Have I mentioned how glad I am you're all on my side? Even if…nothing changes, it's a wonderful feeling."

Her gaze flicked to Brady. Only for an instant, but it was enough to make his pulse jump. And suddenly he was remembering that kiss that never should have happened.

I'm not sorry it did.

Her words echoed in his head, and it took an effort to rein in a body that was suggesting rather hotly that he pursue that.

"I could go back home and get them," Ashley said.

"No!" Brady snapped, so sharply she drew back slightly. He reined in the sudden bolt of alarm that had shot through him. "I just mean you shouldn't risk it until we know exactly what's going on."

"Risk?"

It was Hayley who said gently, "Ashley, you're a wanted felon in the eyes of any law enforcement except Brady."

She paled. She turned a shocked gaze on him. "I didn't look at it that way. I didn't think about what would have happened if someone else had found me. Some other deputy who…wouldn't listen. Or believe."

"That's not important now. What is is how do we…"

His voice trailed off as something occurred to him. She started to speak but stopped when he held up a hand, his brow furrowed as he thought. Then he focused on her again. "Where are your pills?"

"In my bathroom, in the medicine cabinet. Bottom shelf. It's the only thing on that shelf."

"Prescription bottle?"

She nodded. "Labeled as...the real thing."

"That key you had on you...it's the house key?"

"Yes. I didn't want to leave the house unlocked."

Something tugged at him deep inside. And without thinking about it, he reached out and cupped her face in his hands. He heard her suck in a breath at the touch, felt the sudden heat rising in himself at the feel of her soft, smooth skin beneath his fingers. Ignored it for the more important thing at this moment. "Even then, you were thinking that clearly. Remember that, Ashley."

Her eyes widened slightly, as if she hadn't realized that. It was one of the harder things he'd done in these last four days, but he broke the contact. He turned to look at Quinn, trying to think of how to explain the idea that had come to him.

"It might work," Quinn said before he could speak. "But maybe you should let us do it. Nobody would recognize us."

Brady didn't question how the man had guessed. "And therefore would likely call you in as a burglar," he pointed out. "Besides, what if someone's there? Her mother, even?"

"What are you talking about doing?" Ashley said, staring at them both.

He turned back to her. "I'm going to go get those meds."

She stared at him. "You're going to break into the house?"

"No, because you're going to give me that key."

"But what if my mother is there, like you said?"

"Then I'm there officially. Looking for signs you might have snuck back to the house for something, since you took nothing with you. Nobody else knows I have any connection other than prior contact. Which I could play as enough to explain why I'm...interested."

"But she needs to know I'm all right," Ashley said. "I know she has to be half out of her mind with worry."

He hesitated then. Glanced at Quinn, who nodded, then said, "And once her relief fades, if she finds out Brady has known where you are all along and let her worry, her first instinct will likely be to hang him out to dry."

"And," Hayley added, "given her connection to the sheriff, it's likely she could make life very ugly for him if she's upset enough."

"But if I begged her not to, she'd call it off—"

"That's not a bell you can unring," Brady said flatly.

Ashley looked away for a moment, then got to her feet and hurried out of the room. Brady watched her go, wondering if this was simply too much for her, if he just should have snagged the key somehow and done it. He saw Quinn say something softly to Hayley, who nodded and took out her phone and walked toward the kitchen, apparently to make a call. But then Ashley was back. And she held the ring with the house-shaped fob and the single key.

"She put them on that so I'd remember what it was for," Ashley said with a grimace when she saw him looking at the little silver decoration. "She told me I was confused enough to forget."

That suspicion he'd developed stirred anew, but Brady kept it to himself for the moment. He took the key. "Thanks. And for trusting me."

"I think you have that backward."

Hayley came back before he could answer, a relief since he didn't know what to say. "The mayor's office says she's out, they don't know where or when she might be back. They explained she's had a family crisis."

Ashley winced at that. Brady said briskly, "So she could be home or somewhere else."

Quinn nodded. "If you have the option of getting in and

out unseen, I recommend you leave everything else as it is. Just grab a pill out of the bottle and leave it."

He nodded. Hayley got up and went quickly to the kitchen, coming back with a small zip-seal baggie, which she handed to him.

"Once you've got it," Quinn went on, "we'll get it to our guy and find out just what we're dealing with."

Brady thought about asking just how they would do that, but he decided it didn't matter just now. Besides, why would he doubt that the people who apparently had the likes of Gavin de Marco on speed dial could do anything they said they could?

"And Quinn will be in the area," Hayley said. "We'll give you a Foxworth phone, which has a walkie-talkie function, so we can all be in direct, live contact, just in case."

Brady frowned. That would leave Hayley here alone with Ashley.

"I'm trusting you," Ashley said softly.

He looked at her. Realized what she meant, that she was trusting him, so he should trust her in turn. And she had a point. He was in this now—he'd already violated everything he believed in, so what was a little thing like leaving a wanted felon in the custody of a civilian? Although he had a feeling Hayley Foxworth could more than take care of herself. In fact, he knew it, now that he thought about it, because there was no way in hell Quinn would leave his wife in a situation she couldn't handle.

"All right," he said softly. He glanced at his watch. It was late afternoon, and Lieutenant Becker would be off duty soon. "I should call my lieutenant back. See if there are any new developments that might affect this…idea."

Quinn nodded. "Speaker, if you don't mind?"

Brady nodded. "Save time." He pulled out his phone and made the call.

"Crenshaw? About time."

"Sorry," he said. "I've been…in the mountains." Not exactly a lie.

"I figured when I had somebody go by your place and you weren't there." So he'd been right not to go home. Brady saw Quinn raise a brow as if to say "Good call." Becker went on. "Seriously, though, sorry to bother you on vacation. Although why you'd take one in the dead of winter is beyond me."

"Just crazy, I guess." Definitely not a lie. "So what's the status?"

"Suspect is still missing. Couple of sighting reports, but nothing that panned out."

He glanced at Ashley, at her worried expression. "How's the victim?" he asked.

"Physically, she's on the mend. But she's worried sick about her daughter. Fought us on going with the higher charge."

"Does she have any idea where—" he had to stop himself from saying *Ashley* "—she might have gone?"

"A couple, but they all turned up negative. I just thought since you're the only one on the department who's had recent contact with her, and with your…experience with Liz, you might have picked up on something."

He'd forgotten Becker had known Liz. Had warned him about her, in fact. He hastened to head that off before his pitiful romantic past got broadcast to the room. "Not that I can think of right now. I'm going to head into town in a bit—maybe that'll jog something loose."

"Anything," Becker said, sounding very harassed. "The mayor can be a pain in the—"

"I'll bet." He said it quickly; it might be true, but Ashley didn't need to hear it. Not now, with everything else she had to deal with.

He looked at Quinn as he ended the call. "A go?"

"Your call," Quinn said.

Brady nodded. "I'll go change. Better in uniform, I think. That'll be expected."

Quinn nodded, then looked at Ashley. "Can you draw him a layout of the house, where to look?"

She nodded quickly. "Of course."

Brady had turned to go when Quinn spoke again. "I know how this feels, Brady."

He looked back. Saw the understanding in the other man's face. And he guessed Foxworth did know, in a very personal way, what it felt like to go against all your training, all your beliefs.

"The only thing I can tell you," Quinn said quietly, "is that injustice feels worse."

"Good enough," he said. And went to suit up.

Chapter 25

"He's a very special man," Ashley said to Hayley as the other woman watched her husband from where they were sitting at the kitchen counter. She caught herself before reaching for yet another of the delicious cookies Hayley had baked.

"He is. And," Hayley added, with a rather pointed look at Ashley, "so is Brady Crenshaw."

"I know." The words came out barely above a whisper. "I don't know why he decided to help me. I don't know why any of you did."

"Because of those things we believe in and stand for," Hayley said. "We may not get the results we'd like to see for you, but what we will get is you being treated fairly."

She said it with such solid confidence Ashley shook her head in wonder. It had all seemed insurmountable to her such a short time ago, but now...she dared to hope. And then, although she hadn't wanted to, she asked aloud, "I wonder who Liz is. Or was."

Hayley gave her a steady look. "Do you really want to know?"

Ashley blinked. "You mean…you do?"

"Told you Ty was the best."

"You…investigated Brady?"

"I wouldn't say it went that far, but Quinn always likes to know who he's dealing with."

"Oh."

"And Brady is exactly the kind of man Foxworth looks for. The best kind."

She knew if she didn't push, Hayley would leave it there. But she couldn't seem to help herself. "And… Liz?"

"The woman he was engaged to, three years ago."

"Oh." She wasn't surprised—there would have to be someone he was serious about. And what woman in her right mind wouldn't be serious about a man like Brady?

In her right mind…

She nearly laughed out loud. Because being of right mind had nothing to do with being attracted—okay, beyond attracted—to Brady Crenshaw. She was living proof of that.

"It ended a couple of months before the wedding date. Any more than that is his to tell you, or not," Hayley said. "Assuming you're interested."

Ashley sighed. "If there's anything I'm sure of in all this, it's that I have no business even thinking about him that way."

Hayley gave her a rather amused smile. "I think it may be time to tell you about Cutter's other talent."

Ashley leaned down over the dog and kissed the top of his head. Cutter swiped his tongue over the tip of her nose, making her laugh. "I think his existing talents are quite enough."

"Yes," Hayley said with a wide smile. "But there is another one. With an equal track record."

"Oh?"

"He's a matchmaker. And a very successful one."

Ashley blinked. "What?"

"Counting Quinn and me, he's brought together, or brought back together, ten couples."

"He...what? He brought you and Quinn together? I thought Quinn...kidnapped you."

"He did. But the only reason I was there to be kidnapped was Cutter. He fell in love with Quinn at first sight and led me right into it." Hayley grinned. "I, on the other hand, took more convincing."

"I'll bet," Ashley said, thinking this was the craziest thing she'd heard yet.

"So far he's brought together or reunited four of our clients with their perfect match. And two of our Foxworth guys, plus our friend Detective Dunbar. And my brother. Oh, and Gavin de Marco."

Ashley knew she was gaping at the woman now. "Cutter brought them all together...how?"

"He has his ways." Hayley smiled sweetly. "Has he nudged you into sitting next to Brady? Maybe herded Brady toward you?"

"I..." She looked back down at the dog, who looked up at her with those dark, amber-flecked eyes, eyes that suddenly seemed ancient and wise. "Yes."

"I thought so."

"Wait, are you saying he's trying to matchmake us?"

"And he has a one hundred percent success rate."

Ashley felt a little leaping sensation inside. *Wishful*

thinking. She quashed it. "Believe me," she said, "Brady deserves a lot better. Cutter should look elsewhere."

"Did I mention he never gives up?"

Ashley shook her head as she shifted her gaze back to Hayley. "You know what a mess I am," she said miserably. "Why would he wish me on a good man like Brady?"

"I know what a mess your life is right now," Hayley corrected. "And that's as far as I'll go until we have some answers."

And all Ashley could think was what a sad state of affairs her life was when that was a hope worth clinging to.

He would never make it as a burglar, Brady thought, because even with the key and permission of one of the residents, he didn't like this. He was more of an up-front, out-in-the-open kind of guy.

Of course, the fact that that resident was a fugitive and the other was the mayor of this place might have something to do with it. Which thought brought him back to what he'd seen when they had, at Quinn's suggestion, stopped near city hall for Quinn to make a second call to see if the mayor had returned. They'd taken his marked SUV to further the story of this being official if necessary. He hadn't ridden with a partner since his days as a trainee, but he couldn't think of a better choice than Foxworth. The guy was the kind of man who would always have your back.

And in the moment when he'd been told she had just left again, Brady had looked up and seen the woman, exiting the front entrance. She had turned left at the bottom of the steps and proceeded down the street with obvious purpose. And she had looked, to Brady, not worried but angry.

But he'd said nothing. Nor had Quinn, even when he'd

pulled the binoculars out of the unit's equipment box and focused them on the woman striding down the sidewalk. What had begun as a hunch became a certainty when she turned at the two-story building halfway down the block and vanished inside.

His jaw had tightened as he lowered the binoculars. "The shrink's office," he had muttered to Quinn. Who had been not in the least surprised.

"At least we know she's not at home," he'd said mildly as Brady started the unit and they headed for the house. But Brady had guessed the man was pondering the likelihoods just as he was.

Ashley had told him the key would also work on the back door, and given that area was much more hidden from general view than the front, he and Quinn had agreed on that approach. The seven-foot wooden fence that surrounded the backyard wasn't much of a challenge, and within seconds of clearing it, he was at the back door and blocked by the shape of the house from the neighbor's line of sight. He slid the key into the dead-bolt lock and turned it. It was a little stiff, as if this door didn't get used much, but with a little bit more oomph, it went.

He stepped inside quickly and shut the door behind him. He looked where Ashley had told him and saw the alarm panel. He felt a brief qualm as it flashed red at him; if this was where Ashley's mind hit a new glitch, he was going to have some hefty explaining to do. But he quickly keyed in the pass code she'd given him—*It's the date she was first elected*—and the lights turned green. Well, that figured. If there was a date that woman would be unlikely to forget, it was that of her rise to local power.

There would be a record of the entry, but he hoped this would be over by the time anyone thought to look. Unless she'd put a watch on it, of course, and the alarm company had instructions to call her at any unscheduled entry. He could only hope she hadn't thought of that and get himself out of here in a hurry.

Ashley's drawing of the layout was as accurate as the code had been. He tried not to dwell on what that might mean and focused on the task at hand. A minute later he was upstairs and at the door to her bedroom. He paused in the act of reaching for the knob. Looked back over his shoulder at the two other doors in this hallway. Saw that they were a rustic, iron style that matched the rest of the hardware in the house. But this knob was round, shiny, brass, and looked brand-new. His brow furrowed, then cleared as he understood it had probably been changed so Ashley could not lock the door. Her mother would want to be able to check on her. With a shake of his head at having to live that way, he opened the door.

For a moment he just stood there. The rest of the house looked like something out of an interior decorating magazine: fancy furniture and accessories, all color coordinated, carefully placed and likely expensive things on display, and the kitchen had looked like the set of a cooking show. All of it was way too elegant for his casual taste and seemed to him out of place here in the mountains.

But here, in Ashley's room, it all changed. He was willing to bet there was more color and personality in this single bedroom than in the entire rest of this house. Not so much in the walls or furniture, which matched the rest of the house, but in the art on the walls, photographs of wildlife that frequented these mountains, from a dramatic wolf in the shadows of the trees to a less dramatic banana slug, and including a shot of a river otter that could be a twin to the one that occasionally hung out in his own backyard. And what he thought of as a touch of humanity in the shoes kicked off on the floor, the jacket—the green one he'd seen her wearing the day of the crash but that she had not put on that night, because her distressed mind had told her she soon wouldn't be feeling cold, or anything else— tossed over the back of the chair by the window, the book left at an odd angle on the nightstand next to the bed. The bed he had been trying not to look at.

It was tossed, the covers looking as if they'd been kicked aside after a restless night. As if she had tried to sleep, given up...and decided to kill herself instead. He had wondered if he would feel some kind of sexual jolt at the sight of her bed, if he would start imagining her in it, imagine joining her in it, as he'd done more than once at Alex's place. But all he could think of was how desperate she had been that night, and it made him ache inside in an entirely different way.

Get moving, Crenshaw.

He crossed over to a closed door and pulled it open. It was a small walk-in closet, tidy, the only sign of haste a couple of hangers that were at an angle. He closed the door and quickly crossed the room to the second door that opened into the room. The bathroom was tidy as well, towels hung neatly, and on a hook on the back of the door the sweatshirt he'd seen her in that day he'd come by and been shocked by her appearance. It was hard to believe she was the same woman, so far removed from that was she now.

There was only a comb lodged in a hairbrush on the counter. Everything else—lotions, hair clips, makeup, a couple of things he didn't recognize—was on a tray to one side. He only noted this in passing, because he was focused on the mirror above the sink, the one that was hinged and clearly the door to the medicine cabinet he was looking for. He reached out, already mentally searching for the standard orange plastic prescription bottle she'd described. The door to the cabinet swung open easily. He looked at the bottom shelf.

It was empty.

Chapter 26

"But…it's always there."

Ashley stared down at the phone in her hand, from which Brady's voice had issued over the link Hayley had activated with the red button, the link that connected them and Quinn and Brady live.

"The shelf is empty. Only thing in the cabinet is a toothbrush and paste, and little bottle of…some hair stuff."

"You're sure you're in the right room?"

"I'm looking at your banana slug. And your jacket's on the back of the chair by the window." He recognized her jacket? *Trained observer, that's all.* She heard him move over the live connection. "What were you reading?"

"The first of the…" Her voice trailed off as she remembered she had retreated into a childhood treasure, the first of the tales of a boy with a miserable life who found out he wasn't who they'd told him he was at all. "A kid's book," she ended lamely.

"It's okay, Ash. I grew up on them."

Her throat tightened fiercely at the gentle understanding in his voice. And at the nickname he'd whispered in the moment before he'd kissed her that first time. The name she hadn't gone by since her father had used it, despite her mother insisting on the formality of her full name.

Cutter nudged her hand, and Hayley smiled at her. She swallowed and pulled herself together. "You're in the right room, then. But the pills should be there."

"I'll check around."

She heard the sound of movement, of doors closing, and the sliding of drawers. For a moment it flitted through her mind to worry about whether he'd find anything embarrassing, but it seemed a ridiculous thing to worry about right now. Not that there would be anything, not with the dark, swirling mess her life was right now. And if he found them somewhere else, in some odd place, then it only meant this was a pointless exercise, because it would prove her memory really was malfunctioning.

"Nothing," he finally said. "Checked the bathroom and all the drawers in the bedroom." *Well, there you go, Brady Crenshaw digging through your underwear.* Somehow that wasn't nearly as unsettling as she thought it should be.

"What if it was dropped and rolled?" Hayley asked.

"Good point. I'll check the floor."

But he came back again a long moment later. "Nothing."

"This makes no sense," Ashley said.

"Unless they were removed."

That was Quinn, and Ashley frowned at the suggestion. And then was even more puzzled when Brady said, "Just what I was thinking."

"But why—"

"Where's your mother's room?"

"The opposite end of the hall, but she wouldn't take

them. Unless…unless she wanted to keep count, track whether I was taking them."

"Which you weren't. Maybe she suspected that. I'll check."

There was more movement, the sound of a door opening. Then Brady's voice, sounding a bit sour. "You sure a human lives here?"

Ashley laughed in spite of her nerves. "She is a bit compulsive about neatness."

She heard another door, then what sounded like drawers opening, then a pause, then another drawer; she guessed he'd crossed back into the bedroom to check that nightstand. A moment later, the negative came—no sign of the pills in her mother's room, either. Ashley was utterly confused now. "I don't understand. There was at least half a bottle left, fifteen pills or more."

"Damn," she heard Brady mutter. "We need to know what those pills really are."

"Better clear out of there," came Quinn's voice.

"I'll check the kitchen cabinets just in case, but yeah, I think—"

"Wait!" Ashley yelped as a memory hit her.

"What?" came Brady's voice.

"Look, I know this is gross, but it might be the only… go back to my room. I started to take the meds again a week ago, because my mother was pushing. I actually put a pill in my mouth, but changed my mind after she left and spat it out. I tossed it in the wastebasket by the bed. The housekeeper's been there since, but there was nothing else in there, so she might have missed it."

There was a long, silent moment, some more sounds of movement and then a door, and then, "Got it!" Ashley let out a breath. "Good memory," Brady added.

"Well, that's something I've not been accused of lately,"

she said rather wryly. "And sorry you had to pick it up when it's gross—"

"Not. I've tasted your sweet mouth, Ash. Nothing gross about it."

Her breath caught. Had he really said that, on this open line where everyone could hear?

"I see you've done it again," Hayley whispered, and Ashley realized she was talking to Cutter. Who looked rather…smug? Could a dog really look smug?

"Points to you, Cutter. Again." That was Quinn, sounding nothing less than amused. He believed this, too, this… matchmaking thing? The ex-military man seemed far too cool and tough for such fanciful thinking.

But it was only a fleeting thought, because Brady's simple, almost unbearably touching declaration was expanding inside her until there was no room for anything else.

"Foxworth," Brady said as he and Quinn came back in the house, "has some pretty cool toys."

"Necessities to get the job done," Quinn corrected, but he was grinning.

"Oh, absolutely," Brady said, grinning back.

"I gather you met Teague?" Hayley said, and her smile was wide. This was clearly a woman who didn't mind her man buying toys.

"I think it was more that he met the helicopter and, oh yeah, there's a pilot," Quinn quipped.

Brady shrugged, still grinning. The black helicopter coming in to land at the snowy baseball field just outside town had been quite a sight. And he had been a little boggled by the sleek machine and had only belatedly reacted to its pilot. He'd liked the guy right off, though. Quinn had said Johnson was an ex-marine—if there was such a thing—and he could see it in the other man's bearing and demeanor.

He was also clearly a heck of a pilot, setting the thing down without a jolt, even amid the snow he'd set flying. And once more he'd been impressed with Foxworth, not just for the helicopter but because of the fact that Quinn had called for it to pick up one small pill. And had promised they'd have results by tomorrow, if not sooner.

"Boys and their toys," Hayley said, so lovingly Brady half expected them to vanish into their bedroom momentarily.

"And," Quinn added with a pointed look at his wife, "he and Laney have set a date."

Hayley's smile became one of utter delight. "About time. They've been engaged nearly a year. When?"

"May. And he asked if they could do it at Foxworth."

"Perfect! The flowers will be glorious, and we can use the same setup we did for our wedding and—"

Quinn held up a hand in mock self-defense. "You and Laney can plan your hearts out when we get back."

Ashley had gotten very quiet, but then, he had no part in this particular conversation, either. As he'd had none when the other Foxworth…operative, for lack of a better word, had informed his boss of the news. Other than noticing Teague Johnson's besotted grin and feeling a bit…envious.

But then she spoke, hesitantly and more than a little wary. "Is this one of… Cutter's successes?"

Hayley laughed. "Indeed it is. His…third. Second for a Foxworth person, counting us."

Brady's brow furrowed as he looked at the two women. He had no idea what that was about. Wondered if he was better off that way. Ashley looked at him then, and there was something different in her expression, in her green eyes. But it wasn't anger, although he'd half expected she'd be mad at him for what he'd said on that open connection. He hadn't really thought about the fact that Quinn and Hayley were listening. He'd only wanted her to stop sounding so shaky. He hadn't thought about what he was saying, and admitting.

Hell, he hadn't been thinking right since she'd crashed into his life.

He admitted to himself that she wasn't the only one on tenterhooks about what the Foxworth analysis of the pills she'd been taking would turn up. Although he did wonder if she had wrapped her mind around what all the implications were. He kind of doubted it, given she'd had so much to deal with in such a short time.

The only thing he was sure about was he was getting damned tired of keeping himself on a short leash around her. There were guys, he even knew a couple, who would take advantage of her situation, her need for help and comfort, or her mental state to get what they wanted, which would be her in bed. More, they'd walk away afterward whistling happily, without a second thought. He'd never, ever understood that. He'd been told he'd been lucky to have his parents, who had loved each other until the day his father had died and beyond, as an example, but it was more than that. It was something he didn't analyze but knew was bone-deep in him. You just did not treat another person that way.

But that did not seem to be helping him stop thinking about doing just that. About kissing that mouth—which had indeed been sweet—again, about kissing every inch of that silken skin, about tangling his fingers in that long fall of dark hair, about feeling it slide over his own skin, and—

He jerked on that mental leash. Again.

It was going to be a long night.

Chapter 27

Ashley sat looking out the big front windows of the cabin into the night. The remains of the fire that had warmed the room during the day still glowed on the hearth, and the room was still comfortably warm where she sat on the end of the couch nearest the big stone fireplace.

It was a clear night, with a nearly full moon, and outside everything seemed to glow almost eerily. It was cold, she guessed, judging by the way what had been snow melting and running off the eaves had frozen into a jagged yet oddly beautiful line of small icicles.

She was very aware of what was happening. That her mind was racing in that careening way it always had when she'd been faced with a big problem, from possibility to possibility. This was one of the things the drug—whatever it was—had dulled. And when she'd finally given up on sleep and come out here, she'd been worrying if this meant she really did need the stuff.

A sound from the hallway made her head snap around. She'd tiptoed down the hall, not wanting to disturb anyone, although Quinn and Hayley's room was at the back of the house.

Okay, Brady. You didn't want to disturb Brady. He's worried enough about you. And he's already risking so much.

Even as she thought it, he came into the room. She drew back, as if this shadowy corner of the room could hide her. And then she froze, unable to breathe, as he stepped into a shaft of that silvery moonlight coming in through the big window.

He'd just pulled on his jeans, and those were only half zipped, giving her a full view of him down to where a narrow trail of dark hair arrowed downward over abs she'd just known would be rock-hard. With that moonlight pouring over his bare torso, he looked like some Greek statue come to life, powerful, muscled...beautiful.

She thought she'd smothered her gasp, but clearly not, because he spun around. And clearly his vision was well adapted to the dark, because he spotted her instantly.

"I thought I heard something," he said, very quietly.

"I tried to be quiet. I didn't want to disturb...anyone."

"You were. I almost convinced myself I hadn't really heard anything."

"But you had to be sure," she said.

"All things considered, yes."

"Afraid I'd sneak out in the night and run?" She hadn't really meant to say that, didn't believe it, but he had her so disconcerted, standing there, looking like he looked.

"No."

He said it with a quiet firmness that surprised her. "How can you be so sure?"

"Because you have help now. And hope. You're not alone anymore, Ash, and you won't give that up easily."

How on earth had he come to know her so well? The real her, not the woman who had been crumbling to pieces. "No. I won't." Then, with a sigh, she said, "No one's called me that since my dad."

"Do you mind?"

"From you? No. I…like it from you."

He smiled at that. She could see it even in the dark. Then he was sitting beside her, and she could more than see him—she could feel him, the heat of him, and smell that impossible scent, that mix that reminded her of sitting outside on the patio here, with the snow-covered pines all around.

"No matter what we find out, you won't be alone again, Ash. I promise you that."

And this man's promise, you could take to the bank, as her father used to say. She knew it was true, on some gut level that didn't need her brain to process—it simply was. And her throat tightened at the fierce gentleness in his voice, at the way he was looking at her, so steadily that she could almost feel it. Even in this shadowy corner, she could see the determination in his face, in the set of his jaw. And the strength to carry it out in the muscle of his body, his arms, his neck, his broad, powerful chest…

"Hey," he said, reaching out to brush at her cheek with his thumb. Only then did she realize tears were starting to spill from her eyes. "Don't, Ash. Please. It'll be okay. One way or another, it will be okay."

She couldn't seem to stop, and the next thing she knew, he was pulling her into his arms. And with his solid warmth wrapped around her, she found the strength to speak. "It wasn't that. It's just…it's been a long time since I've been so sure that someone will keep a promise."

He went very still for a moment. She looked up at him, so very, very aware of his bare skin beneath her cheek, aware of her palm pressed to the flat, hard ridges of his belly. She could feel the power of him as if it were suddenly made tangible, and heat blasted through her as she thought of what it would be like if she slid her hand downward, if she caressed that hardened flesh she could feel pressing against her thigh.

That proof that she was not alone in this wanting seared her to the core.

And then he was kissing her, hungrily, deeply, as if he'd longed for it as much as she had. She opened for him, wanting to taste him, to trace the even ridge of his teeth with her tongue, even as every nerve in her body blazed to life as they never had before this man.

She moved, pressing against him. Never breaking the kiss, they slid down until they were lying on the couch. She was practically on top of him, but he was holding her, so tight, so close she was barely aware of it. The shaft of moonlight that had poured over him fell across them here, and he seemed more beautiful to her than ever. More everything. Yes, more, she wanted more, she needed more. She needed all of him, in every way she could think of and a few she couldn't—yet. She wanted to—

He broke the kiss. She heard him suck in a breath as if he'd forgotten how until now. She knew the feeling.

"We've got to stop, Ashley. You don't want this."

She didn't like him going back to her full name. Wondered if it was his way of putting a barrier between them. But then the sense of what he'd said registered. And reality slammed back into her. A bitter reality. "Oh, I want it. But I see why you don't."

"Stop it," he said, rather fiercely. "I want it, want you, more than I've ever wanted…anything. But it's not right. Not now."

"How can this—" she reached up to trail a finger over

his mouth, felt with satisfaction that he shuddered slightly under the touch "—be not right?"

"Your life's in chaos right now, and it's not right, not fair to you to…go where we were going."

"But you said it will be okay."

He grimaced. "Hoist with my own petard," he muttered, and despite herself, despite everything, she laughed. It startled him—she could feel it. That quickly the mood changed. The fire was banked. Far from out, but banked. She was afraid that he would get up, that he would leave.

"All right, we'll wait," she whispered. "But please. Stay."

"You have a lot of faith in my restraint."

"I have a lot of faith in you, Brady Crenshaw."

She felt his arms tighten around her. He shifted them until they were spooned together and pulled her into the curve of his body. She'd never felt safer, more protected.

And after a few minutes of simply savoring his closeness, she slipped into a blissfully dreamless sleep.

"You're up early," Brady said, glad he'd gotten up from the couch and headed in here to start coffee. Otherwise Quinn would have found him draped all over their client, half-naked.

And hard as a rock, don't forget that.

He was glad the kitchen island was masking him from the waist down. But all thought of anything else fled when he saw the expression on Quinn's face. It was grim.

"I got the report from the lab."

Brady glanced at the clock on the microwave. "At 6:00 a.m.?"

"What is it?" Ash asked as she joined them. Her long hair was tousled, her eyes still a little sleepy. She had slept, at least, and he was grateful for that. Even if lying there awake, holding her in his arms for hours without pursuing the impossible heat that flared between them, had been more exhausting than his highest-level workout.

"I think we'll all need coffee for this," Quinn said. "Hayley'll be here in—"

"Two seconds" came Hayley's voice from behind him, the promised two seconds before she came into the room.

Quinn got mugs, and Hayley poured, as if they were truly welcome guests and not people in trouble who had been foisted upon them by chance.

Or chance and a dog.

He nearly laughed at his own thought, especially when he glanced at the animal and found him…smiling back at him. Which was impossible, he realized, but that's what the dog's satisfied expression looked like.

When they were all seated around the dining table, Quinn set down his laptop, which was already on. He glanced at Brady, but when he started to speak, his gaze was fixed on Ash, as was Hayley's.

"These—" he gestured at the document showing on the screen "—are the test results on the pill. There are two things of crucial importance. First, it was a combination of drugs not commercially available."

Ash's brow furrowed, and Brady frowned. "You mean… what? This was some kind of custom-brewed thing?"

Quinn nodded. "The shape and size aren't unusual for an illicit pill factory."

Ash's eyes widened. "Illicit…you mean they were what, some kind of homemade thing? He gave me some crazy drug he made up?"

Her voice started to rise a little, and Brady reached out to put a hand over hers. "Let's hear it all, then I'll blow up with you."

She sucked in an audible breath, but nodded.

"The second thing, and the most important," Quinn said, looking at Ash steadily, "is that this combination of drugs, in a healthy person, would likely cause every one of your supposed symptoms."

"You're not crazy. You never were."

Ashley sat, still feeling stunned. She was back on the couch, Hayley beside her. Brady was up and pacing, but he had stopped in front of her to declare the words once more. And all she could manage to do was look up at him.

He began pacing again. "I knew it. Deep down I knew it all along. Because the woman I saw that day at the accident was no way on the edge the way you thought you were."

How had he seen past the surface others saw, the craziness others saw? Because when it came down to it, she had sensed from the beginning he doubted she was truly mentally ill. He had doubted it even when she had been convinced. He had always had that expression of puzzlement when the subject came up, as if he just couldn't accept it. She'd recognized it because in the beginning, she'd worn the same expression all too often.

"But…" Oddly, she felt more at sea now than she ever had when she'd believed it. Her processing speed seemed to have slowed to a crawl.

"I always thought the haze, that layer between me and the word, was…me. That it was just made worse by the meds, because I'd read where that wasn't unusual."

"But it's been gone since you quit?" Hayley asked.

She nodded. "I was worse for a while, when I was on the pain pills from the accident, but since I never started up the…whatever this was again, yes, the fog is gone."

"What you thought was the effect of the pain pills could also have been withdrawal from the others," Brady said.

Even as she acknowledged the sense of what he said,

her mind was spinning. This was— She cut off her own thought when she realized she'd been about say it was crazy. She doubted she would ever use the word casually again. Wondered if that was how people who truly had mental health problems felt when they heard people toss the word around so easily.

People who truly had problems.

She was not one of them.

It still seemed impossible. She was reeling nearly as much as the first time she'd had to believe she was one of them.

"I don't understand," she said, almost desperately. "Why? Why would he do this?"

"Right now I don't give a damn why," Brady snapped.

"There's a word for this," Hayley said, and she sounded furious.

Brady nodded, then turned around to look directly at Ashley. And when he spoke, his voice was flat, yet fierce. "You're being gaslighted."

Chapter 28

"That's impossible." Ashley looked more stunned than ever. Brady hated to see that look on her face, but he understood. And he was, inwardly, feeling a tiny, growing kernel of relief.

She wasn't mentally ill.

It rang over and over in his head, like some cacophony of mountain squirrel chatter. But this was not the time to even think about the fact that what had been holding him back with her had just vanished. Right now she was even less ready for that than before. He resumed his pacing, needing to burn off at least some of this pulsing, raging anger.

"Why would he do such a thing?" She sounded bewildered.

"Because the psychiatrist needs a psychiatrist?" Brady suggested sourly.

"But…why?" She shook her head. "Maybe it's just some drug he was trying, thinking it might help."

"Using you as a guinea pig?" Brady's jaw clenched, and he had to consciously relax it. "That wouldn't move him up much in my book."

"But why else would he do this?"

"For one thing, it kept you coming to him," Hayley said.

"Because you trusted him." Brady practically spat it out, the thought of how that trust had been abused made him so livid.

"I know." She said it as if he'd accused her.

He stopped in his tracks, his gaze locking on her. "Ash, don't. This is not your fault. None of it."

"He's right," Hayley said, gently. "You had no reason not to trust him."

"But…he has a lot of patients. And all that money you said he has. Why would he need to make sure I kept coming?"

"Now that's an interesting question," Quinn said.

Brady was glad the other man sounded calm and collected, because he knew he himself was not. Not by any stretch. Pacing wasn't enough to keep his growing anger in check. What he needed was about a five-mile run. Uphill. Through the snow. But as he turned to stride back across the great room, he risked another look at Ash. And stopped dead again.

She was sitting there, looking dazed, and…shivering. Tiny little shudders were visibly rippling through her. In that moment Cutter, who had been quietly on his bed in front of the fireplace, watching intently, got to his feet. He walked over to Ashley, sat at her feet and, as he did whenever he apparently sensed she was on the edge, rested his chin on her knee. She automatically lifted a hand to stroke the dog's head, and the shivers subsided.

Nice trick, dog.

Except it should have been him. He should be the one offering support, comforting her.

His gut knotted. It was true, the main thing that had held him back was gone now, but that didn't mean everything was magically resolved. He told himself he didn't even know who she really was, who she would be without this cloud hanging over her. Neither did she.

Cutter shifted then, turning his head to look directly at Brady. Then he got up and walked to him, gave his right hand a rather adamant nudge with his nose and then continued over to sit politely by the back door, at first staring at Brady, then shifting his gaze to Ashley, then back again.

Brady was moving again before he even thought about the absurdity of taking directions from a dog. And when he did think it, he quickly jettisoned the thought; he'd seen enough police K-9s work to know some dogs had extraordinary skills, both mental and physical. Maybe that was it—he just needed to start thinking of Cutter like one of them.

He walked over to her and held out a hand. "Come with me. We'll take him outside. Just for a little while, until your mind slows down."

She looked up at him, then glanced at Cutter, as if despite her turmoil she'd understood what the dog was doing.

"Good idea," Hayley said.

He saw Ash glance at the other woman, who was giving her an oddly amused smile. And even more oddly, Ash was...blushing? His brow furrowed. Women, he thought, were sometimes impossible to understand.

But she took his hand.

"Don't think about it, just for a few minutes. Just look at the snow and try and picture what it's like here in spring, when everything's coming back to life."

Brady's voice was soothing, and she felt more of the tension drain away, just as it did when she petted Cutter. She gave an inward laugh, wondering how he'd feel about her comparing him to a dog.

"What?" he asked, and she realized something must have shown outwardly.

"Just thinking how…calming you and Cutter are."

She saw him glance at the dog, and for a moment she wondered if he really would take offense. But then he was looking back at her and said, with a crooked grin she found endearing, "I've been compared to worse."

She laughed. And his expression changed.

"Damn, that sounds good, Ash."

She knew what he meant. It was the first time she'd laughed and not felt that sense of confusion afterward, that sense that she had no business laughing, or that people would think her even crazier for laughing in her condition.

"It feels good," she admitted. And it felt even better with him right here, on her side, as he'd essentially been since he'd pulled her out of the car on the side of the mountain. She just hadn't known it. "It's strange, though. All your pacing, the finger tapping—you shouldn't be calming. Are you always wound so tight?"

"Only when something really matters."

She studied him for a moment. "Would you tell me… about Liz?"

He frowned. Then shrugged. "Not my favorite subject. She was my fiancée, but she hated my job and, eventually, me."

"She couldn't handle your work?" She could understand that, Brady risking his life for a job few would.

"She was…fragile, I guess." He grimaced. "Although my mother said manipulative. Among other things."

"She didn't like her?"

He let out a long breath. "She said she didn't want a partner, or even protection. She wanted a servant." His mouth twisted wryly. "And she was right."

And looking out for her child, no matter how old he was. Like a mother should. Her mind wanted to veer back into the chaos that had descended on her, so she was grateful when Cutter came back from his ramble through the snow, his nose and muzzle decorated with the white stuff.

"Find something interesting out there?" she crooned to him, gently brushing the snow away. Then she leaned down and kissed the top of the dog's head.

"If I go roll in the snow, will you do that for me?" Brady asked. Startled, her gaze shot to his face. "With the kiss somewhere other than the top of my head," he elaborated.

"I…" She couldn't get out another word, because the images that shot through her mind had stolen all her breath. And then it hit her, amid all the roiling of her emotions, that perhaps, just perhaps, her imagination wasn't out of control. Because maybe now, she had a chance to truly grab at that gold ring. Because if she truly wasn't going mad…

Joy at even that chance shot through her, and she said recklessly, "I would kiss you…anywhere."

Shock registered on his face, his usual somber expression vanishing, but then it was replaced with something she couldn't put a name to except…hunger. It took away the breath she'd momentarily regained, and she felt her heartbeat in a way she never had before as it kicked up and began to hammer in her chest.

"Sorry to interrupt," Quinn's voice called from the doorway, "but Ashley, there's something you need to hear."

"Well, I'm sure that'll be good news," Brady muttered with more than a touch of sarcasm. When she looked at him rather sharply, he shrugged. "Nothing that interrupted what you just said could be good enough news."

She felt her cheeks heat, and her worry about his tone vanished. "Hold that thought," she whispered.

When they were back inside, Quinn wasted no time in niceties, for which Ashley was grateful.

"Dr. Sebastian has gone over your father's records."

Ashley opened her mouth to ask how they'd gotten them so quickly, even after she'd given permission—which she had been sure would clash with her mother, who had once said she never wanted the world to know how bad her father had been—then shut it again, remembering Brady telling her something about not asking too much about how they got things done.

"According to those records, he was prescribed the same medication you were supposedly on."

"I remember he was taking something. Mom was always reminding him to take his—" Belatedly it hit her. "You think it was the same fake stuff?"

"Don't suppose you remember what it looked like?" Quinn asked.

She shook her head slowly. "No."

"Twenty years ago," Brady said briskly. "And you were only eight."

"And scared to death for my daddy," she whispered. "My God, he did it to him, too, didn't he?"

"Can't be sure, but it's very possible," Hayley said. "And if he succeeded once, he'd likely be more willing to try again."

"With me."

She turned around, rather wildly looking for someplace to sit down before she fell down. Before she could decide, Brady was there, wrapping his arms around her, holding her, enveloping her in his strength and warmth. She trembled, feeling as if she would like to burrow into this safe haven and stay forever.

"My father wasn't mentally ill," she whispered.

"And neither are you," Brady said roughly. His tone was underlaid with something else it took her a moment to recognize. Anger. Again. For her.

He was angry again, on her behalf. And that stopped the reeling of her mind. Then her head came up, as the inevitable conclusion hit her. "If this is right…then he…that *bastard* is responsible for my father's death."

Brady's arms tightened around her. When he spoke, his voice was grim. "As responsible as if he'd pulled the trigger himself."

Chapter 29

"Why?" Ash asked, sounding bewildered.

They'd gone back to the table, in part for the quick coffee access. But also, Brady suspected when Hayley, with help from Cutter—or maybe the other way around—had shepherded them there, because it felt more…official to Ash. More like a meeting to decide what to do rather than just constantly being hit with things she had to absorb and process. So he didn't protest, just took the chair beside Ash. Which, he noted with a touch of amusement, Cutter seemed to have herded him to.

"I suppose there are those who just get some twisted, evil need satisfied," Hayley said as she filled mugs. "But…"

"Otherwise, follow the money," Brady said acidly.

"Usually," Quinn answered, his tone more mild. But he didn't have the personal stake in this that Brady had. His future didn't depend on the outcome.

And yours does?

Even as the question rang in his mind, he knew the answer. Because the possibilities were there, glowing in the distance, and it did all depend on what happened, depended on his gut feeling, that instinct he'd had since he'd first looked into frightened but steady green eyes, that Ashley Jordan not only wasn't mentally ill but was much, much more than she first seemed.

"But I still don't understand why he would do this," Ash said. "I mean, taking extra money for testifying, I sort of get that, that's simple greed, but what could he possibly get out of…making me believe, and my father believe, we were mentally ill?"

"Assuming you're the only ones," Quinn said.

Ash's eyes widened. "You mean he could be doing it to other patients? Making them think…they're going insane? What a horrible thought."

"Indeed," Hayley agreed.

"What on earth would he get out of…doing something like that?"

"That," Quinn said, sounding just as grim, "would likely be something for Dr. Sebastian to analyze."

Brady, who'd fallen silent but had kept pacing, suddenly stopped and looked at Quinn. "Or your Ty." Quinn gave him a quizzical look. "You said there was money in that offshore account that didn't correlate to Andler being paid for his court testimony, right?"

Quinn's expression went suddenly unreadable. But after a moment he let out a low whistle. "Now that would make him a real piece of work."

"Yeah," Brady muttered.

"But it would make sense of it."

"Yes." Brady's voice was beyond grim now, just like he felt.

"The question is, by who?"

"The why would be easier to find, I'd think."

Quinn nodded. "I'll get him started."

"Someone want to explain to us non–mind readers in the room?" Hayley suggested as the two men finally stopped.

"Thank you," Ash muttered.

Brady grimaced as he looked at them. "You mean those of you who don't have twisted imaginations?"

"That, too," Hayley said, but she smiled at him when she said it.

Quinn answered. "What Brady wants us to consider is the possibility that Andler isn't getting paid over and above just for his testimony, but for doing to other patients what he's done to Ashley and quite possibly her father."

Brady saw the horror in Ash's eyes. They looked more shocked and terrified than when her own life was in danger, when he'd pulled her out of the car on the mountainside. He found that significant, but this was not the time to analyze it.

Ash whispered. "Why would anybody do that?"

"Follow the money," Brady repeated sourly.

"We are," Quinn said.

"You mean people would pay a psychiatrist to convince someone they were crazy?" Ash sounded beyond shocked now.

"Or convince someone else," Brady said grimly.

"You mean…like a court," Hayley said slowly.

"Exactly."

"Good way to get someone out of the way," Quinn said.

"Wait," Ash said, coming out of her apparent shock enough to think now. "Are you saying someone paid Dr. Andler to do this…to me? Who?"

Brady thought there was only one obvious answer, but

Ash clearly wasn't there yet. But Quinn was, he noted, seeing the man exchanging a glance with his wife, who then looked at Ash with a world of sympathy in her eyes as she got there, too.

"Whoever has something to gain," Brady said bluntly, feeling there was no room for subtlety here, and no amount of careful wording was going to lessen the jolt for her.

"But—"

She stopped when Quinn held up a hand. He picked up the laptop and turned it around so Ash could see the screen. "I need you to read that list, see if anything looks even vaguely familiar."

"What is it?"

"Please, Ashley, just read it, then we'll talk about it."

Her brow furrowed, but she began to read. Brady watched her, somewhat cravenly wishing for Quinn to be the one who dropped the final bomb on her, because he didn't want to do it. He didn't want her to think of it every time she looked at him.

There was only one very brief moment when her expression changed, when the furrowed brow cleared and the tiniest smile flickered for an instant. But then she went on, until she reached the end of the page. She looked up at Quinn, slowly shaking her head.

"I don't see anything I recognize. What is it?"

"A list of where the deposits to Dr. Andler's offshore account came from."

Brady let out a low whistle. "I do *not* want to know how you managed that."

"Did he not mention his massively intimidating sister is a financial genius, with contacts all over the world?" Hayley said lightly.

"And that's all anyone needs to know," Quinn put in.

Brady shelved his curiosity and turned back to Ash.

"If you don't recognize any of these people or entities, what did you react to? You almost smiled there for a second."

She looked surprised. That she'd shown a reaction, or that he'd noticed? "I... It was just one of the things listed here is the Amalfi Group, like the Amalfi Coast in Italy."

"And that's significant?"

"Not to this," she said. "It's just that's my mother's favorite place. I think her family's from there, way back. Alexander was originally Alessandro, I think."

And here they were. A glance at Quinn told him the other man had reached the same conclusion. He understood why Ash didn't see it, however. What he suspected was the truth was horrible. He tried to imagine finding out the same thing himself, but couldn't. He supposed she felt the same way. And he was not looking forward to the moment when she realized.

But he was dreading the possibility of having to tell her.

"Let's look at this from a different angle," Hayley said, her voice taking on such a gentle tone Brady thought she must be thinking the same thing. "All we truly care about right now is you, so let's focus on that."

Ash gave her a fleeting smile. "Thank you for that." She glanced at Quinn, who had retrieved the computer and was typing something, then settled on Brady with that vivid green gaze. "All of you."

He put a hand over hers where it rested on the table. He felt the little snap he always felt when he touched her but tried to ignore it. It wasn't easy, not when she looked at him as if she'd felt the same thing.

"I know this whole thing is terrible, but you need to think, Ash. Who would have something to gain by you being declared incompetent?"

"You mean financially? No one. I mean, there's a trust I'll get access to when I turn thirty, but it's not huge.

Certainly not worth the kind of machinations you're talking about."

"There's a trust?"

She nodded. "My father set it up. There was a bit of family money."

"You didn't think to mention this before?" Brady asked, his voice tense.

Her brow furrowed. "Why would I? It has nothing to do with…anything."

Was she really that naive? Or was it just so foreign to her nature that it would never occur to her the lengths people would go to to get their hands on a chunk of change? He guessed it was the latter. Because he knew, down deep, that at her core Ashley Jordan was that basic building block of civilization—a decent human being.

"Just how big is it?"

"I…haven't looked at it in a long time, but a couple hundred thousand or so, I think."

So a lot, but as she'd said, not a multimillion-dollar prize. "Who's in charge of that trust until you turn thirty?" he asked.

"My mother, of course. She makes the investment decisions, and she's good at it. Why?"

Brady took a deep breath, then said what had to be said. "And who gets the money in that trust if something happens to you?"

"I… She's my beneficiary, so…" He saw by her expression that she had at least gotten the implication, but he could also see that she was a long way from accepting it as fact. "No. No, Brady. She wouldn't."

"I get it, Ash. She's your mother. But—"

"She may not be the warm, comfortable, homebody sort of mother, but she loves me. Ask anyone. She's always made that clear."

"I'm sure she has," he muttered.

It was Hayley, still in that gentle voice that told Brady she knew exactly what they were doing to Ash and how much it was going to hurt, who said, "That's very often part of the gaslighting process, Ashley. The front of being loving, caring, so that no one will believe what they're really doing."

"But…she's always looked out for me, worried about me."

"And told others how worried she is about you?" Brady suggested. "Afraid that perhaps you'll go the way your father did?"

He saw by her expression he'd hit home. So he pushed harder. "Those texts. There was something…off about them."

Hayley nodded. "I showed them to Dr. Sebastian. She said they were nearly classic gaslighting, telling you she's the only one who really cares about you, that you have no friends, nowhere else to turn, belittling you."

"Does this trust have a name?" It was the first time Quinn had spoken since he'd taken the laptop back, and he did it in that businesslike tone that seemed to pull Ash out of the murk. She gave the man a smile that looked half sad, half almost embarrassed.

"The Murphy Trust. He named it after our dog at the time."

"Ah," Quinn said. "That explains why it didn't come up in our initial searching."

Quinn typed in something else, as if he were telling someone—probably the redoubtable Ty, or maybe the genius sister—what she'd said. Silence descended around the table as they waited. Brady belatedly realized he was still holding Ashley's hand. And again had to corral his mind, which wanted more than anything to shout that the barrier between them was gone. But this wasn't the time any more than it had been before.

But he didn't let go of her hand.

After a few silent minutes, Quinn looked up from the screen. There was more, Brady could sense it. Could see it in the way the man was looking at Ash, as if deciding how to say it.

"Just do it," Brady muttered.

Quinn grimaced, but apparently agreed. "My sister, Charlie, happens to be in our headquarters office today, so she's made some calls. When, exactly, was the last time you looked at that trust?"

Ash seemed embarrassed. "A very long time ago. I tried to ignore it, partly because it hurt to think about my dad, and partly because I didn't want to be…one of those trust-fund kids who knew they didn't really have to earn a living."

Brady smiled. "Good for you."

She smiled back, then said, "Besides, I knew it was in good hands, so I didn't bother about it, since it would be years before it would be mine. Foolish, huh?"

"That trust has grown," Quinn said. "By a factor of about twenty-five."

Ash blinked, clearly shocked. "It's worth millions?"

"Five, at the moment."

Brady drew back slightly. When he'd said follow the money, he hadn't expected it to be quite that much. But he had no time to dwell on it, because Quinn was continuing, and his voice was ominously grim.

"And those investments you mentioned? One of them is more than an investment, it's wholly owned."

"Meaning?"

"The trust—and the administrator of it—controls it completely."

"You mean the trust owns a business? What kind of business?"

"Ty hasn't got down into it enough yet to determine the details. But Charlie has a name." Quinn's voice turned nearly as gentle as his wife's had been. "It's the Amalfi Group."

Chapter 30

Ashley felt a chill envelop her, oddly from the inside out. Was aware of the cold sweat and the touch of queasiness, but as if from a distance, as if she were observing, not feeling.

And then Brady spoke, and his voice was so full of barely suppressed fury it broke through her shock.

"The perfect solution," he bit out, "if you draw your twisted line at murdering your own daughter. Just have her declared incompetent and committed to a psychiatric facility."

She registered his tone. Once more he was angry on her behalf. And she clung to that, as if it were a physical thing she could touch. As if it were an anchor keeping her from flying apart.

"This is…guesswork, right?" she asked Quinn, desperately.

Brady grabbed both her hands. She shifted her gaze to

his face, saw the wrath in his vivid blue eyes, in the set of his jaw. "Ash, it's a trail lit with freaking neon lights, and it leads straight to her."

"But…my mother?"

She saw and heard him suck in a breath. His voice was gentler then, as if he'd reined in the anger. "I know it's hell to process, that your own mother would do this to you, and for money."

"For any reason," she said, still shaking her head in disbelief.

"But Ash, don't forget the good news." His voice was almost urgent. "You're not mentally ill. Not crazy. Not going crazy. Not losing it. None of that was real."

A tiny spark of joy kindled within her. But it was not enough to lighten the burden they had just dropped upon her. At least, not yet. She stood up suddenly. Brady rose the minute she did. He looked ready to fight. Someone, or something, although there was nothing he could do. Still, he was ready to, and that meant so much, and in a strange way added to the pressure she was feeling.

"I…need a minute alone," she said. "No, several minutes. I have to think and I can't. I need…"

What she needed was for all of this to go away. But it wouldn't. And if she didn't get some room to breathe in the next instant, she just might burst.

"There are lots of decisions to make," Quinn said. "But none that have to be made this instant."

"Go outside," Brady said. "But put your jacket on, it's snowing again."

"Yes," she said. "Yes, that's what I need."

"Take Cutter. Or rather," Hayley amended, "don't fight him going with you, since he's already made up his mind."

She glanced down to see the dog at her feet, looking up at her determinedly. She wasn't certain that, even with his uncanny ability to comfort, the animal could help her with this, but he certainly couldn't hurt. Nor would he expect her to talk, to make sensible thoughts out of the bedlam in her mind. And she marveled for a detached moment at how sanity could possibly seem more chaotic than her mind had been for the last few months.

But it wasn't. Not really. Because one key element was missing. She was shocked, possibly in shock. She was reeling from possibility of the worst imaginable betrayal. She was feeling crushed by the weight of it all. And the thought of those decisions Quinn had mentioned was far beyond daunting.

But she wasn't afraid. Not anymore.

"None of this will stand up in court, will it." It wasn't really a question, because Brady already knew the answer.

He was pacing again, pausing at one end of his established track to glance outside and make sure Ash was all right.

"Cutter will see to her," Hayley had assured him. "And make her come back inside if she gets too cold." At Brady's look, she had laughed. "He knows what shivering means."

"Some will," Quinn said in answer Brady's observation. "Methods won't."

Brady rubbed the back of his neck. "I never liked the mayor much, but this…"

"Is beyond the pale? Unnatural?" Hayley suggested, her tone overflowing with revulsion.

"I was heading for perverted," Brady said with a grimace. He turned on his heel to head back across the room and found Quinn in front of him.

"I need your opinion. Of all of us, except maybe Cutter, you've got the best read on Ashley."

He blinked. "I do?"

One corner of the other man's mouth quirked. "You do. For reasons you will eventually understand. But I need to know how much you think she can take."

Brady drew back slightly. "Hasn't she taken enough already?"

"More than anyone should have to, yes. But what I need to know is if the relief of learning she's not descending into a mental hell is enough to counterbalance what we suspect about her mother."

Brady's brow furrowed as he studied the man who apparently had more expert resources at his fingertips than Brady had known existed. "To what end?" he finally asked. "Those decisions you mentioned?"

Quinn nodded. "If she wants to take legal action, we need to go one way. If she doesn't, then some things become not a concern, and the goals change."

Brady considered that for a moment. "You're saying it's her decision."

Quinn nodded. "Which is why I gave you the chance to opt out. Because that's not the way you would do things. Not by the book."

"Right now," Brady said grimly, "I'm ready to throw that book into a snowdrift, because I know damned well what would have happened if you people hadn't come along when you did."

"I think," Hayley said, giving him a warm smile, "she would have had help the moment you knew something was off about her situation."

"Thanks for the compliment," Brady said, "but there's no way I could have marshaled the forces you guys have."

Quinn only smiled. Then said, "Speaking of forces, it might be helpful to know what the official status of the search is. Anybody you could get that from without giving yourself away?"

Brady thought for a moment. "Yeah. Hang on."

He pulled out his phone and called up the number for Rich Larios, one of their half dozen detectives and a good friend. Rich answered on the second ring.

"Hey, Crenshaw, how's the life of leisure?"

I wish I knew. "Great. I should try it more often."

"As I keep telling you. So what's up?"

"Just wanted the name of that ski run in Snowridge you were talking about."

"The Ridge Route Run. If you can't say it, you're too drunk to ski it."

Brady managed a laugh. "Thanks, man. What's up there?"

"Quiet. Except for pretending there's a chance we'll find the mayor's daughter alive."

"No trace yet?"

"Got a vid of her walking past Benny's at 7:55 p.m. on Sunday, but then poof. So after a week, you know the chances when you're dealing with someone with her mental history. But the mayor being the boss's good buddy, you know the drill."

"Yeah. Sucks. Don't put too much energy into it."

"Copy that," Rich said, clearly heartfelt. "Enjoy the skiing."

He ended the call and looked once more at Quinn. "They're expecting to find a body, if anything," he said grimly, trying not to think of how close that had come to being reality.

"And would have," Hayley said, "if not for you." She looked at her husband. "Can we give her time to process and make up her mind? Until Sunday, maybe?"

Quinn was silent for a long moment, clearly considering. "I don't like making your colleagues spin their wheels," he said to Brady.

"This is a pretty quiet gig," Brady said. "They might be pissed, but it won't hurt them any. The budget, on the other hand…"

"Foxworth will see to that." He looked back at his wife. "All right. We'll hold off, make decisions on Sunday and start—" he glanced at Brady "—marshaling those forces you mentioned on Monday morning."

"Go tell her," Hayley said. "Tell her not to think or worry about it for tonight. It will take some pressure off her, something she surely needs right now."

Brady wasn't sure how you stopped thinking about something like this, but maybe she could at least stop worrying about it for a while.

Brady's words, as they so often did, rang in Ashley's head as she lay in bed staring into the darkness.

Try not to think about your mom. Just think about being well.

Could you?

He'd paused then, and answered honestly. As she'd known he would.

No.

Somehow that honesty made it possible for her to at least try what he'd suggested. Although it had put her in another complicated position, because the only thing strong enough to jolt her mind out of that rabbit warren of thoughts was…him.

The memory of how he'd held her, so gently, helped, but it was the memory of his kisses, and of the feel of that long, strong body pressed against her, that was the only thing powerful enough to shove everything else out of her mind, at least for a while. And his restraint, his refusal to pursue what had flared to life between them when he felt it was unfair to her, perversely only added fuel to the fire. The fire in her, anyway. He seemed too busy tamping it down or trying to ignore it. For very noble reasons, yes, but—

Reasons that didn't exist anymore. He'd held back because of something that she now knew wasn't true. She wasn't delicate, fragile, on the edge of crumbling.

Suddenly something new, strange and wonderful was coursing through her. As if someone had put her fate back into her own hands. As, in fact, they had. The Foxworths, true, but it was Brady who had saved her for them to do it. Brady who had seen something wrong, or something in her, enough to inspire him to go against everything he believed. For her.

Her restlessness had transformed from an exhausted merry-go-round of fruitless, careening thoughts to a sort of energy she hadn't felt in…maybe ever. And abruptly she simply could not stay here, curled up in the dark, another second. She rolled out of the bed and pulled on the socks she had been using as slippers against the chill and the sweatshirt on the foot of the bed since she had no robe.

She would go back out to the great room and sit by what was left of the fire again. She wanted to be there, where he'd come to her. Not because she hoped he would do so again—no, Brady had made up his mind, and he would not risk that again—but so she could savor the memory, there, where he'd kissed her so fiercely and things had nearly spiraled out of control. She wished they had. Because just the thought of Brady Crenshaw out of control, over her, gave her a thrill she'd never experienced before.

The reality would be…overwhelming. In the best possible way. She—

She stopped dead in the hallway when she saw a shadow move. Smiled when she realized it was Cutter, standing outside the media room door.

Brady's door.

"Hello, furry one," she whispered as she bent to pet him. "Making your rounds?"

Hayley had told her the dog often did that when he was on a case. It had sounded so funny to her she'd almost laughed, but she was beginning to realize it had not at all been a joke.

Cutter swiped his tongue lightly over her fingers. "Want to come out and sit with me?" she asked him, still whispering and very aware that they were right outside where Brady was sleeping. Another memory arrowed through her, searing her as if it were aflame. Brady, bare-chested, jeans low on his narrow hips, stepping into that shaft of moonlight. When she caught herself wondering if he slept naked, she knew she had to move or she was liable to do something stupid.

But when she tried to move, the dog got in her way. She smiled at him and stepped around him. Or tried to, but he was there again. A third time, and this time she was watching him, saw that he moved the instant after she did, and she couldn't see how it was anything but purposeful.

"You don't want me to go out there?" she asked, feeling silly. She had the thought that perhaps Hayley and Quinn were out there, and the dog was protecting their privacy. They certainly hadn't had much chance to enjoy their anniversary trip alone, although they had had some time before all this had descended on them.

Cutter moved again, this time gently nudging at her. Not, as she had half expected, back down the hall toward her room but…toward Brady's door.

"Oh, don't tempt me, dog," she muttered. "There's nothing I'd like better."

"Than what?"

Brady's sleep-roughened voice came from barely two feet away, where he'd just opened that tempting door. He wasn't naked, as she'd imagined, but the snug-fitting knit boxers were damned close. For a moment that seemed to spin out forever, she stared at him, and the broad, strong expanse of his chest, the ridges of his abdomen, the trail of dark hair that arrowed downward like an invitation.

And feeling reckless for the first time in her generally staid life until now, she answered him honestly.

"Than you."

Chapter 31

The hunger in her eyes, visible even in the shadows of the hallway, nearly did him in. But then she whispered, "Wanting you is the first thing I've been utterly, absolutely sure of in a long time," and he was lost.

But still, feeling he had to, he only stood aside, leaving the decision to step through to her. She made it without hesitation. He caught a glimpse of Cutter, who oddly had plopped down in front of the doorway as if it were his place. Or like a guardian.

But then she was in his arms, and all other thought fled. It was all he could do to close the door quietly instead of slamming it in his haste.

The reasoning side of his brain gave one last warning, to remember what she'd been through and take care. But it was the last cogent thought he had before his body took charge. He would take care and give more than he took because that's the way it should be, but take he would.

He felt as if he'd been holding back since the first moment he'd looked into those green eyes of hers, and now he was done with it.

She came at him so hungrily it became elemental in an instant. The slow savoring he'd on occasion imagined would have to wait; this was an urgency beyond anything he'd ever felt. It was impossible not to respond in kind when the woman you'd been panting for made it so damn clear she was as hot for this as you were.

As hot for you as you were for her.

She was kissing him, not hesitantly but ardently, sliding her tongue over his lips and then farther, licking, tasting, until a vision of her doing that to other parts of him nearly put him on his knees. He tasted her in turn and felt his entire body tighten even more.

Her hands slid over him, her fingers stroking over his chest and down his belly, and for the first time in his life he realized how utterly arousing it could be to be the one who was practically naked, while she was still clad in a sweatshirt and heavy winter socks.

And then she was doing exactly what he'd imagined, following the paths her hands had traced with her mouth, her tongue leaving trails of fire over his skin. He had to slow her down or this was going to be, humiliatingly, over before it really started. He knew the perfect way. He reached for the hem of that sweatshirt and tugged. He hated the simple logistics that said to get it off her he'd have to break that kiss, but the temptation of baring luscious female curves topped all else. And then she was helping him, pulling off not just the sweatshirt but the T-shirt beneath it.

He groaned aloud as her breasts were bared now to his gaze, and for his hands. With a split second of thanks that she'd already shed her bra and he didn't have to deal with it, he reached to cup them. She sucked in an audible breath the moment he did, and when he ran his thumbs over her nipples, she moaned. Then she slid her hands down his back and beneath his waistband. Almost without his volition, he lowered his head to take her mouth again in the instant her hands cupped his ass in a possessive way that snapped the last thread of his restraint.

He ripped off the pajama bottoms she had on and an instant later had his boxers on the floor beside them. And then she was backed up to the door, pressed against him from lips to knees, and he knew he couldn't wait another second. When he reached to lift her legs she practically climbed him in her effort to help. He barely managed to stroke her with a finger, and when he did, it was so obvious she was slick and ready for him, he swore under his breath.

"Ash," he whispered.

"Hurry," she whispered back.

"Those shots you were getting," he began.

"From a real, honest doctor. It's all safe. Please. I've been waiting for you all my life."

He broke. Drove forward, surging into her to the hilt. This time the oath wasn't under his breath—he nearly shouted it in the same moment she cried out his name with a resonance that echoed in his ears. She was hot, tight and fit him perfectly. And he realized he'd underestimated the power of being wanted so fiercely in return.

He began to move because he had to, stroking her from within as he held her against the door. She wrapped her legs around him, shifting to take him deeper, adding the motion of her hips to his thrusts until it took everything he had to hold back the boiling tide.

And then she cried out his name again, then again in a tone of wonder, and her body convulsed around his, gripping, squeezing until that tide breached his control. Even his vision dimmed, and he was barely aware of holding on as waves of incredible sensation billowed through him, and with an echoing groan of her name in turn, he poured himself into her.

Nearly drained of strength, it was all he could do to keep her safe as they slid downward. His heart was still hammering, and he heard another low moan from her as, limbs entangled, they collapsed on the floor.

And he'd never wanted anything in his life more than to simply live in this moment endlessly.

"Morning-after regrets?"

Ashley gave him a sideways look as he lay on his side next to her, his head propped on one hand, studying her rather intently. It was morning, barely—she could tell by the light. Although the sun rose late here this time of year, so timewise it was probably later than it felt like. The fold-out bed in the media room was more comfortable than she would have expected. More importantly, it had served their purposes sufficiently after he'd gently picked her up and brought her to it, making love to her all over again, the second time slower and more gentle. The third time had been a sleepy, cuddling affair that turned heated quickly, so quickly it had taken her breath away.

"I should be asking you that."

"After the most amazing night of my life?"

She let out a relieved breath. "It was all that and more."

"If it got any better, every circuit would be burned out instead of temporarily fried," he said with the crooked grin she had seen far too little of.

"But you were the one who…wouldn't. Before."

"It wasn't right."

And there was Brady Crenshaw in a nutshell. "Thank you."

"For what? Waiting?" The grin again. "If I'd known what I was missing—"

"I meant for the first nightmare-free sleep I've had in longer than I can remember." She grinned back at him then, delighting in the feeling of lightness that she'd awakened with. "For what time we slept, I mean."

"Well, if I'd known it would help that much…" he said with a suggestive leer.

She reached for him then, unable to quite believe her life had turned around so completely that this beautiful man was hers to touch, to stroke, to kiss. And this time, with a boldness she had never expected to feel again, she took the lead, doing that touching, stroking, kissing, until tough, strong Brady begged her to end it and she straddled him, taking him as deep into her as she could, savoring the stretching, the fullness, moving until all control shattered and he grabbed her hips and locked her to him as he arched up beneath her with a groan of her name in the same moment she gasped out his.

When she could move again, after collapsing atop him, he held her gently in place. "Stay there. It feels…perfect."

"Yes," she whispered. "It does."

For a few long, silent moments, she just lay there, listening to the steady beat of his heart, feeling the heat of him warming her enough to make up for the fact that the covers on the bed had long ago been tossed aside.

And then he spoke quietly into the dim, dawn light. "Tell me about the nightmares."

A little to her own surprise, she didn't cringe at the thought. Telling Dr. Andler—her mind sparked with anger at just the name, but she set it aside for the moment—about it had been beyond difficult, but now, to Brady, it came out easily.

"It's really only one, with slight variations. In it I'm a child again, in a dark house, and down the hall I see a monster walking toward my father's den. I know it's bad, that I need to warn him, but I'm frozen, I can't even scream."

Brady muttered an oath under his breath and pulled her tighter against him, and it comforted her more than anything had since this living nightmare had started. More than anything had ever, she realized. It felt more than right, it felt perfect.

"What does the monster look like?" he asked.

She gave a weary shake of her head. "I never see more than a shadow."

"But you know it's a monster."

"In the dream, yes."

"Is it an animal? Like a tiger or a snake? Or something unreal, like a dragon or hydra?"

"A troll or an ogre, maybe," she said dryly.

"So it's a human shape? Or could be a human exaggerated by a child's fear?"

She blinked. She hadn't really thought about it in that way. "I…suppose so. But whatever it is, it freezes me to the spot, and I can't move or even scream."

He hugged her again. "I'm sorry, Ash. I can't imagine going through that every night."

She shook off the chill that thinking of the nightmare always brought. "Not last night," she said with a smile as she stroked a hand down his rib cage and savored the way he sucked in an audible breath and clenched his jaw. And using everything she had learned of him during the night, every way he liked to be touched, every caress that drove him wild, she pushed him to the edge until he rolled them both over and drove into her fiercely, just as she'd wanted. Craved. Needed. As she never had before.

And then, amazingly, she slept again. And the nightmare did not come.

Chapter 32

"That," Quinn said, "is a nice sound."

Brady, who had just come out of the shower in time to hear the laughter from the kitchen, looked that way in time to see Hayley and Ash grinning at each other over the rims of two coffee mugs.

"Yes," he said. "The best."

"I don't even care if we're the subject."

Brady blinked. "You think we are?"

"Given how things changed overnight, I'd say it's a good guess."

"Changed—" He broke off when he realized what Quinn meant. He knew, which meant Hayley also knew, where Ash had spent most of the night.

The other man was looking at him steadily, but there was nothing of accusation in his gaze. "Not a surprise, Crenshaw. I am amazed—and impressed—that you waited until she had herself back again."

Brady stared down at Cutter, who had arrived to sit at—actually on—his feet and grin. There was no other word for the dog's expression. "Had to," he muttered. "Would've been…wrong."

"Yes. And that you waited says a great deal about you. You ever get tired of wearing that badge, come see me."

Brady's head came up sharply. Saw in Quinn's level gaze that he meant it. "I'll keep it in mind," he said. "I like what you do."

He looked over at Ash again and this time caught her watching him. And the smile on her face brought last night crashing down on him until all he wanted to do was grab her and cart her back to his bed.

Quinn laughed. And at Brady's sharp look, he merely gave a half shrug and said, "Cutter told us this was coming almost from day one."

Brady looked down at the dog again. It wasn't only a grin, it was a smug grin. An expression he would have laughed at applying to a dog just…two and a half weeks ago.

He looked back at Quinn. "What are you talking about?"

Quinn proceeded to tell him of a one hundred percent track record Cutter had in another realm besides helping and comforting people. If it had been anyone other than Quinn Foxworth, he wouldn't have believed a word of it. Even then he couldn't help saying, "You're as reality based as I am, but you believe it?"

"Ten for ten is pretty solid evidence." Quinn grinned at him. "Make that eleven for eleven, now."

"But he's—"

"A dog. Yeah. I noticed." Brady gave him an exasperated look. "I get it. I know how hard it was for me to believe. And," he added pointedly, "how much better I felt when I just gave in to the inevitable."

Quinn was having far too much fun with him over this. "Why do I get the feeling you enjoy this?"

"Because it reminds me of what it was like to find Hayley."

Quinn's voice had gone quiet, and the expression on his face as he looked over at his wife sent a flood of memories through Brady. Memories from last night, accompanied by a rush of heat. It had been the most amazing night of his life, and he wanted a long, unbroken string of them. Nights spent with Ash in his arms, the woman who had come to him last night, wounded but whole, the heavy burden she'd been carrying shifted, free of the fear at last. True, she had an entirely new ordeal to deal with, and he couldn't imagine a worse betrayal. Except the kind she thought she'd been dealing with, the betrayal of her own mind.

But now he knew she had the capacity to do it.

More importantly, she knew she had the capacity to do it.

"Hope they don't get stuck somewhere," Brady said as the Foxworths drove off into the snow that had just begun to fall again. "So Hayley just suddenly wanted to go skiing?"

"They don't even ski." Ashley said it blandly, smiling inwardly as Brady looked bewildered.

"But she said—"

"They wanted to give us some time. Alone."

He went still. She saw his expression change, saw the sudden anticipation. But he only said, "Oh."

She wondered why, then understood he, being Brady, wouldn't assume anything. Given the situation, that her life was so tangled, he was still leaving the decision to her. He wouldn't make the first move. And she found herself longing for the day he did; then she'd know the worst was over.

But for now she merely said, "And they left Cutter in case we…needed direction."

Brady glanced over to where the dog was plopped on his bed, watching them alertly. After what Ashley had told him about how the dog had practically herded her to his door last night, he wasn't sure he doubted anything he'd heard about the animal anymore.

"I'm beginning to think that dog isn't really a dog," he muttered.

"Hayley says she won't be surprised if they find out one day he's an animagus."

Brady blinked. "A shape-shifting wizard?"

She smiled, widely. "You really have read those books."

"You didn't believe me?"

She lowered her gaze. "I thought maybe you just wanted to make me feel better."

"Well, I did, but it's true."

"How about now?"

His brow furrowed. "What?"

She looked up at him again. "Want to make me feel better now?"

The heat that flared in his gaze sent her pulse racing. "I've been wanting that since we got up."

He might not make the first move, but once she had, he wasted no time. And she was suddenly reminded—as if she'd needed it—just how strong he was when he swept her up into his arms and carried her back to the bed they'd vacated just a couple of hours ago. And he proceeded to prove to her that he knew exactly how to make her feel better, taking his time until there wasn't an inch of her that didn't feel treasured. Loved.

She shied away from the word even mentally, in her own version of not wanting to assume. She simply gave herself over to the pleasure of his touch, the stroke of his hands and the feel of his mouth as he sucked at her nipples while stroking the very core of her, which was already hot, slick and ready. But when he moved next, it wasn't as she expected. He replaced the fingers that had been caressing her with his mouth and tongue, until she was biting back a scream at the sheer intensity of it. And then she remembered she didn't have to hold back—the house was empty except for a dog who'd made it clear this had been his plan all along.

She screamed Brady's name as she burst into heat and sensation. And she had never felt anything more perfect than when he slid into her as her body was still convulsing, driving her upward again before the last throes had even faded. And when he let out a low, heartfelt oath as he shuddered above her, she grabbed him and held on, wanting him so deeply inside her that he would stay forever.

Brady woke to Ash curled up in the curve of his body, his arm around her just under the soft curve of her breasts. To his amazement, after the day they'd spent, his body made clear it was ready for more. He'd thought the need would slow down now that it had been sated a bit, but obviously he was wrong.

Or he had underestimated the power of the attraction between them.

But she was sleeping so soundly that he didn't move, didn't want to wake her. Peaceful sleep had been nonexistent for her for a very long time. So he lay still, only shifting his head so that he could look out the window, where he could see snow was still falling, albeit lightly.

He wondered what Hayley and Quinn were really doing, since the skiing was evidently a pretense. Maybe, when this was over, he should offer to take them skiing, if they had any real interest. He was no instructor, but he'd taught a youth class once and it had gone fairly well. Maybe—

There was a loud, sudden crack of sound, familiar to mountain-raised Brady as a branch overloaded with snow giving up under the weight. But he had only a moment to categorize the sound before another wiped all other thought from his mind.

Ash screamed.

The sound of it was a physical thing to him, stabbing him as if it were a blade. He pulled her hard against him, wrapping around her as it came again.

"Ash, it's all right. Wake up, it's all right."

She went rigid against him. He shifted so he could see her face. Her eyes were wide-open, and the look of horror in them stabbed him all over again.

"It's all right," he repeated. "The noise was just a branch breaking with all the snow."

"The nightmare." She shuddered, and he felt it ripple almost violently through her. Apprehension began to steal over him; there was more to this, he could sense it. But he tried again to calm her.

"It's okay, Ash. There's no monster, it was just your dream."

She looked directly at him then, and he felt an even deeper qualm when none of the horror in her gaze faded. She lifted her hands, steepling them in front of her face as if praying, but pressing them to her mouth as if to stifle another scream.

"It wasn't a monster," she whispered. "It never was."

"Ash?" he said gently when she stopped.

"And it wasn't a dream. It was a memory. It was real."

He was afraid to say anything that might disrupt this. He didn't have to hear the words to know how critical, how crucial this was. So he just held her, and waited.

"It was real," she said again. "I was really in that dark hallway. Outside my room. I'd heard Dad in his den in the middle of the night and was worried, so I got up to go check on him."

At eight years old, she's looking after her father. The thought roiled his gut even more. Still, he waited. She went on in a sort of numbed tone that told him she was barely hanging on.

"I opened the door and saw her go into the den." He didn't ask who—he knew. "Brady," she said, and he could hear the heartbreak in her voice, which damned near broke his in turn. "She had a gun. I don't think I recognized it back then, it was just a shape in her hand, but now I remember."

The branch breaking, he realized. It had been almost as loud as a gunshot. It must have triggered this, this flood of memory.

"Ash—"

"He didn't do it. Brady, he didn't do it!" She was clutching at him now. "He didn't kill himself."

He was familiar enough with the way people grasped at things when they were in shock, the way they fixated on anything except the ugly core of what had happened. And he supposed in the end this would be what would be most important to her. At least he hoped so; much better for this realization to be the most important to her. This one, not the other.

Not the ugly fact that her mother had murdered her father.

Chapter 33

"Quinn? Where are you, really?"

Brady's voice was sharp, commanding. As he must sound snapping out orders in an emergency. Ashley knew she was seizing on this to avoid thinking about the rest, but she couldn't seem to help it. Her mind was darting around, looking for anything to think about except the reality she was now face-to-face with.

He listened to Quinn's answer. "Good. Head back. Now."

He ended the call—was it a call if he'd made it using the Foxworth phone they'd left for them, the one with the walkie-talkie function?—before Quinn could have done anything more than agree. She wondered—seizing on this now—how many people there were in the world who would dare give a man like Quinn Foxworth orders like that. Not many, she guessed. And yet Brady had, and Quinn had apparently accepted it. Which said as much about Brady as it did about Quinn.

"They're on their way back." He set down the phone and resumed his pacing. And Ashley resumed watching him, the way he moved, the long, powerful strides, the barely leashed strength of him. He looked fierce, almost dangerous, and she realized that he could be, if necessary, just that. And she found that of all the things, all the places her desperate brain had darted off to, the only one that had to power to truly distract her was Brady, and the wonder they'd found together.

"Brady—"

He held up a hand to stop her. "Wait until they get here. I don't want you to have to go through this more than once."

She lapsed into silence, but it was with a sense of realization, of how different this felt, Brady's protective instinct, compared to…others. Her mind shied away from it so vigorously it almost made her dizzy, and she knew he was right. Getting through this once would be about all she could handle. Even Cutter's comforting only took the edge off.

Hayley and Quinn didn't waste any time once they arrived. They all sat around the table, and Quinn looked at Brady and said simply, "Go."

Brady sucked in a breath. "Details of how later, but the bottom line is, Ash's nightmares were born in reality. She saw her mother go into her father's den with a handgun and moments later heard the shot."

Hayley gasped, but Quinn's expression shifted to one very similar to Brady's—fierce, determined. And somehow, hearing it said flatly like that, with utter conviction, by the one man she trusted above all others, made it real. Truth. And suddenly her mind settled, quit caroming around and arrowed toward the undeniable truth. And something new, something hot and fierce, began to bubble up inside her.

"Well, that tears it open," Quinn said. "Lay it all out," he said, his order as clear as Brady's had been. And as quickly, Brady showed the same respect and complied.

"My theory is this. Her mother realized from the description of the recurring nightmare that started six months ago that Ash had witnessed her going in to murder her husband. And so she started this…campaign to have her declared mentally ill, so if she remembered completely, it would be dismissed."

The memory of all she'd gone through, all the treatments, the crippling drugs, all the fear and horror at what was happening to her, rose up and tried to swamp her. But it hit the rapidly rising wall of that new factor, that thing she'd never felt during this entire ordeal until now. Cutter nudged her, and she looked at the dog. Oddly, his expression seemed almost approving. And she remembered suddenly that day at the clinic, when her mother had arrived and the dog had growled and put himself between her and Ashley. *You knew even then, didn't you?* She leaned over and kissed the top of the dog's head.

"And incompetent to manage the trust fund," Quinn said grimly.

"Especially that," Brady said, sounding just as harsh. "Bottom line, the murder was for the money, but gaslighting Ash was to save herself from getting caught."

"I suppose I should be grateful she didn't just kill me, too."

Everyone stopped dead and stared at Ashley as she spoke icily. She didn't wonder why; they'd been dealing with such a broken soul, this cold fury must have startled them all.

"Ash?" Brady said after a moment. "I know this is horrible, but we have to—"

"What it is is evil." She said it in that same icy tone.

"That…woman murdered the sweetest, most loving man in the world, for money, and it wasn't even that much at the time. Worse, she made it look as if he'd killed himself, which to an eight-year-old means he hadn't loved her enough to stay. And she got away with it, for twenty years. But when there was just a chance she might be found out, she tried her best to destroy her own daughter's mind and heart."

Brady was staring at her, with a touch of what she could only call awe. And that warmed her as much as that new force growing within her. "She put you through the worst kind of hell. That you're even still functioning is a miracle and testament to your strength."

"I haven't been strong, but I am now." She finally gave a name to that new, solid wall of emotion that was holding everything else—pain, misery, fear, all of it—at bay. "And I am furious."

The slow smile that lifted one corner of Brady's mouth—that luscious, wonderful mouth—showed her there was still room for one more emotion in her newly fierce heart.

"What you are," he said in a tone that matched the smile, "is glorious."

Brady wondered, for just a moment, if he'd known. If somehow, on some level, he'd known this Ash existed. If he'd sensed that beneath the pain, the anguish and the nearly broken spirit, this fierce, strong woman lived. Maybe that was what had drawn him. Maybe it wasn't that he hadn't learned his lesson with Liz—maybe he had, and completely.

In the end, it didn't matter if he'd known. What mattered was that his fear that this ugly truth would destroy her was not only unfounded but seemed absurd in the light of the way she'd come back fighting. Now that she knew, now that she was sure of herself, Ashley Jordan seemed… indomitable. The kind of woman who could take what life threw and spit back in its face.

The kind of woman he'd never expected to find.

"What do you want done, Ashley?"

Quinn's quiet question snapped him out of the reverie he'd slipped into, visions of last night and this afternoon spinning out into a lifetime of the same sweet wildness filling all the days of the rest of his life.

"What are the options?" Ash said, so briskly it almost made him smile all over again.

Quinn answered in the same way. "Firstly, you do have the option of doing nothing. We can build you a package of proof that you're mentally fine and help you get started somewhere else, if that's what you choose."

Brady stared at Quinn, not quite able to believe what he was hearing. Quinn turned his head as if he'd felt it, and said quietly, "This is one of those points where our goals diverge. We do what Ashley wants."

"Just let her get away with it? She murdered my dad!" Brady felt relieved at Ash's reaction. Just the sound of her outrage at the idea reassured him she was going to be okay. He relaxed again.

Quinn looked back at Ash. "It's just one option. And one I didn't expect you to take. So, next. I'm not certain we could prove your mother guilty in a court of law of the murder of your father. Gavin is the best, so anything's possible, but a twenty-year-old crime where it's entirely reasonable that her DNA would be all over anyway, and with the only new evidence an eight-year-old's suppressed memory, would be a difficult challenge." Quinn's mouth quirked. "Of course, that's what Gavin likes best."

Brady had to rein in what he was sure would be a silly

grin as Quinn talked so easily of Gavin de Marco. The guy had written the book on blowing up criminal cases.

"I hate thinking she'll get away with it," Ash said.

"There's a court of law," Brady said, drumming his fingers on the table restlessly, "and there's the court of public opinion. And from what I've seen, in your mother's case, the latter might be almost as bad."

Ash looked at him and after a moment nodded slowly. "Yes. Yes, you're right. Her image has always been paramount to her. If we can't put her in jail for murder, that would be the next best thing."

"Gavin can see to that. He's got an incredible amount of juice, and the media will have what we couldn't prove spread around as quickly as what we can prove. Which is that she paid and probably planned what was done to you, her own daughter."

"And take out that disgusting excuse for a psychiatrist in the process?" she asked.

"Indeed," Hayley said determinedly. Then she looked at Brady. "A wild card in this is your boss. You've said he's tight with Mayor Alexander. How tight?"

Brady stopped his tapping. A wry smile lifted one corner of his mouth. "Not tight enough to go down with her, if that's what you're asking. Once the torpedo hits, he's more of an every-man-for-himself kind of guy."

"Good to know," Quinn said with a grin. He glanced back at Ash. "Is there anybody else we need to worry about? Extended family or powerful friends?"

Her brow furrowed. "My grandparents died before I was born. She has a brother she doesn't have any contact with, but that's it."

"By his choice, if he's smart," Brady muttered. Ash glanced at him, and he thought he saw a flash of…something, appreciation maybe, in her eyes before she went on.

"She has the usual sort of political friends, but no one she's really close to." She grimaced. "She always said taking care of her job and me took all her time."

"Another layer to the guilt and confusion," Brady said, feeling the anger surge in him again. He turned and covered Ash's hand with his own. She instantly turned hers to wrap her fingers around his. Even that small gesture had the power to steal his breath, and it was a moment before he could speak. "Do you want the confrontation, Ash? Do you want to face her down and tell her you know it all, what she's done, what she is?"

He thought he already knew the answer. And then he saw it in the narrowing of her gaze and the tightening of her delicate jaw in the moment before she spoke.

"Damned right I do."

And Brady couldn't help but smile widely as he nodded at her.

Chapter 34

Ashley thought she'd understood the power of Foxworth, but by Monday afternoon, she knew she'd underestimated.

The amount of background and research and evidence they'd put together in such a short time astonished her. The arrival of Gavin de Marco Monday morning was the icing; that a man with his reputation came immediately when Hayley had called spoke volumes. Even Brady had appeared a little awed when they'd shaken hands.

The man wasn't just dramatically good-looking—he radiated competence and charisma and got up to speed so swiftly she understood why he'd become famous around the world as the man to go to if you were in a jam. She'd never heard why he'd quit the world of criminal defense, but she was sure his years on the top of that heap probably gave him great insight into what the more twisted denizens of the world—including her mother—might do. And yet he was kind, tactfully making sure she knew what she was in for.

"There's enough to put her away for a while," he told her. "Perhaps long enough for us to come up with further evidence about your father's case. But I can't promise that."

"I understand." Then, hesitantly, she glanced at Brady before looking back at the attorney and saying, "I don't want Brady in trouble over this."

Gavin only smiled. "He won't be. He saved them a lot of humiliation, saved a life, uncovered a crooked, drug-dealing physician and solved a cold murder case, all of which got by them because the sheriff succumbed to political pressure. I dare them to try and twist him up over that. And I'll be happy to take them on if they do."

She took a deep, relieved breath.

The lawyer studied her for a moment. "How bad do you want this meeting to be?"

Her mouth twisted. "The loving family reunion, you mean?"

He nodded. "Right now, do you want to do this publicly, see her broken and humiliated in front of witnesses and the media, or do you want a private confrontation? It will all become public, but do you want to become public yourself? It's your call."

Ashley blinked. Foxworth was definitely different. "I just want…to say what I need to say to her. As tempting as the other sounds… I don't want to be an act at the circus." Gavin smiled in understanding.

"I wouldn't have your restraint," Brady said from where he sat close beside her. Wonderfully close. "But that would show her you know she's the crazy one, not you, and that you're far above her level. And that she didn't, could never break you."

She looked at him and smiled. "Yes. That."

"Then we're agreed?" Gavin asked, with a glance at Hayley and Quinn. "We take her down now for the gaslighting and bribery and fraud, let her know we'll be turning over what we have to the authorities to reopen Ashley's father's case—she doesn't need to know that might come to nothing, let her worry about that, too—and that her daughter will be under Foxworth protection until she's safely locked away?"

Ashley nodded, although she hadn't really thought of that—that her mother might try to do away with her after all. But she had little doubt, not anymore, that Nan Alexander would do anything she thought would save her.

"I don't want you alone with her," Brady warned.

She looked at the man in whose arms she'd spent the last three nights, feeling magnificently light and free despite it all. And from that new, unshadowed intimacy, she'd drawn all the strength she needed.

"I don't need to be," she said. "And I'm angry enough it's probably best I'm not."

"I'll be there," Gavin said. Then with an assessing look at Brady, he added, "And you, I think."

"In uniform?" Brady asked.

Gavin grinned as if he'd read his mind. "Absolutely. And if you could get me a few minutes with your boss, I'll see to that, too. As Ashley said, we don't want any of this rebounding on you."

"That'll be the biggest name-drop of my career," Brady said with a laugh. Clearly he wasn't worried.

"You're sure it won't?" she asked anxiously. "Because if it could hurt Brady, I won't do it."

Brady's head came around, and he stared at her. "What?"

"I'll just take option one and go away."

"Ash—"

"No, Brady. I won't have her hurting someone else I love."

She saw the shock spread across his face. It wasn't the way she would have wanted to say it, but she wouldn't take it back. And then he lowered his gaze to stare at their clasped hands. But he was smiling. Almost embarrassedly, but smiling.

She looked at the others. Gavin showed no reaction, but she would have expected that. Hayley and Quinn were both smiling as if she'd only confirmed something they already knew.

And Cutter simply gave her a look she could only describe as smug. And in that moment, she believed every word they'd told her about this uncanny dog.

Brady felt odd in full dress. He'd been going to go simply for the standard working uniform, but de Marco had said go full-bore dress uniform, complete with honors. So his badge, gleaming name tag, top-ranked marksmanship medal, training officer pin and the two medal of valor pins were on display. He'd even dug out his hat, pulling off the plastic rain cover for better effect.

It had also felt odd, going back to his place to get the gear. He'd found himself looking around his home critically, wondering if Ash would like it.

I won't have her hurting someone else I love.

The words that had been circling wildly in his mind since she'd said them made another round. He hadn't had the chance to really respond, and maybe that was just as well. There might be a better time for it.

He tapped his finger on the steering wheel of his marked SUV. Stared at the front door of the house where he'd been once before and had been greeted by a haunted, tortured woman who bore little resemblance to the woman who had warmed his bed, his body and his heart. The woman who deserved so much more than she'd been dealt, who had been nearly broken but had come back fighting with a courage that humbled him.

The Foxworth phone beside him beeped. He glanced at the screen, saw the texted Ready. No trouble with the boss, then, but he hadn't really expected any, not with the arrival of Gavin de Marco. The man had instilled dread in better men than Sheriff Carter.

He sent back Copy. Contact in two.

He got out of the vehicle, settled his uniform jacket and drew himself up to his full six feet. Then he walked to the door of the mayor's house, where she had been in essence imprisoning her daughter. The woman had arrived about a half an hour ago, after sucking up some oxygen at a meeting of the local merchants.

She answered the door herself. He might have expected at least a maid, such were her delusions of grandeur, but Ash had told them no one lived in. Now that made sense. *Don't want any witnesses around while you gaslight your own daughter.*

He reined it in and put on his best *I've got bad news* face.

"Mayor Alexander," he said, taking his uniform hat off politely.

Then he spotted something over her shoulder that nearly blew everything up. Packing boxes, full of what appeared to be clothing and other personal items. And on top of one was the same jacket he'd seen in Ash's room. She was packing up her stuff? She didn't even know where her daughter was, if she was even alive, and she was packing up her stuff?

It took every bit of determination he had to keep his expression even when she spoke. "Deputy…Crenshaw, isn't it? You helped my daughter the day she had that awful accident."

"Yes. And I'm afraid she's why I'm here now."

He was watching carefully for her reaction to his phrasing. There was just enough delay, and a fraction of a second's calculation in her expression, to tell him she'd been expecting this. An instant later her face showed nothing but distress.

"You've found her."

"I'm afraid so." *And you should be afraid. Very afraid.*

"She's dead, isn't she." It wasn't a question, and he didn't think he was wrong about the split second of relief that flashed in her dark, cold eyes.

"We need you to come to the sheriff's office."

She actually did pale at that. "Why?"

"I'm afraid there will be some details to handle."

"Oh. Of course."

"I will drive you, Madam Mayor. I've been instructed to offer you every courtesy."

He didn't think it was possible, but his loathing grew at her preening reaction to that ploy. And as he drove the vicious woman, he allowed himself a brief fantasy about dropping her off—literally—the lookout where Ash had nearly jumped. But what was coming would be even better, and he had to smother a smile of anticipation as they pulled into the back parking lot and he escorted her into the building.

"We'll be using the sheriff's private conference room," he said, thinking he'd arrested and brought in fried meth heads and drunks who had puked all over themselves with less repugnance than he felt now. Being obsequious to her was turning his stomach.

He pulled open the door to the conference room, seeing that his boss had decided to vacate the area. Covering his bases, Brady guessed, in case this didn't go as planned.

But there were two uniformed deputies standing at the other door, and he gave them a nod.

But it would go as planned. He knew that the minute they stepped inside and the two men already there stood up. One, holding a folder, was Gavin de Marco, whom the mayor gave a puzzled look, as if he were familiar but she couldn't place him. The other was Dr. Andler, who gave her a look Brady could only describe as terrified as, at a word from de Marco, he scurried out that other door into the hands of the two deputies.

He felt the woman beside him falter just for an instant when she saw the doctor run. But then she steadied herself, and he could just imagine how her mind was racing, trying to think of how she was going to turn this away from herself.

"You notified my daughter's doctor before me?" she said, going on the offensive with her tone.

De Marco didn't even look at her. Instead he spoke to Brady. "This is her?"

Brady almost smiled at the disdain in the man's voice. "It is." And then, dropping the formality and letting a little bit of his glee about what was about to come at her show, he said, "Nan, meet Gavin de Marco. You may have heard of him? And of who he works for, the Foxworth Foundation?"

She looked utterly shocked. De Marco didn't offer to shake her hand, didn't even nod at the introduction. Instead he said, in a voice that gave even Brady a chill, "Yes, that Foxworth. The ones that helped take down a corrupt governor. So let me say up front, a small-town mayor is no challenge at all."

Nan Alexander sank down into a chair at the small conference table, looking shaken at last.

Oh, we're just getting started, you pitiful excuse for a human being.

At de Marco's nod, Brady walked to the door the doctor—who he knew had poured out his guts in the hope of lighter consequences—had used and opened it. Ash was just outside, looking a little pale but determined.

"You can do this," he said softly. "I don't have a doubt in the world. Just remember you're fighting for yourself, and for the father who can't, because of her."

She drew in a deep breath, steadied herself and nodded. Took a step toward the doorway, but stopped when he spoke again from right behind her.

"Oh, and Ash?" She looked back. "I love you, too."

Chapter 35

Her mother rose to her feet, one hand pressed against her chest. Ashley knew better than to believe it was in relief at seeing her, but there was a split second when she wavered.

You're fighting for yourself, and for the father who can't, because of her.

Brady's words about what she was facing, and the fact that he was solidly at her back, steadied her.

I love you, too.

And those words made her able to smile in the face of her mother's treachery and evil.

"Hello, Madam Mayor."

She was delighted that it came out evenly, almost casually. Gavin de Marco gave her an approving nod and sat down as if content to watch. Brady looked as if he were stifling a grin.

"Ashley, I don't know what they've told you, but—"

"Don't bother."

"But—"

"I remembered, *Mother*. Just as you were afraid I would."

"Honey, you're just confused—"

"Do not even try. Sit down."

Her mother looked as if she would protest, and Brady took a step toward her as if to enforce the order. She sat.

"I'm going to give you a list. You will stay silent until I'm done. Is that clear?"

Ashley had the pleasure of seeing her mother's uncertainty for the first time. "There's no need to be rude, dear."

Ashley nearly laughed out loud at that. She glanced at Brady, who was again stifling a grin. And then he winked at her, and she knew she could, as he'd said, do this.

She walked to the opposite side of the table from her mother, put her hands down flat on the surface, leaning toward her.

"One, I know you and Dr. Andler have been drugging me with some home-brewed concoction that caused my symptoms—"

"Don't be—"

"—and I have the chemical analysis to prove it." There, Ashley thought, she'd winced at that one. "And the tea you've been forcing down me is being analyzed as we speak." *Bingo*, Ash thought as the woman's expression flickered again. She went on. "Two, you conspired with him to further the illusion that I was mentally ill, with things like the missed appointments—changing the date in my phone and on an new appointment card he gave you—and the fire in the kitchen, the snow tires and a dozen others I could name. Three, I know you intended to have me either declared incompetent or committed to an institution."

"For your own safety—"

"I said silence. Four, I know about the payments from the Amalfi Group." Nan Alexander went white then. And glanced fearfully at Gavin, who allowed himself a small smile. "Yes, Mr. de Marco and Foxworth are very, very thorough. So I think we can do away with the farce that this was out of any concern at all about me."

"Ashley—"

Ashley cut her off again. "Fifth, and now we're getting to the really good stuff, I know you did the same thing to my father."

The woman—for that was how Ashley was now starting to think of her, that or just Nan—gasped. "You know he was unstable!"

"You mean he wouldn't dance to your tune?" Brady said, the first time he'd spoken. Nan frowned as she glanced at him, as if she were trying to figure out exactly how he fit into all this.

He's the man who saved me. And if I get some kind of justice for my father, it will be because of him.

"You meant for me to overhear that discussion with Andler, didn't you? You were setting me up to believe he was becoming violent. Violent enough that he would have to be sent away."

"Of course not."

"My snow globe," Ashley said as it suddenly occurred to her.

Her mother blinked. "What?"

"You're the one who smashed it. Tell me, was it to further the perception that Dad was becoming violent, or simply to hurt me because you knew I treasured it so?"

Nan didn't answer, but it didn't matter—she could see both were the truth. When she did speak, she said only, "This is all absurd. I don't know what you think you're doing, but you can't prove any of this."

Ashley straightened up at that, and Gavin moved. He took a group of pages out of the folder he held and silently slid them across the table. They came to rest neatly in front of the woman, and Ashley wondered with an inward smile if he'd had to practice that or if he was just naturally that good. She knew what it was, a copy of the offshore account records showing the Amalfi deposits to Dr. Andler. And then he took out another, thicker sheaf, these stapled together, and did the same. They edged the others to one side as they hit, and she decided he was just that good.

Gavin still didn't speak, and when she glanced at him, he merely nodded. This was her show, unless and until she'd had enough and wanted out, then he would take over. But she hadn't had nearly enough yet.

"That," she said with no small amount of enjoyment, "is Joseph Andler's full confession. That he was paid by you to help gaslight my father, and then me. That he helped you perpetrate the fraud that he was unstable and suicidal. And that later he did the same thing again, to me. Nothing to say now, *Mother*?"

She resumed her position with hands on the table, leaning in even closer now. And her voice was harsh as it came out through nearly clenched teeth. But this had been building for twenty years under the surface, and it erupted now. "But I haven't gotten to the very bottom of your nasty, evil soul yet, have I? You tried to drive my father to what I nearly did. You tried to drive him to suicide. But when that didn't work, when he was too strong for you to break, you made the ultimate decision."

"I never wanted you to die."

"If you're expecting gratitude, forget it. Because remember what I said before? I mean it. I remembered. You were afraid I would, from the moment I told you about the nightmare. And then you saw me watching those videos of Dad, so you guessed it would surface soon. That's what started all this. You didn't realize until then I'd seen you, did you? You didn't know I'd seen you with that gun, going into the den to kill my father."

Her mother shot to her feet. Brady took one step forward. "Please," he said. "Please do something truly stupid. I really want to see you destroyed in a court of law, when your brilliant, gutsy daughter takes you apart publicly. And Gavin de Marco makes sure it's front-page news."

Through the glow in her heart caused by his words, Ashley saw the moment when the woman who should have been the one to protect her and instead had been the one to try and destroy her, broke. She sank back down into the chair. It was as if whatever propped up her twisted psyche had collapsed. And suddenly it was enough. She had seen the nasty truth in her mother's now flat, expressionless, almost inhuman eyes.

There was nothing left to do except move on.

Brady stood at the kitchen island as Hayley poured coffee, watching Ash as she, Quinn and de Marco sat in the great room of the lodge discussing what came next. Her mother—although she didn't deserve the term—was in custody facing a multitude of charges, none of which were murder. Yet. But Brady had the feeling if there was any way it was possible, Foxworth would pull that off, too. They wouldn't give up until they found a way.

"Quinn is still hunting down a mole who nearly got us killed on the mission where he and I met," Hayley said, apropos of nothing. Except his thoughts, and he gave her a startled look.

"Was I that obvious?"

"No. I just know both of you want her to pay for her

worst crime, Ashley especially. And I wanted you to know we don't quit."

"I'm glad."

It was a moment before Hayley said quietly, "She's going to need some time."

"I know."

"She needs to know she can stand on her own."

"She went through six months of pure hell and came out fighting. She'll be all right."

"Yes, she will. But…"

Brady turned to look at her as she hesitated. "Are you telling me to leave her alone? That…what happened between us isn't, wasn't, real?"

"Oh, I know it's real. I've been there myself. Besides, Cutter says so."

Brady glanced over to where the dog was sprawled on his bed, looking utterly relaxed for the first time since this had started. Obviously the dog considered his work done.

"I swear, you've got me believing he's what you say he is."

"He is. And the only thing I'm saying is give her time to level off. She's been in the pit, and now she's flying high. It will take her time to find her own normal."

"I can't let her go through this alone."

"Of course not. But keep in mind you're also a major witness in this."

"Oh." He had to admit he'd forgotten that aspect.

"Gavin will run interference on that, but it might be wise to keep the true nature of your relationship under wraps until her mother is locked up."

How they were going to manage that, he didn't know, but he only said, "You sound certain she will be."

Hayley nodded. "Oh, I am. We've got the evidence, and Gavin will lay it out so completely that all the prosecutor has to do is show up. Not to mention just the sight of his face in a courtroom still has a very powerful effect for whichever side he's on. And in this, he's on Ashley's."

Brady smiled at that, although underneath he was wondering how he would get through this if he had to take a step back from her. But as he watched her, as he saw the clever, quick, beautiful woman who had blossomed since that moment she'd realized the truth, he realized he had to look at the long game here. And for him, that meant the rest of their lives together.

And for that, he could—and would—do whatever it took.

Chapter 36

Ashley looked out over the incredible vista and drew in a breath of air that carried the crisp scent of new snow and not even a hint of the spring that would arrive officially in just over a month. The Foxworths, including Cutter—who, oddly, seemed just an ordinary dog now, taking a last roll in the snow before leaping into the back of their vehicle soaking wet—had left Monday, heading home after their unexpectedly extended anniversary trip. They, and Gavin, had stayed until it was clear her mother, now clearly broken, would not be fighting the charges, although they promised they would be back and at her side at the hearing that would be coming, or if she needed them. As had Gavin when he'd left yesterday.

More importantly, she knew the man at her side now would be there, and that was all she really needed. She had been worried for a while, when he seemed to have pulled back, but there had been so much to do in the aftermath, she'd had little time to think about anything else. And then she had realized that was exactly why Brady had backed off—to give her room to come to grips with the complete wreckage of what had been her life. Yet he had still been there, every step of the way, radiating such utter confidence that she could do whatever was necessary that she couldn't help but believe it. It had been a long ten days, but she had plowed through all the grim detail work, made the decisions necessary and at last, today, had called a halt.

It was, after all, Valentine's Day. And so she asked him to bring her here, to where her life had hit its lowest point…and turned around so miraculously.

"You know the biggest irony in all this? That night, when you found me here, I thought about what I was doing, how it would hurt my mother to go through another suicide," she said as she leaned against him where they sat on the stone seat. She felt him go very still, as if even thinking about it made him tense. "But that wasn't what stopped me long enough for you to grab me."

"What did?" His voice was low and a little rough.

"I didn't want to do what you said—ruin this place for you. You'd done nothing but be kind to me, and I simply couldn't do that to you."

He went still. "You didn't—and don't—owe me anything, Ash."

"And that you say that and mean it is why I knew, even then, that there was a reason to hang on."

His arm tightened around her. For a moment he didn't speak, as if he couldn't. And when he finally did, his voice was light, teasing. "And here I thought it was because you fell in love with me on the spot."

"That, too," she said, only she said it with utter seriousness.

"I'm sorry you had to go through this."

She sighed sadly. "Once I'd had my say, once I saw in her face it was all true, I wanted to walk away. I took no pleasure in seeing her crushed when the formal charges were filed."

"Even though she tried to destroy your life and you yourself?"

"I thought I would enjoy it more."

Again his arm tightened. "You needed it, Ash. But that doesn't mean you wanted it. You're not anything, not an iota like her. And you proved that. And how strong you really are. I am so damn proud of you."

She looked up at him then, his words filling her with a joy she'd never felt in her life. "Thank you. That means more to me than anything she ever did or said. Or anyone else, for that matter."

It was a long silent moment before he asked, "Have you decided what you want to do with her house? You know it'll be yours in the end, as damages, if nothing else."

She grimaced. "Is burn it to the ground on the option list?"

Again he gave her that one-armed hug. "I can make that happen if you really want it."

She sighed. "No. That would be a waste. But I will not live there."

"Maybe you could put it to another use."

She leaned back to look at him more directly. "Like what?"

"I don't know." He shrugged. "Maybe a halfway house for people really going through what she made you think you were."

Her eyes widened. And then, with a dawning smile, she held his gaze and said, "I love you, Brady Crenshaw."

He blinked, as if he didn't realize what had made her say it. But that was Brady—he just went about the business of helping people and thought it was nothing special. "I love you, too," he said after a moment.

They sat there until the wind kicked up and with it the

chill. They got back in his car—his personal vehicle he'd picked up at some point, a smaller SUV—and he started the engine and turned on the heat. But before putting it in gear, he turned in the driver's seat to look at her.

"If you're not going to live in that house," he began.

"I know. I'll have to find someplace else." She looked out the window, back toward the lookout. "But I don't want to leave the mountains. I won't let her take that away from me."

He said, sounding a bit hesitant, "I know a place up the road from Alex's." Her breath caught. His words came back to her instantly…*my place up the road*. Was he saying what she thought he was? "It's not as grand, but it's solid and comfortable. With a big fireplace like you loved there. Kitchen probably needs a few newer amenities, but—"

"Does it have the most important one?" she interrupted.

He blinked. Asked with a slight frown, "What's that?"

"You."

His expression cleared. And his slow smile was as brilliant as any sunrise she'd ever seen or ever would see in the future. "Yes."

She smiled back at him, letting everything she was feeling show. "I'd better pack, then."

And then he was leaning over and kissing her, fiercely, possessively, and she reveled in it, kissing him back just as fiercely.

"So," she said when he finally put the car in gear, "is there room for a dog at your place?"

He flashed a grin at her then. "*Our* place. And yeah, I'd say there is."

"Good," Ashley said.

Although she seriously doubted there was another dog in the world like Cutter Foxworth.

* * * * *

Get 4 FREE REWARDS!

We'll send you 2 FREE Books
<u>plus</u> 2 FREE Mystery Gifts.

Harlequin Romantic Suspense books are heart-racing page-turners with unexpected plot twists and irresistible chemistry that will keep you guessing to the very end.

FREE
Value Over
$20

YES! Please send me 2 FREE Harlequin Romantic Suspense novels and my 2 FREE gifts (gifts are worth about $10 retail). After receiving them, if I don't wish to receive any more books, I can return the shipping statement marked "cancel." If I don't cancel, I will receive 4 brand-new novels every month and be billed just $4.99 per book in the U.S. or $5.74 per book in Canada. That's a savings of at least 13% off the cover price! It's quite a bargain! Shipping and handling is just 50¢ per book in the U.S. and $1.25 per book in Canada.* I understand that accepting the 2 free books and gifts places me under no obligation to buy anything. I can always return a shipment and cancel at any time. The free books and gifts are mine to keep no matter what I decide.

240/340 HDN GNMZ

Name (please print)

Address   Apt. #

City   State/Province   Zip/Postal Code

Email: Please check this box ☐ if you would like to receive newsletters and promotional emails from Harlequin Enterprises ULC and its affiliates. You can unsubscribe anytime.

> ### Mail to the **Reader Service:**
> **IN U.S.A.:** P.O. Box 1341, Buffalo, NY 14240-8531
> **IN CANADA:** P.O. Box 603, Fort Erie, Ontario L2A 5X3

Want to try 2 free books from another series! Call 1-800-873-8635 or visit www.ReaderService.com.

*Terms and prices subject to change without notice. Prices do not include sales taxes, which will be charged (if applicable) based on your state or country of residence. Canadian residents will be charged applicable taxes. Offer not valid in Quebec. This offer is limited to one order per household. Books received may not be as shown. Not valid for current subscribers to Harlequin Romantic Suspense books. All orders subject to approval. Credit or debit balances in a customer's account(s) may be offset by any other outstanding balance owed by or to the customer. Please allow 4 to 6 weeks for delivery. Offer available while quantities last.

Your Privacy—Your information is being collected by Harlequin Enterprises ULC, operating as Reader Service. For a complete summary of the information we collect, how we use this information and to whom it is disclosed, please visit our privacy notice located at corporate.harlequin.com/privacy-notice. From time to time we may also exchange your personal information with reputable third parties. If you wish to opt out of this sharing of your personal information, please visit readerservice.com/consumerschoice or call 1-800-873-8635. **Notice to California Residents**—Under California law, you have specific rights to control and access your data. For more information on these rights and how to exercise them, visit corporate.harlequin.com/california-privacy.

HRS20R2

Love Harlequin romance?

DISCOVER.

Be the first to find out about promotions,
news and exclusive content!

f Facebook.com/HarlequinBooks

🐦 Twitter.com/HarlequinBooks

📷 Instagram.com/HarlequinBooks

📌 Pinterest.com/HarlequinBooks

ReaderService.com

EXPLORE.

Sign up for the Harlequin e-newsletter and
download a free book from any series at
TryHarlequin.com

CONNECT.

Join our Harlequin community to
share your thoughts and connect
with other romance readers!
Facebook.com/groups/HarlequinConnection

HSOCIAL2020